Outnumbered. Out of luck.

The Sioux rushed straight at him wielding a tomahawk, and it was clear that his intention was to kill. The tomahawk swept downward and Hawkes ducked as the blade bit deeply into the tree behind him. The mountain man lurched forward, thrusting with his knife, but the Dakota warrior was agile and danced out of harm's way. Hawkes stumbled and fell to one knee, cursing.

Drawing his own knife, the Dakota lunged. Hawkes twisted his body, taking the impact and driving his knife up into the warrior's belly even as the Indian's blade plunged into his shoulder. Snarling at the pain, Hawkes twisted the knife and eviscerated his foe, feeling hot blood gush over his hands.

Heaving the dead brave aside, Hawkes instinctively rolled, struggled to his knees, and looked up in time to see the butt of a rifle an instant before it struck—and then the world blacked out. . . .

MOUNTAIN COURAGE

Jason Manning

A SIGNET BOOK

SIGNET
Published by New American Library, a division of
Penguin Putnam Inc., 375 Hudson Street,
New York, New York 10014, U.S.A.
Penguin Books Ltd, 27 Wrights Lane,
London W8 5TZ, England
Penguin Books Australia Ltd, Ringwood,
Victoria, Australia
Penguin Books Canada Ltd, 10 Alcorn Avenue,
Toronto, Ontario, Canada M4V 3B2
Penguin Books (N.Z.) Ltd, 182–190 Wairau Road,
Auckland 10, New Zealand

Penguin Books Ltd, Registered Offices:
Harmondsworth, Middlesex, England

First published by Signet, an imprint of New American Library,
a division of Penguin Putnam Inc.

First Printing, October 1999
10 9 8 7 6 5 4 3 2 1

The events described in Part One of this novel transpire after Gordon Hawkes leads Brigham Young and the Saints down the Mormon Trail in 1847 but before he becomes involved in the Mormon Rebellion of 1857—all of which is recounted in *Mountain Massacre*.

PART ONE

1851

Chapter 1

When Gordon Hawkes went in search of his brothers, the Absaroke Crows, he had a pretty good idea where he could find them. He rode north from his remote mountain home near the Uinta Range as spring turned to summer, and some days later he arrived at the Wind River Valley. To the south rose the stunning Wind River Mountains, still heavy with snow, while the impressive Owl Creek Range formed the northern rim. The valley was as pleasing to the eye as any Hawkes had seen—and he had seen many in more than fifteen years of travel and exploration in the Shining Mountains. The grass was lush, the streams frequent, the game plentiful. Here the Crows retreated to escape the heat of summer. They had already concluded the spring buffalo hunt. In the autumn they would venture out onto the High Plains once more to seek out the buffalo, in order to lay in stores of meat for the long winter.

By then Hawkes would be gone, back at his isolated cabin, far removed from the main trails. He seldom stayed away from home for very long. Every summer, though, he came down from the high reaches to trade his plews for a few necessaries, usually at Fort Bridger. And most summers he paid the Crows a visit too. He was an adopted member of the tribe, and they always made him feel welcome. A man needed to feel that way every now and then, and Hawkes was most assuredly *not* welcome among his own kind. Not with a pair of murder charges still hanging over his head.

But he did not seek out the Absaroke solely for his own benefit. He had his family in mind as well. As they rode along the banks of the Wind River, in the sun-speckled shade beneath the ash and elder trees, Hawkes turned in his saddle to look back at his wife, Eliza, and their two children, fifteen-year-old Cameron, and Grace, soon to turn seven. They enjoyed these sojourns among the Indians as much as he did. Remaining isolated from all human contact wasn't healthy, especially where the children were concerned.

"I know how difficult it must be for you," he had told Eliza once years ago, "being married to a fugitive from justice. Forced to live in hiding, far removed from other people."

"You haven't heard me complain, have you?" she had replied, with that gentle smile that always left him marveling at his good fortune.

Eliza never complained about anything. His willowy, pale-skinned wife appeared quite delicate at first glance, hardly the kind of sturdy pioneer woman one would think likely to survive the hardships of frontier life. But Eliza was in fact both physically and emotionally strong. She had proven many times over that she could handle anything life threw in her path. But she didn't have to speak out for Hawkes to know the truth. She did get lonely, and so did the children. And so every summer he ventured down from his mountain hideout, fully cognizant of the risks involved but convinced that the benefits outweighed them.

Little Grace rode behind him, her bare legs and feet dangling. She was the spitting image of her mother—the yellow hair, the fine, high cheekbones, the blue eyes big and bold and afraid of nothing, the slender build. Garbed in a blue gingham dress that Eliza had made for her over the summer, Grace rode a gentle paint pony that Red Bear, chief of the Mountain Crow, had given her last year as a gift. Hawkes knew his little girl was very tired. The trail from the Uintas was not an easy one. But Grace could tell that they were drawing near their destination, and excitement gleamed through her weariness. There would be plenty of Crow children for her to play with, and she had many friends among them. There was something about Grace that drew people, both young and old, to her. A purity of heart, a gallant spirit, an infectious good cheer.

Behind Grace rode Eliza. More often than not, the frontier aged people in a hurry, but this fate had not befallen Eliza. She'd had her fair share of hardships, sure, not the least of which was the death of her parents, murdered by Flathead Indians. But though she was more than thirty years old, Eliza looked ten years younger. She was more beautiful today, thought Hawkes, than when he had first laid eyes on her. Eliza's formidable strength of will had two sources—her unquenchable love for her husband and her unbending faith in God. The daughter of missionaries, she exhibited some of the proselytizing zeal that had consumed her mother and father and that ultimately had led them to their doom. All her previous attempts to convert some of the Absaroke had met with poor success. But the Crows liked her, and tolerated her efforts in that regard, and Eliza would not be deterred by past failure.

And then there was Cameron. As Eliza was reflected in Grace, so Hawkes saw himself in his son. Cameron was a tall, strapping lad. You grew up quickly in the mountains. Hawkes had taught his son all he knew about how to survive in the wild country, and Cameron had been a ready pupil. He could ride like a Plains Indian, shoot with the best of them, and read sign as well as the most accomplished scout. He was strong, smart, resourceful, and resilient.

All his life Cameron had been associating with the Crows. In fact, he'd spent more time with the Absaroke than with people of his own race. While he had made a number of childhood friends, these days he was exhibiting a good deal more interest in the young Crow maidens. Hawkes had first noticed this development last summer. Cameron was growing up and would soon be a man. The years were flying by at a rate that astonished Hawkes. In no time at all Cam would be full-grown, and he would marry—in all likelihood an Absaroke woman—and before long Hawkes would find himself a grandfather. Shaking his head, the mountain man felt the inexorable current of life washing over him.

Turning his attention back to the trail ahead, Hawkes could sense that the Crow village was near. Through the trees, way up yonder in the middle distance, a herd of Indian horses grazed out in the open. He could smell a faint odor of woodsmoke, and he knew that in a matter of minutes they would see the skin lodges. He had no worries regarding the reception they would receive. In recent years, hard feelings between the red man and the white had increased on the High Plains. More and more immigrants were pouring into the frontier, pushing the Indians aside in their quest for a new beginning. The Crows were not immune to this pressure. But Hawkes and his family were assured a friendly welcome nonetheless.

Nearly twenty years had passed since Hawkes had boarded ship in Dublin harbor with his father and mother, bound for America. Thomas Hawkes, a poor potato farmer, had dreamed of a better future in the promised land. But Hawkes had watched his father die of ship's fever. Consumed by grief and a tragic addiction to opium, his mother had tried to bind him over to the ship's captain in return for the seaman's assurances that he would look to her needs. The boy was uninterested in a life on the high seas, especially one subject to the sadistic whims of Captain Warren, and so he had escaped the ship at New York, aided by a Scots adventurer named William Drummond Stewart.

In the company of Stewart, Hawkes had made his way to New Orleans, there to be falsely accused of the murder of a Creole planter. He and the Scotsman fled to St. Louis one step ahead of bounty hunters and joined a westward-bound expedition of the Rocky Mountain Fur Company. In competition with the American Fur Company, the RMFC had hoped to stymie its rival's quest for dominance in the fur trade by building an outpost on the Yellowstone River. In saving the life of a Crow chief's young son, Hawkes improved relations between the RMFC and the Absaroke and at the same time forged a personal bond with the tribe that endured to this day.

Emerging from the trees at a bend in the river, Hawkes saw the Crow village for the first time now, dozens and dozens of skin lodges stretching for at least a mile along the opposite bank, where there were relatively few trees. On this side of the river the vast horse herd grazed, nearly three thousand head by his calculation. Red Bear's band numbered about eight hundred souls, with a good two hundred warriors, each of whom owned between ten and thirty ponies. A Crow male's material worth was measured largely by the number of horses he owned.

A mounted pair of those warriors were crossing the river at a good ford marking the eastern extremity of the village. Other Absarokes on foot dropped what they were doing and begin to drift toward the ford. Hawkes was certain that his arrival came as no surprise. They would have known long ago, probably as soon as he entered the valley, that he was on the way. Their scouts were many and always ranged far afield. He knew this to be the case even though he had seen no sign of them. The Crows had many enemies, on all sides. Their land was prime beaver and buffalo country, much sought after by more powerful tribes like the Dakota Sioux and the Cree-Assiniboine. Then, of course, there was the Blackfoot Alliance—the Blackfoot, Blood, Piegan, and Gros Ventre tribes—to the north. For many years the alliance had been the implacable foes of the Absaroke. Thus it was the habit of Crow chiefs, even deep within their own country, to ring their villages with scouts of keen eye and stout heart.

As the warriors drew near, Hawkes checked his horse. He sat tall in the saddle, a lean and sinewy man, his sandy hair and beard already touched with gray though he was only two years on the far side of thirty. Bareheaded and clad in buckskins, he rode with his Hawken Plains rifle sheathed and tied to the saddle beneath his right leg. There it remained, unheeded by its owner, who was more than confident that the Crow braves posed no threat to him or his family.

As with all Plains tribes, the Crows had a number of warrior societies. By the regalia and paint worn by the two braves, Hawkes could tell at a glance that they were members of the Fox Clan. He also knew that each year one warrior society was selected to serve as tribal police, and he assumed that this responsibility currently rested upon the shoulders of the Foxes. Were a stranger to approach the village it would be the duty of the Foxes to determine his purpose and, if necessary, prevent his entry. In this case, though, the warriors were coming merely to welcome their visitors and escort them into the village. In addition, tribal police were charged with apprehending and punishing those who violated the Absaroke codes of conduct. During buffalo hunts they were responsible for making sure that every hunter received his fair share of the meat. They were to prevent unauthorized raids against other tribes that might be contemplated by young hotheads out for revenge or loot or glory.

These two Absarokes wore beaded hide breechcloths and leggings adorned with beaded bands, fringe, and hairlocks. Each was clad in his war shirt, which was heavy with quill- and beadwork, trimmed with animal fur, and fringed the full length of the sleeve with buckskin and hair. Each also wore a medicine bag tied to his shirt, to provide him with protection from the weapons of his enemies. The shirts of both braves bore long, colorful beaded bands on each shoulder. These signified that the men had distinguished themselves in battle, as did the coup feathers dangling from their hair, which was cropped short in front but allowed to grow quite long in back, divided into thick cords and stiffened with clay. Their faces were painted, red on one side and yellow on the other, and they wore fox skins around their necks and waists.

This ceremonial dress confirmed to Hawkes that his arrival had been expected. In dressing so, the warriors demonstrated their respect for him. They were armed, of course—no brave ventured even a short distance from the village unarmed—but Hawkes wasn't the least bit worried about the knives, war clubs, short bows, quivers of arrows, and trade rifles that these braves carried. Such men would feel naked without their weapons. As members of a warrior society, they were "made to die"; when initiated they had sung a song in which they expressed the fervent desire to die in battle in defense of their people. In this way they would bring honor to their clan and their families and secure a place for themselves in the Other Side Land. Hawkes knew of no finer fighters among the Plains tribes, with the possible exception of the Dakota.

Checking their ponies, the warriors raised their rifles high over their heads and uttered short, sharp cries that resembled the barking of foxes. In this way they showed their pleasure at seeing Hawkes, greeting him as a fellow Crow warrior. Hawkes knew one of them—He Smiles Twice. It was He Smiles Twice who rode closer, checking his pony alongside the mountain man's gray mustang.

"White Crow, brother of the Absaroke, you and your people are welcome."

Fluent in the Absaroke tongue, Hawkes solemnly thanked He Smiles Twice for his courtesy.

"Red Bear will be happy to see you," said He Smiles

Twice. "There is to be a great peace council at Fort Laramie."

"Peace council?"

"Yes. It was Broken Hand's doing."

Hawkes nodded. Thomas Fitzpatrick, known among the Indians and mountain men as Broken Hand, had agreed to act as an Indian agent for the government in the Upper Platte region. Fitzpatrick had been a trapper and explorer, and his feats were as legendary as those of Jim Bridger and Jedediah Smith. His purpose in agreeing to represent the United States government was to somehow bring peace to the High Plains and end the incessant warfare between various tribes. Hawkes considered the quest quixotic at best. To be productive, such a peace council would have to include representatives of all the principal tribes, and Hawkes could scarcely imagine an Absaroke reaching any kind of workable agreement with the tribe's perennial foes of the Blackfoot Alliance—or a Dakota and a Mandan, or a Hidatsa and an Arikara doing the same. But if indeed there was a council scheduled, perhaps Broken Hand had wrought some sort of miracle.

"When will this take place?" asked Hawkes.

"Soon," replied the Crow warrior. "Red Bear will want to speak to you about it."

"I see." Hawkes glanced over his shoulder at Eliza. She was looking at him, her face a stoic mask, but her eyes were deep-blue harbors for a sudden anxiety. She, too, knew the Absaroke tongue passably well, so she understood all that had transpired between her husband and the Crow warrior. And her first thought had been identical to his own—that it was entirely likely that Red Bear would try to involve him in this upcoming peace council in some way. The wellspring of her anxiety consisted of more than a wife's dismay at the likelihood of a long separation from her man. She knew how potentially dangerous it was for Gordon to leave the relative safety of the high country. Six years ago he had left her side, bound for Independence, and had not returned for a year and a half, during which time he had been gravely wounded, was accused of yet another murder he did not commit, and had been of some assistance to Brigham Young's Mormons in their trek westward to the promised land. Hawkes was well aware that this experience was still fresh in her mind—eighteen months of loneliness and worry, of wondering whether he was alive or dead.

He Smiles Twice turned his pony and, rejoining the other warrior, led the way across the rocky ford and into the Absaroke village. Hawkes wanted to help the Crows in any way he could, but he prayed that Red Bear would not impose on him to go to the Fort Laramie council. He did not want to be put in the position of having to choose between his loyalty to the Absaroke and his commitment to sparing his beloved wife the torment of another long separation. He would have to disappoint Red Bear. He would have to say no.

Chapter 2

Standing in the hot September sun, sweating beneath his buckskins, Hawkes kept his eyes on the congregation of Indian representatives and the envoys of the United States government who had gathered just outside the main gate of Fort Laramie. But his thoughts were elsewhere. He missed his wife and children, missed them terribly. More than a month had passed since he had bid them farewell, leaving them with the Absaroke in the Wind River Valley. He rued the day when he had entered the Crow village. As soon as he had heard mention of this peace council he should have turned right around and headed for home. But he hadn't, and as a consequence, here he was.

"Ain't never seen so many Injuns all in one place before," said Broken Hand Fitzpatrick.

Hawkes glanced at the tall, rail-thin, bearded man who stood beside him. Fitzpatrick was leaning on his rifle and gazing out beyond the cluster of Indian delegates, army officers, and government agents in broadcloth suits. Hundreds of skin lodges stretched as far as the eye could see across the dusty sagebrush plain. There were ten thousand Indians here, from nine different nations. The Crow had set up their lodges beyond Laramie Creek, along with the Hidatsa, the Shoshone, and the Arikara. The vast Dakota Sioux village stood off to the northeast, isolated by their own choosing from the other tribes. The Cheyenne, with their warlike cousins the Arapahoes, were encamped due west.

"Never has there been this many of 'em gathered in one place before," mused Broken Hand. "Good thing it's to make peace, and not a war. Lucky for us."

"You really think this treaty will stick?" asked Hawkes.

Broken Hand pursed his lips. "Last year I seen near to fifty thousand gold seekers pass through these parts on their way to California. Add them to the thousands of others bound for Oregon and a new start, and you had thousands of buffaloes kilt, the grass grazed down to the roots, and a plague of cholera among all the Injun villages in my district. The Injuns come and begged me to tell the Great Father to keep his people on their own land. The old chiefs wanted to keep the peace all the same, but as time went on it got harder and harder for them to stop their young bucks from raiding the wagon trains. I seen it coming, Gordon. Something weren't done and soon, them braves out yonder would be painted up for war, not decked out to smoke no peace pipe."

Hawkes nodded. Fitzpatrick had answered his question, admittedly in a roundabout way—Broken Hand didn't know any better than the next man whether the treaty even now in the process of being signed would be worth any more than the paper it was written on. But at the very least it had forestalled massive bloodletting—for the time being.

The proceedings were about to be concluded, and

for that Hawkes was grateful. The negotiations had been dragging on for days. Most of the talks had taken place at Horse Creek, some miles away, but the final signing ceremony, which Hawkes and Fitzpatrick were witnessing at this moment, had been moved back here, in the shadow of Fort Laramie's stout adobe walls. The whole business had taken as long as it had for several reasons. For one thing, the Indian delegates had haggled interminably over the size and composition of the annuities they would receive in return for abiding by the treaty's terms. For another, each tribe had, of course, felt compelled to air its grievances against not only the whites but often another tribe. Several times Hawkes had expected the talks to break down completely, and on two occasions he had predicted violence. But thanks in large measure to Broken Hand's influence—he was highly regarded by nearly all the Indians present—peace had been maintained. The Indians trusted Fitzpatrick. They were confident that he had their best interests at heart.

Another reason the council had dragged on for the fortnight was the late arrival of the Absaroke. Red Bear and most of the other Crow chiefs had harbored grave doubts about participating in the council, and the debate was so prolonged that when Red Bear, Iron Bull, and the other leaders finally came to an agreement and embarked on the journey to Fort Laramie, they were already several days past the intended departure date.

All told, nearly a thousand Absaroke made the trek, with several hundred people from Red Bear's village accompanying their chief. Such an event, of tremendous significance to the tribe's future, was one that many Absaroke had no desire to miss. Others, however, preferred to remain behind. Hawkes had debated whether to bring his family along, deciding in the end that it was too dangerous. He had expected harsh words and hard feelings to precipitate a fight. In short, he had underestimated Thomas Fitzpatrick, and the commitment of David Mitchell, superintendent of Indian Affairs, to a positive outcome for the council.

Hawkes tried to mask his impatience. He wanted the council to conclude so he could head back to the Wind River Valley. The sooner he got started, the sooner he would be reunited with his family. But dozens of Indian leaders had to make their mark on the treaty document, and each signature was inevitably accompanied by a short speech by Mitchell, who then presented the signatory with a silver medallion stamped with the likeness of the president, Millard Fillmore. On the other side, two men, one in hat and coat, the other in buffalo robe and feathers, clasped hands in friendship. The medallion hung from a red, white, and blue ribbon. It was all very formal, very solemn. And Hawkes couldn't shake the feeling that, ultimately, it was also very pointless.

At last it was done. Mitchell signed the document, rolled it, sealed it, placed it in a metal cylinder, and handed the cylinder to an army major who stood at his shoulder, resplendent in dress uniform, saber at his side and dragoon cap under his arm. The superintendent then shook hands with each chief in turn, and the chiefs joined their mounted warrior escorts and departed for their various encampments.

"Well, that's it, then," said Fitzpatrick, his expression and tone of voice registering satisfaction. "Now we can celebrate a job well done. There's to be a big shivaree in the fort tonight, Gordon. I'll expect to see you there."

"Can't do it, Fitz," said Hawkes. "I'm making tracks."

Mitchell was coming toward them, looking every bit as elated as Fitzpatrick. A short, stocky man with a deeply creased face and chin whiskers, he had been a fur trapper himself in his early years. The superintendent wore a dusty, sweat-stained black broadcloth suit. He had tried in the first days of the council to maintain some degree of sartorial dignity, but since then he'd given it up as futile. Hawkes had come to admire the man for his zeal, persistence, and grim determination. Dealing with Indians, especially members of nine different tribes, could test the faith of one of the Twelve Apostles, not to mention the patience of Job. But Mitchell had a bulldog quality about him. Come hell or high water, he was going to take a treaty back to Washington.

"Gentlemen!" he exclaimed, his voice hoarse and raspy from too much dust and too many speeches. "Gentlemen, we have done it at last! We have accomplished a great feat. This day will go down in the history books, mark my words. We have brought peace to the frontier. We have secured safe passage for our fellow citizens who are bound for Oregon and California, while at the same time resolving conflicts among the tribes that have, in some cases, raged for generations." He extended a hand to Fitzpatrick. "You deserve the lion's share of the credit, Tom. Without you, none of this would have come to pass."

"Dunno about that," mumbled Fitzpatrick, overcome by modesty.

"And permit me to extend my thanks to you as well, Mr. Gordon," said Mitchell, turning to Hawkes and proffering a hand. "Without your able assistance, I am not sure but that the Crows would have departed from these proceedings a long time ago."

Hawkes shook the superintendent's hand. As far as every white man here was concerned, his name was Henry Gordon, since his own name was associated with a pair of murders back East. Up until now the alias had served him well. So far as he knew, the authorities were aware that Gordon Hawkes had gone west following the death of the Creole planter, Anton Remairie. Ten years later he had suddenly reappeared in Independence, Missouri, where they believed he had taken the life of an attorney named Ira Taggert, and then disappeared once again into the uncharted wilderness. Many more knew the name Gordon Hawkes than actually knew anything about his appearance. There was always a risk involved, of course, in associating with his own kind, but it was a risk he found himself increasingly willing to take. As the years passed he remained undetected.

"The Absaroke have never wanted anything but peace. They have always been friendly to whites. They're just cautious. And I can't say that I blame them," Hawkes replied.

Mitchell nodded sympathetically. "I know, I know. But you must admit, Mr. Gordon, we have been more than fair to your Crow friends. We have identified their lands as those that lie west of the Powder River, east of the Wind River, north of Rattlesnake Hills, and south of the Musselshell. By this treaty, the United States government solemnly guarantees those boundaries, as we do the boundaries herein established for all the other tribes. In return, we have obligated ourselves to provide the Crows with annuities worth fifty thousand dollars, including provisions, merchandise, and farm tools."

"Yeah," said Hawkes. He wouldn't have been able to conceal his skepticism even if he had wanted to—which he didn't. "You honestly think you can turn these people into farmers, Mr. Mitchell?"

"Clearly you do not."

"No, sir. That will never happen. They'll take your hoes and turn them into lances. And they'll use your pickaxes as war clubs."

"But surely you can see that their future depends on learning to till the land. There is but one constant, sir, and that is that everything will change. The nomadic life of the Indian is doomed to end. Eventually the vast herds of buffalo will be no more. In their place will graze our cattle and our sheep. Whether it is a future you look upon with satisfaction or consternation, it is nonetheless inevitable. And to survive in that world the Crows, along with all the other tribes, must adapt to changing circumstances."

Hawkes glanced at Fitzpatrick. He was unable to decipher Broken Hand's expression. The mountain-man-turned-Indian-agent hid his true feelings on the subject of the Indians' future behind a mask of impassivity.

"Well," said Hawkes, "maybe you really believe all that is possible. Frankly, I don't. You will never turn the Absaroke into plow pushers. But they will keep the peace, so long as they are left alone. They'll abide by that agreement just as long as everyone else does. You don't have to worry about that." He looked beyond Mitchell at the distant, teeming Indian encampments. There was a lot of activity now, and a dun-colored haze of dust bled the blue out of the sky. "But I'll tell you what you do need to worry about."

"The Dakota," said Fitzpatrick quietly.

"That's exactly right," agreed Hawkes. "They won't be long satisfied with their tribal boundaries. For years now they've been pushed westward by whites encroaching on their land. They just happened to be right smack in the way of what you call progress, Mr. Mitchell. You're pushing them right into the other tribes."

Again Hawkes looked at Fitzpatrick. "You know I'm right," he continued. "You know the Dakota better than me. Never had much to do with them. But I've watched them up close these past weeks. They are a proud people, and strong, and they have a fondness for war."

"Their principal chiefs have signed the treaty," said Mitchell.

"Sure they did. Because you promised them that the lands they now occupy will be theirs forever."

"That's the agreement," said the Indian Affairs man. "All we want is peace on the plains. And safe passage for our people who are bound for points west."

Hawkes sighed. "You were talking about the future a minute ago. Just how far into that future are you looking?"

"I'm not sure I know what you mean," said Mitchell, wiping his face with a soiled handkerchief.

"Look around you. Maybe you don't have a high opinion of this country, but once California and Oregon fill up, folks will think to look twice at this land, and they'll begin to see the possibilities. They'll know what the Mormons have done down in Desiree. Brigham Young said the Saints would make the desert bloom, and in a few short years they have done just that. You're worried about keeping the tribes within their boundaries. But how will you keep white settlers from crossing those boundaries, sir? And when that happens—and it surely will—your treaty won't be worth the paper and ink it took to make it."

Nonplussed and more than a little annoyed, Mitchell stared at him. Hawkes could understand why, and he regretted his words. The superintendent had toiled long and hard to make the peace council a successful endeavor, and at this moment of triumph Hawkes had rained on his parade.

"Well, Gordon," said Mitchell, wearing a tight smile, "you are a hardened skeptic, aren't you?"

"I guess so. And I could be wrong."

"I hope you are, sir. I sincerely hope that you are."

"Me, too," said Hawkes, but he knew in his heart that he wasn't. He tried to tell himself that even so— even if a long and bloody war between red men and white men was inevitable—it would not affect him or his family. He could remain aloof from it all, safe and secure in his high-country hideaway.

Parting company with Mitchell and Fitzpatrick, he returned to the Absaroke encampment. Already preparations were well under way for the departure of the Indians. The skin lodges were coming down. Travois were being loaded up. It was time for the great buffalo hunt. Excitement hung in the air. Red Bear invited Hawkes to come along, but he declined. The Absaroke chief thanked him again for his help during the peace council.

"You are the only white man that I trust completely, White Crow," admitted Red Bear.

"If you don't trust them, why did you sign that treaty?"

Red Bear looked about him at all the activity in the encampment. Behind him, his wives and daughters were removing the buffalo-hide lodge covering from its skeleton of poles. Hawkes reflected again on Mitchell's assertion that in order to survive, the Indian would have to give up his nomadic ways and become a "civilized" tiller of the soil. Back East, the Cherokee and certain other tribes had managed to do just that. But the Cherokee were not Plains Indians.

"I put my mark on the paper," said Red Bear sadly, "in return for a year or two of peace for my people. That is all."

Hawkes nodded. The Absaroke chief was a realist. He too was a hardened skeptic, and he knew better than Mitchell what the future held. But then, he had good reason to. Red Bear had signed the treaty to buy some time. Nothing more or less than that. Hawkes just wondered how *much* time had been purchased.

Within the hour he was riding west, putting Fort Laramie behind him, heading for the mountains, accompanied by thoughts of a happy reunion with Eliza and the kids—an anticipation tempered by an ill-defined dread that kept nagging at him. Not dread for himself, but for the Absaroke and their future. He resolved to linger a while in the Wind River village, to share just a handful more idyllic days with his Indian friends, knowing that such days were now numbered.

Chapter 3

A vivid mountain sunset had brought a rosy blush to the darkening sky when Cameron Hawkes slipped out of the Absaroke village, then paused at the edge of the trees to watch and wait. He had told his mother only that he was going to take a walk. Guiltily he wondered what she would think if he had told her the truth—that he was here to meet Walks in the Sun, the Crow girl with whom he had fallen madly in love. He hated to mislead his mother, but he feared she would sternly disapprove, perhaps even prevent him from keeping the rendezvous. She would say that he was too young. Only fifteen, Cameron did not want to hear his mother remind him that he was just a boy who could not know the true meaning of love. Because he *did* know. His heart knew. He longed for his father's return, because he had always been able to talk to his father about everything.

As the day drew to a close and the night shadows slowly deepened in the valley, Cameron watched the village and the many pinpricks of yellow flame that marked the cook fires, aching all the while for his first glimpse of Walks. It was difficult to arrange a little time alone with her. He had known her almost all his life—she was one of the many Crow children he had played with during the summers when his father brought him and his mother down out of the mountains. Oddly, he had paid no particular attention to her—until this year. Returning one day from a hunt, he had happened upon her and a few other girls who were collecting firewood in these very woods. It was the first time they'd seen one another this summer, and when she turned to look up at him and smiled, his world changed forever. Cameron's cheeks burned as he remembered that moment—a moment of indescribable joy and wonder, as well as pure terror. He hadn't been able to say anything, or do anything, for that matter, except flee the scene, kicking his horse into a gallop and making for the village.

One might have thought that such behavior on his part would have convinced Walks that he wasn't worth further effort. Certainly Cameron hadn't expected her ever to acknowledge his existence again, much less smile at him. Much to his surprise, though, she continued smiling. In fact, she seemed to go out of her way to be in a position to smile at him. Every time he turned around, Walks in the Sun was there, watching him, her eyes harboring a beguiling blend of girlish wonder and womanly wisdom. Not one to make the same mistake twice, Cameron acquainted himself with her daily routine and conspired to be somewhere in the vicinity when she went out to collect firewood or gather water. Walks liked to take long strolls along the river's edge in the early evening, and he often managed to be there too.

They tried always to meet away from the village, but of course they could not conceal their attraction for one another from others for long. The friends of Walks in the Sun were the first to notice it. And then there were the young men of the village, many of whom had their eyes on Walks because she was one of the prettiest girls in Red Bear's band. Some of her would-be suitors came to resent Cameron, but he didn't care. Most of the young Absaroke who looked at Walks were older than he. It was Crow custom that a young man did not marry until he was about twenty-five years old and had counted coup in battle. At the same time, Walks was fast approaching the marrying age. At this point Cameron couldn't bear to think of her being married to another man. And it had become increasingly obvious to all concerned that Walks had no interest in anyone but him. That in itself was wonderful from Cameron's point of view, but as a practical matter it didn't count for much in Crow society. By no means was Walks completely free to decide for herself which man she would take as a husband.

As the night shadows deepened he began to worry. Where was she? What was keeping her? Maybe she wasn't coming. Maybe she just wasn't able to get away. It would be impossible to conceal from her own family forever the fact that she was in love. And it was unlikely that her parents would approve of her choice. For one thing, he was white, and that was a crucial factor, in spite of the fact that his father was the adopted brother of the Absaroke. For another, he was just a boy, untested in battle. He had certainly never counted coup! And third, he had no material possessions to speak of. He had no horses to offer Walks in the Sun's father in return for his daughter's hand. Her parents would want to be sure that she was well provided for by a man who would bring glory, and prosperity, to the family.

Cameron shook his head, trying to drive such

thoughts from his mind. He didn't want to think about the future in a practical, logical way. What did logic have to do with love, anyway? His lanky frame propped up against a tree, he leaned his head back and shut his eyes. Being in love was such wonder—and such agony too. Not long ago he had looked forward to spending time with his Crow male friends, hunting and riding and fishing. Now none of that appealed to him. All he had been wanting to do lately was be with Walks. When he was with her it was like being in paradise. Nothing else mattered. But when they were apart, the ache in his heart was almost more than he could bear. All he could think about were her dark eyes, her smiling lips, her warm skin, her slender body. Just the thought of her excited him. It was a miracle that his mother had not noticed the change in him. Fortunately she was preoccupied with her task of trying to convert the Absarokes to Christianity.

"Cameron!"

His eyes snapped open. Walks in the Sun was running toward him, her beautiful face luminous with joy. For one heart-stopping moment he thought she might fly straight into his arms—but then she pulled up short, and Cameron couldn't decide if he was disappointed or relieved. She cast an anxious glance over her shoulder, in the direction of the village.

"What's the matter, Walks?" he asked. "Is there something wrong?"

"My sister," she said, and then looked at him and laughed softly. "She thinks she is wise in the ways of love just because she is older than me and will soon be Long Hair's woman."

"What has she done?"

"She has done nothing. But she thinks I left tonight

to meet with a man. She asked me if this was so. I told her to mind her own business." Again Walks laughed. Usually her laugh was enough to make Cameron grin like a fool from ear to ear. But this time he was frowning instead.

"What if she tells your mother?" he fretted.

"Tells my mother what? She does not know anything." With a mischievous gleam in her eye, Walks tilted her head to one side and glanced sidelong at him through a cascade of raven-black hair. "What would you do, Cameron, if my mother told me never to be alone with you again?"

Cameron almost told her the truth—that he would feel like dying, because life would hold no meaning for him anymore if she were not a part of it.

"I don't know," he said glumly. "Guess there wouldn't be anything I could do about it."

She gazed earnestly into his eyes for a moment. Mortified, Cameron sensed that his response was not the one she had wanted to hear. Then she touched his arm.

"Come, I want to go down to the river."

He walked along beside her, through the trees to the river's edge.

"It is said that evil creatures live in the water," said Walks, watching the river tumble over its rocky course. "There is a place in Big Horn Canyon, where a beast that is half man and half wolf lives in a waterfall. When people come too close he jumps out of the falls and kills them, dragging them back into his cave, where he eats their flesh. All water creatures eat people. That is why it is always a good idea to throw some meat into a river before you cross it. The water creature will eat the meat and not be so hungry."

Cameron didn't know what to say. Of course all that was complete nonsense, and he thought about trying to convince Walks that there really were no water creatures.

"But you do not believe in these things," she said, smiling at him. "You are a Christian. You do not think there are any water creatures."

"Well," said Cameron, trying to be diplomatic in his answer, "there is evil in the world, sure. It's all Satan's handiwork. His goal is to corrupt the soul and crush the spirit of every person."

"There are spirits in all things. In that tree. In the stone beneath your feet. And there are spirits from the other world. There are spirit horsemen who sometimes appear when Crow warriors are battling their enemies. Our men never see them, but the enemy does, and they are terrified and run away."

"I don't know that there are that many differences between what you believe and what I believe, really," said Cameron. "For example, the Absaroke believe they are descended from Man Alone . . ."

"Yes. Magah-Lawathus. He gave us our language."

"Well, Christians believe that we came from the first man, whose name was Adam. And the first woman was called Eve."

"No," said Walks. "The first woman was called Red Woman. She was very bad. Her bones were made of stone. One day the Absaroke captured her. They tied her to a stake and burned her. All her flesh melted away, and her bones made of stone were so hot that they exploded when a cold rain fell on them. The arrowheads that we find are all that is left of Red Woman's bones."

"I have heard about how your god, First Worker,

created the world," said Cameron. "How in the beginning the world was covered with water. First Worker sent a duck below the surface, and the duck returned with clay in its bill. First Worker took some of the clay and formed it into a cake and threw it out upon the water and created the land, the plains and the mountains, so that the water was confined by the land into rivers and lakes. Then First Worker made the grass and the trees grow upon the land. He took the little clay that he had left and made a man and a woman. Soon there were many people and they separated themselves into tribes. In the beginning the tribes all spoke the same language, but one day First Worker made it so that they all spoke with different tongues."

Walks nodded, smiling. "Yes, that is how it happened."

"Well, you see, the way we look at how it all began is really a lot like that. God made the earth and he made Adam and Eve, the first man and woman, out of clay. He breathed life into them, and for a while they lived in the Garden of Eden, a place free from want or worry, a paradise on earth. But then they broke God's law and ate forbidden fruit, and God cast them out of the Garden. They suffered a great deal, but they had children, and their children had children, and so on." Cameron glanced at Walks, and the way she was smiling at him made him blush furiously, and he could only hope that it was dark enough that she couldn't tell. "Anyway, at first everybody spoke the same language. But one day, when the people gathered together at a place called Babel, God made it so that they spoke different languages."

"Why did your god do that?"

"I have to admit I'm not too clear on that part."

Cameron looked sheepishly at his moccasin-clad feet. "Guess that must strike you as odd, since my mother puts such great store in religion. But my point is, I don't know why you couldn't say that my God and your First Worker aren't one and the same. We may call Him by different names, and the stories we tell about His work might be a little different in some of the details, but that doesn't mean He isn't the same God."

Walks considered his words carefully. "Your mother does not believe they are the same. She tells us that unless we forsake First Worker and accept her god we will not cross over to the Other World when we die."

Cameron frowned. "Yeah, I know she does."

"Would I have to believe in your god, Cameron, if I wanted to be your woman?"

Cameron nearly strangled on the lump that suddenly formed in his throat. "Well, I . . . I don't . . . I mean I . . ."

"Because your father, when he was a young man, not much older than you, took an Absaroke girl as his woman."

"Yes, that's right," said Cameron. "Her name was Mokamea. She was given to him by the chief whose wife and son my father saved from the river."

"Did they believe in the same god?"

"I don't know." Cameron swallowed hard. "Walks?"

"Yes, Cameron."

"Your sister thinks you're in love, doesn't she?"

"Yes, she thinks so."

"Um, are you?"

Walks reached out and placed her hand on his chest. Cameron was sure she could feel his heart racing beneath the buckskin of his hunting shirt. He stared at her, scarcely daring to breathe, not believing that he had actually had the gall to ask such a question. But she was not looking into his eyes. Her gaze roamed all over him, taking in every inch of his rangy frame.

"Yes," she said, barely above a whisper. "I am in love."

Cameron wanted to shout with joy. He took her hand in his and held it tightly, and their eyes met. He thought hers reflected the love and the passion that he knew shone brightly in his own. But the moment was too fleeting, for then Walks looked away, and though she did not pull away, Cameron let go of her hand.

"But soon you will have to leave, as you always do," she said pensively. "When your father returns he will take you home."

Cameron knew with absolute conviction that he could not endure the long winter of separation from her that lay ahead, the many months that would have to pass before he could see Walks in the Sun again.

"Maybe," he said, a hollow desperation echoing in his voice, "maybe I could stay."

"They will not let you stay, Cameron," she said, a sorrowful reproach.

He knew who she meant by "they"—his own folks. His mother's reaction to such a notion was an ironclad certainty. She would be dead set against it. As for his father, Cameron couldn't be sure.

"Then I'll think of something," he promised.

She stood there in thoughtful silence for a long moment, gazing at the river, listening to its song as the water rushed over the rocks, and he dared not intrude on her thoughts.

"Your father might come back tomorrow," she said softly.

"I guess he could. But it could be a good while yet."

"If it is tomorrow, then tonight would be . . ."

She didn't finish her thought, turning to him instead and putting her slender arms around his neck, pressing her willowy body against his. Her warm breath on his lips aroused his passion, and he kissed her, tentatively at first, then more boldly. Her enthusiastic response fed the fires within him, and he took her in his arms and kissed her again, this time even more feverishly. Breathless, she pushed away from him, and for an instant he was afraid that he had gone too far. But then she lifted her buckskin dress over her head, letting it drop to the ground, and stood there naked before him, watching him shyly. Stunned, Cameron stared at her. The night shadows accentuated the flare of a hip, the curve of a breast. Her lips were slightly parted, and she was breathing rapidly, as though she had run a long distance.

"Cameron," she whispered.

She did not need to say more. It was a beckoning, and he fumbled with his own clothes, shedding them clumsily, and took a step closer to her. Suddenly, with a nervous laugh, she turned and ran. He gave chase, and they sped through the dark woods, but didn't go far, because Walks in the Sun did not run as swiftly as she was capable of doing, and when he caught her they fell to the ground, their bodies entwined, kissing one another hungrily, their skin hot with desire as they discovered the ecstasy of two bodies becoming one and the wonder of two souls in communion.

Chapter 4

Gordon Hawkes rode into a storm of trouble when he returned to the Wind River Valley. Still miles away from the Absaroke village, he was met by three warriors, all of whom were members of the Fox Clan, who seemed to come out of nowhere to intercept him. They weren't belligerent, but they didn't come across as all that friendly either. All they would tell him was that, for the moment anyway, he could not proceed. One of the braves rode away in the direction of the village. Hawkes didn't cotton to people telling him where he could and could not go. He had lived the free mountain life far too long for that kind of thing not to stick in his craw. On top of that, he missed his family terribly; a throbbing and persistent ache had taken up residence in his heart.

Now, to make matters worse, he worried about their well-being. Had something happened to Eliza or one of his children? He gave serious thought to challenging the warriors who had detained him, but good sense prevailed. They were charged with keeping him away from the village, and they would go to any lengths to carry out that duty. Hawkes knew that if he took these men on he would not come out the winner. So he dismounted and settled down in the shade with his back to a tree and spent his time striving to control the anxiety that threatened to seize control and lead him to rashness.

Fortunately he didn't have to wait long. The third warrior returned in less than half an hour, accompanied by He Smiles Twice. Hawkes could tell that both men had pushed their ponies hard. He jumped to his feet as He Smiles Twice executed an agile running dismount, and he could tell by the expression on his friend's face that something was definitely wrong.

"My family," breathed Hawkes, his heart pounding against his rib cage.

"They are well," said He Smiles Twice.

Hawkes drew a long breath, trying to calm himself. "Thank God. Then what has happened?"

He Smiles Twice took him by the arm and led him deeper into the trees that grew along the river, until they were well out of earshot of the other Fox Clan warriors.

"My friend, you know that an Absaroke who seeks a woman to be his mate places much importance on her purity."

"Yes, I'm aware of that. So?"

He Smiles Twice looked away, his brows knit as he concentrated on finding just the right words.

"Crazy Dog has a daughter who is called Walks in the Sun. She has seen fifteen summers. Soon she will be of an age to marry. But Crazy Dog is very angry and wonders what man will want to take his daughter as a wife now that she is no longer pure."

"Dammit, get to the point," snapped Hawkes. "What does this have to do with me?" He made sign with sharp gestures to reinforce his words. "Talk straight."

He Smiles Twice nodded gravely. "Your son has lain with Crazy Dog's daughter."

For a moment Hawkes was speechless. His first reaction was to think this was all some kind of joke. Indians were notorious pranksters. But a search of the Absaroke warrior's features persuaded him that He Smiles Twice was in earnest. His second thought was that there had to be some colossal misunderstanding.

"How do you know this to be true?" he asked.

"Your son said it was true, White Crow. And since he is your son I know he would not lie."

Hawkes turned away. If Cameron said it was so, then it was so. *Poor Eliza*, he thought. He was well aware that his wife's aspirations for Cameron did not include an Indian wife or a life spent in the mountains. She wanted him to marry a good Christian woman and live and prosper in the white man's world. He knew all this even though they had not talked over such matters to any great extent; for a number of reasons Hawkes simply preferred to avoid the subject. But he could see that they were going to have to talk about it now.

He Smiles Twice put a hand on his shoulder. "There is more that you should know. Crazy Dog's son, Raven, has said he will kill your son. We have kept him from doing it. But Raven will not let the matter rest. He stirs up trouble among some of the others, those who stand against closer friendship between the Absaroke and the *masta-cheula*, the white man."

Hawkes nodded. It was inevitable that this incident would not remain confined to the personal level. Some of those who had remained behind in the Wind River Valley when Red Bear rode off to the peace council at Fort Laramie did so because of their supreme indiffer-

ence, if not outright hostility, to the idea of a peaceful
coexistence between white interlopers and red neighbors. The Crows had more or less kept the peace with
the whites, but that didn't mean there wasn't a small,
and vocal, minority who opposed this policy. Here,
then, was a perfect excuse to stir up trouble—the deflowering of a Crow maiden by a white man. Hawkes
was well aware of the presence of this faction among
the Absaroke. He realized that he and his family were
a particularly handy target for their animosity. As
White Crow, Hawkes posed a real threat to them, for
he represented the good relations that had thus far
prevailed between the *masta-cheula* and the tribe. That
it was his son standing in the middle of this present
controversy only added to their fervor.

Hawkes turned to He Smiles Twice. "What do you
want me to do?" he asked, his composure regained, his
voice as calm as a summer's evening.

"It is for me and my brothers in the Fox Clan to keep
peace among our people. This we will do. But we need
your help, White Crow."

"I understand," said Hawkes gently. "I will not
strike a blow except to defend my own. You have my
word. But it is up to you and your brothers to keep
Raven and the other troublemakers under control."

He Smiles Twice nodded. Hawkes turned to his
horse, but then he thought of something. He faced the
Absaroke again.

"Thank you," he said. "You could have brought my
family out of the village to meet me."

"I would not show you such disrespect, White
Crow."

"For that I am grateful." For He Smiles Twice to
have done such a thing—escorting Eliza and Cameron

and Grace out of the village—might have seemed a sensible course of action, one almost certain to prevent a confrontation. But it would have been a grave insult to Hawkes. Though his skin was white, Hawkes was considered by most to be a full-fledged Absaroke warrior, and one did not deny a warrior his right to take care of his own family and to face his enemies.

As Hawkes mounted, He Smiles Twice went to his own pony, and with a final nod at the mountain man, turned his mount to gallop back to the village accompanied by the other three Fox Clan warriors. Hawkes would be permitted to enter the village alone, without escort or bodyguard—another gesture of respect.

Steeling himself, Hawkes kicked his horse into a canter, following in the wake of the Crow braves.

His arrival in the village did not bring any untoward attention. A number of the Absarokes stopped what they were doing and came forth to greet him and welcome him home. There were no urgent queries regarding the outcome of the peace council, because Red Bear had sent a messenger ahead to carry the news of the treaty signing to those who had stayed behind in the Wind River country. Hawkes kept his eyes peeled for trouble but saw nothing to cause him concern.

Arriving at the skin lodge that had been erected for his family before his departure for Fort Laramie, Hawkes noticed a pair of Fox Clan warriors standing together a short distance away. As he dismounted, Cameron emerged from the skin lodge.

"Hello, Pa. I can see you've heard about what's happened while you were gone."

"Yes, Cam, I have."

Grace burst out of the lodge and flew into his arms.

Laughing, Hawkes swept her off the ground and planted a big kiss on her cheek.

"How's my little princess? Did you miss me?"

"Yes, I did, don't be silly," scolded Grace. "What did you bring me from Fort Laramie?"

"Now, what makes you think I brought you anything?"

"Oh, dear! You mean you didn't?" Grace looked crestfallen.

Hawkes chuckled. "Well, okay. Maybe I did."

"Good! What is it? Tell me, please!"

"It's in my possibles bag. I'll fetch it in a minute."

"No, now! I want it right now! Please?"

"That's no way to be, Grace," said Eliza, coming out of the skin lodge.

Hawkes gave Grace another peck on the cheek before putting her down. Going to Eliza, he wrapped his arms around his wife and pulled her close to him. She curled her arms around his waist and rested her head against his chest. Hawkes experienced that rare sense of wholeness, of contentment, that he knew only when he was with his beloved wife.

"I missed you so much," she said softly. "I'm so very happy you're back, safe and sound."

"Did you bring Mommy something back from Fort Laramie, too?" asked Grace.

Hawkes had to smile. "Yes, I believe I did."

"Oh, good," said Grace. "Mommy, can I go play now?"

Hawkes felt a sudden tension stiffen Eliza's slender frame.

"You'd better stay close by, Grace," she replied.

"But why? I'm tired of sitting in that smelly old tipi!"

"It's okay, Grace," said Hawkes. "You run along and play."

Grace beamed at him and scampered away in search of her friends.

"Gordon, it simply isn't safe," whispered Eliza.

"No one would dare harm a hair on her head," he replied.

Eliza stepped back and glanced at Cameron. "I suppose," she said to Hawkes, "that you are aware of what has happened while you were away."

"He Smiles Twice told me."

Eliza nodded. "You will want to talk to Cam." With that she went back to the skin lodge.

"Let's take a walk," Hawkes told his son.

Cameron glanced at the two Fox Clan warriors.

"Come on," said Hawkes and started walking.

Cameron fell in alongside him, throwing a look over his shoulder to see if the Fox Clan warriors were going to follow.

"Don't worry about them, son."

"I'm not worried."

Hawkes threw a sidelong glance at him.

"Well, okay, maybe I am, a little," confessed Cameron.

"They aren't your problem."

"You're mad?"

"No, not mad. Some disappointed, though."

"We're in love, Pa, Walks and me."

"That's good. I'm glad. Hate to think you'd stir up this much dust over a girl you didn't love."

"Didn't mean for this to happen. It just did. I—I couldn't help it."

"You could have. You just weren't using your head."

"Maybe not. But you did the same thing."

"Not exactly the same. For one thing, Mokamea and I were brought together by an Absaroke chief. She was his daughter. From what I hear, Crazy Dog didn't give his blessing to you and Walks."

"Well, no . . ."

"And besides, that business with Mokamea was a big mistake. I found out soon enough. But I was a young fool and didn't know any better."

Cameron's lips tightened as he became even more defensive. Now he was being labeled a young fool. Why was it so difficult for adults to understand that just because a person was young didn't automatically mean he or she had no common sense? But Cameron also knew he could not afford to push his father too far. He had to remain calm and employ reason in his argument. He had to make someone see his side of things.

"Have you and your mother talked about this at all?" asked Hawkes.

"No. She doesn't want to talk about it. Pa, I never set out to hurt anybody. I never wanted to make trouble for you or Ma. But I . . ."

"I know. You're in love with her."

"Yes, I am." Cameron studied his father's face. "Don't you believe me?"

"I believe you, Cam. But being in love sometimes just isn't enough. It just can't stand alone on its own legs."

"Not enough?" Cameron frowned, trying without much success to figure out exactly what his father meant. "Feels like it's all that matters. I want to be with Walks for the rest of my life, Pa. And she feels the same way about me. I know she does. I can't leave her here. I'm going to stay. I've got to!"

Hawkes stopped in his tracks. "You're going to stay?"

"Yes. Either that or she leaves with me."

Hawkes took a long look around. Here he stood with his son in the middle of the Absaroke village, with a hundred pairs of eyes on him, talking about his son's future and perhaps his very life—and he felt like laughing. In spite of this predicament, he couldn't help but marvel at Cameron's stubborn resolve to have things his own way regardless of the consequences. Eliza had remarked on more than one occasion that Cameron was a lot like him in so many ways. Hawkes hadn't really seen it—until now.

"Cam," he said, "there is just no way on earth that I would let you stay here."

Cameron's face turned red. He clenched his fists. "Nobody and nothing is gonna keep me and Walks apart."

"You can't stay here, son. You'll end up dead."

"I'm not afraid of Crazy Dog or his son."

"You should be. Do you think that just because you're my son you won't come to harm?"

Cameron looked at the ground, pondering his father's words. "Okay, then. She and I will have to run away together."

"That won't happen, either."

"I won't be apart from her. I—I can't!"

"Has she said she would go with you?"

"No. But she doesn't have to tell me. I know she would."

"That may be so. But if you loved her you wouldn't let her run off with you. If she left without her father's permission she would be banished from the tribe forever. Do you want her to be an outcast, shunned by her own people?"

"Well, no, I guess not."

"'Course you don't. Best thing for you to do is leave it alone for a while. Let everything die down."

"And not see her again until next summer? I can't go that long."

"Yes, you can. Between now and then we'll get some plews together. Get our hands on some ponies. By next summer you'll have something to offer Crazy Dog."

Cameron seized at this thread of hope as though it was a lifeline. "Do you think he would even listen?"

"Could be. Especially if Red Bear asks him to."

Cameron drew a long breath. "That's the only way, isn't it?"

Hawkes put a hand on his son's shoulder. "That's how I see it. I know that from where you're standing it looks like you'll have to wait forever. But it won't be as bad as you think."

"But—but what if something happens between now and next summer? I mean, what if Walks . . ."

Hawkes smiled. "She loves you, doesn't she?"

"Yes."

"You sure?"

"I'm sure."

"Then she'll be here, waiting for you, next year."

Cameron sighed in pure anguish and said, "I have to see her one more time before we go."

"Don't know if that will be possible. If not, we can make sure she gets a message from you. How's that?"

"What about Ma?"

"We'll have all winter to work on her," said Hawkes, grinning. "Between us we should be able to convert her."

"She just thinks I'm being foolish. She'll say that by next summer I'll be over this infatuation. But she's dead wrong. I know this is real."

"Okay." Hawkes draped an arm around his son's broad shoulders. "Come on, we'd better be getting back. I think we should head for home in the morning. Sticking around here any longer won't do anybody a lick of good, especially not you."

Cameron nodded sadly.

They had just turned and begun to retrace their steps when a shout of warning caused Hawkes to whirl around. Two men were running straight toward him. He recognized one as a Fox Clan warrior. The other, running in front, was a young brave, and there was hate in his eyes and a knife in his hand. Hawkes didn't need a formal introduction to know that this had to be Raven, Crazy Dog's son and Walks's brother. Pushing Cameron away, Hawkes instinctively laid his hand on the pistol in his belt. The U.S. Model 1836 flintlock fired a .54-caliber ball, and at close range it could drop a charging grizzly if the shot was well placed. Hawkes judged that he could draw and fire before Raven got close enough to use that knife.

But he decided to leave the gun alone and instead engaged the Absaroke bare-handed. As Raven closed in, Hawkes blocked the knife stroke with his left arm and drove a fist into the young man's face. His nose spurting bright-red blood, Raven landed flat on his back. Hawkes stepped on his wrist and pried the knife out of his fingers, then knelt on Raven's chest and put the blade to the Absaroke's throat.

"This time you live," he said with a fierce calm. "But if there chances to be a next time, you will surely die."

The Fox Clan warrior arrived and tried to pull

Hawkes off the fallen Raven. Hawkes shrugged the man off, stood, and tossed the knife aside contemptuously. In an instant several more Fox Clan warriors appeared on the scene. A crowd was quickly gathering. It was obvious by the resentment on their faces that some of the young men converging on Hawkes and his son were on Raven's side of the issue. Raven was helped to his feet. Bleeding and reeling, Crazy Dog's son was led away. The Fox Clan warriors formed a protective circle around Hawkes and Cameron. Turning to his son, Hawkes could see that Cam wasn't too happy with him either.

"I'm old enough to fight my own fights," said Cameron.

"Maybe so," conceded Hawkes. "But are you old enough not to have killed him? Let's get out of here before somebody does get killed."

Cameron followed in his father's wake as the crowd, ominously subdued, parted to let them pass.

Later that day Hawkes and his family left the Absaroke village. He Smiles Twice promised to deliver a message to Walks from Cameron. "Tell her I love her," said Cameron, feeling perfectly wretched. "Tell her— tell her that I will be back, and that I'll be thinking about her every minute that we're apart. Tell her . . . well, I guess that's all."

He Smiles Twice thanked Hawkes for refraining from taking Raven's life.

"I hold no grudge against him," said the mountain man. "It is a matter of honor with him, and I understand that. But if he or anyone else comes after us, I will have no choice—I will kill them."

"No one will follow you, White Crow."

He Smiles Twice was right. Though he took extra

care in checking his back trail, Hawkes saw no sign of pursuit. Cameron kept an eye on their back trail, too, hoping against all reason that he would see Walks, rushing to be with him. By the third day he had given up hope.

PART TWO

1858

Chapter 1

When Fort Union came into view, Gordon Hawkes checked his mountain mustang and sat in the saddle for a spell, resting his arms on the saddle horn, gazing at the distant outpost and sorting through the memories that came rushing toward him like a stampede of ghost horses.

Located on a low bluff at the mouth of the Yellowstone River, Fort Union was the biggest and most bustling trading post on the frontier. From the outset it had been owned and operated by the American Fur Company. More than twenty years earlier, Hawkes had visited it for the very first time. Back then he had been in the company of Robert Campbell's Rocky Mountain Fur Company expedition. The RMFC had intended to build an outpost to rival Fort Union. While the post had been built, it had never come anywhere close to Fort Union in terms of importance or volume of trade.

These days, the Rocky Mountain Fur Company was nothing more than a fond memory. In the epic contest between the two enterprises, it had come out on the losing end. With the benefit of hindsight, Hawkes could see that the RMFC had been doomed from the first. It had never been much more than a loose alliance of strongly independent trappers and traders, united by precious little except varying degrees of animosity toward the American Fur Company. The latter, on the other hand, was an efficiently run organization that demanded, and received, complete and utter loyalty from its employees. No one in the Rocky Mountain Fur Company had ever considered himself an *employee*. The leaders of the American Fur Company had always kept one goal in mind—the domination of the western fur trade. That goal had been accomplished.

Twenty years earlier, Fort Union had been run by a man named Kenneth "Redcoat" McKenzie, and to this ruthless and brilliant Scotsman belonged much of the credit for the success of the American Fur Company. Born in Inverness in 1801, McKenzie had first come to America in the service of the British fur outfits. It was he who had erected Fort Union and used the post as his headquarters during his highly successful campaign to expand the influence of the company over the various Plains tribes. His greatest accomplishment had been a treaty between the company and the Blackfoot Alliance, a diplomatic coup that opened up a vast new beaver country—country that had always remained off limits to the RMFC. But McKenzie had made the mistake of opening a distillery at Fort Union and providing whiskey to the Indians, in violation of the laws of the United States. When word got out, the company's reputation was sullied and McKenzie was forced to resign.

As of late, Fort Union was run by Alexander Culbertson, a Pennsylvanian of Scotch-Irish descent who had fought the Seminoles in Florida before joining the American Fur Company. With McKenzie gone, Culbertson was the most powerful man in the Missouri fur trade, and he ensured the profitable alliance between the company and the Blackfoot Alliance by marrying a Blackfoot woman. Being neither as arrogant nor flamboyant as McKenzie, Major Culbertson was well respected by nearly everyone who came in contact with him. But then, he had no need to be as ruthless or predatory as his predecessor. The company no longer had any rivals to contend with. Its hegemony over the fur trade was unchallenged. Since beaver hats were now out of fashion, having been replaced by headgear covered in China silk, the company had turned its attention to the harvesting of buffalo.

At the moment, one of Gordon's companions, Robert Meldrum, was studying the distant outpost and its immediate environs with a spyglass. Meldrum had lived with the River Crow on and off for twenty years, and had married into White Bull's band. With his dark hair, dark complexion, and Indian clothing, he would have passed for an Indian but for his thick beard. He had fought bravely with the River Crow against their Alliance enemies and was said to have taken five Piegan scalps in one battle. But from the start he had been in the employ of the American Fur Company, which often assigned employees the task of living among the Indians so that they might act as go-betweens. For this reason, Red Bear and the Mountain Crow did not entirely trust Meldrum always to have the tribe's best interests at heart. And that was why Gordon Hawkes, who sat his mountain mustang and eyed Fort Union without enthusiasm, was here.

"Can't see the river from here," said Meldrum, "but I see steam rising, so I reckon the riverboat is there.

And there sure seems to be a good deal of hustle and bustle up along the bluff."

"Then we should hurry," suggested Plenty Coups, the third member of the party, "before Redding sells all of the goods that belong to us to your friend, the one called Culbertson."

Not amused, Meldrum lowered the spyglass and peered at Plenty Coups. "That's just a wild rumor, my friend. You ought not to put so much stock in it."

Plenty Coups smiled, but there was no warmth or humor in his expression. The product of the union between a French voyageur and a Crow maiden, he was a warrior of great repute among the River Crow and of considerable value to the tribe because he spoke fluent English and French. Hawkes had met him once before, at the Fort Laramie peace council seven years ago, but only briefly. Now, having been on the trail with the man for the past two weeks, he had come to respect Plenty Coups's intelligence. The warrior's fighting prowess he could take on faith; the eagle feathers woven into his long mane of hair vouched for that.

"I know this much," replied Plenty Coups, "and so do you, Round Iron—in the past few years my people have not received everything that the White Father promised us at Laramie."

Meldrum—called Round Iron by the Crow because he had once been extremely generous in handing out the worthless iron medallions circulated by the American Fur Company as tokens of friendship with the Indians—simply smirked and moved his shoulders in a what-can-I-do shrug. "You seem to forget, Plenty Coups, that they are my people, too."

"So you say."

Hawkes had learned early on that there was no love

lost between Meldrum and Plenty Coups, and he was in no mood to suffer through another verbal sparring match between the pair. So he gathered up the reins, tapped his heels against his mustang's belly, and put the horse in motion.

"You two pick that bone later," he said. "I came here to take care of some business."

Their arrival at the fort did not attract much undue notice. There was always a lot of coming and going at Fort Union this time of year. Dozens of trappers, traders, scouts, buffalo runners, and rivermen made this post their base of operations. Culbertson kept a small army of American Fur Company employees as a kind of garrison, and many had wives and families with them. The majority of their wives were Indian. In addition, a regular army detachment had set up camp here, their tents in a neat row beneath the eastern wall.

On the other side of the post, and some distance removed, stood about thirty tipis. Hawkes could tell by their lodge markings that this was a Sioux encampment. The Dakotas had expanded westward in the past few years, just as he had known they would. They were not content to remain within the boundaries established for them by the Fort Laramie Treaty; instead they insisted on encroaching on a wide corridor of land set aside by the treaty terms for use as a passageway for American emigrants bound for California and Oregon. The problem for the United States government was the fact that the Sioux nation was powerful and warlike. Short of waging war, the government had no way of compelling the Sioux to abide by the boundary lines drawn on a map. The fact that the White Father was turning a blind eye to their activities only emboldened the Dakotas.

Hawkes knew full well that it was the presence of
the Sioux that was responsible for his being here now.

As they reached the bustling post, he could see the
river below the bluff. A shallow-draft riverboat was
moored to a dock down there, gray-black smoke bil-
lowing from its twin stacks. The vessel was apparently
on the verge of embarking, no doubt bound downriver
with a load of company furs destined for Independence. Hawkes could only hope that this same boat
had brought the government annuity that was ear-
marked for his Crow friends. In addition to the steam-
boat, there were keelboats and mackinaws and canoes
on the river.

They found Culbertson in the fort, supervising an
inventory of the post magazine. Culbertson knew Meldrum, who introduced him to Plenty Coups and then
to Hawkes, who, of course, was known not by his own
name but rather by the alias Henry Gordon. Few and
far between, in fact, were those on the frontier who
knew his true identity.

"Pleased to make your acquaintance, Mr. Gordon,"
said Culbertson, a tall, spare man whose grip was
strong as he shook hands with Hawkes. "I've heard
about you. You're one of the few white men who has
managed to earn the trust and respect of the Mountain
Crows."

"It's for them that I've come here," said Hawkes.

"Oh, yes, the annuity. It arrived several days ago.
Mr. Redding, the Indian Affairs man, should be
around here somewhere. Come to my quarters for a
drink or two while I send someone to locate him."

Culbertson's quarters included the very same room
in which Hawkes had first met Kenneth "Redcoat"
McKenzie more than twenty years earlier. Bearskins

covered the floor and maps adorned the walls. The big stone hearth stood cold. Though well worn, the ornate furniture looked out of place on the frontier. Meldrum sank his weary frame into a velvet-upholstered wing chair, but Hawkes and Plenty Coups preferred to stand while Culbertson's half-breed daughter, a dark-haired and fair-skinned beauty in a calico dress, served them drinks. Meldrum, Hawkes, and Plenty Coups settled for Tennessee sour mash, while Culbertson indulged his proclivity for cognac.

"I will try to assist you in every way possible to get that annuity to the Crows," said Culbertson pleasantly. "Is it your intention to take it overland or by river?"

"I saw half a dozen keelboats down on the river," said Hawkes. "Could you spare a couple of them?"

"They do not all belong to the company, but yes, I think we might be able to work something out, Mr. Gordon."

"How much would that cost us?"

"Why, nothing."

Meldrum hiked an eyebrow. "Did you say what I think you said, Major?"

Culbertson chuckled. "Do you think me a poor businessman now, Robert? In fact, my primary task is to maintain good relations between the company and all the tribes. We fare well with the Sioux nation. And thanks largely to the efforts of my predecessor, we also remain friendly with the Blackfoot Alliance. But we have not yet won over the Crows, now, have we, Robert? This, in spite of all you've tried to do over the years."

"It's the Mountain Crows that have been difficult to win over," said Meldrum, glancing at Hawkes.

Hawkes nodded. "That's right. But you have yourselves to blame for that. The Absaroke have been the mortal enemies of the Blackfeet for generations. Since you made friends with the Blackfoot Alliance you couldn't very well expect to be friendly with the Crows too. That's not realistic."

"But the Fort Laramie Treaty has brought the tribal wars to an end," said Culbertson. "The Crows no longer have anything to fear from the Alliance."

"That's what you think. And even if it was true, the Sioux pose an even greater threat to the Absaroke now."

"The Dakota are a threat to us all," remarked Plenty Coups gravely.

"Why do you think the Absaroke have refused to come here to get their annuity?" Hawkes asked Culbertson. "Because now the Sioux stand between them and this post."

"I am aware of no blood having been spilled between the Sioux and your Crow friends, Mr. Gordon."

"There hasn't been—yet. And it's something the Absaroke want to avoid at all costs."

Culbertson mulled this over. He knew perfectly well that there was some truth to what the mountain man was saying. In 1853 Agent Redding's predecessor, Alfred Vaughn, had brought that year's annuity to Fort Union but arrived too late. He discovered that the Crows had made the long journey from their homeland only to leave in disgust, believing that the government had failed to live up to its end of the bargain. Though Vaughn sent messengers out to bring the Crows back, the Absaroke had refused to return.

In 1854 Vaughn had transported both that year's annuity and the previous year's consignment to Fort Sarpy, a location considerably closer to the Absaroke homeland, but the tribe did not show up, and again Vaughn had to dispatch agents to bring them in. Some had come that time, albeit reluctantly. The following year, Vaughn had once again tried to transport the annuity to Fort Sarpy, but this time an attack by a Dakota war party had forced him to hasten back to the safety of Fort Union. He had reported the attack to his superiors, but Washington had declined to act on the information. Culbertson knew why. The government wanted to maintain the fiction that the peace accomplished by the Fort Laramie Treaty could still be relied upon by the thousands of immigrants streaming westward.

The American Fur Company had a big stake in maintaining that fiction as well. Quite simply, war was bad for business. Very bad. So Culbertson found himself in something of a quandary. He knew in his heart that Gordon was right. The Sioux nation could not be trusted. In fact, the Dakota were powder kegs waiting for a spark. The Crow were quite right not to put their faith in the government's treaty promises to keep the peace, and they were also right to avoid all contact with the Sioux. For one thing, they could not possibly win an all-out war with the Dakota. The Sioux nation was just too strong. *Hell,* mused Culbertson, *it would take the full might of the entire United States Army to quell a Sioux uprising.* But, knowing all this, Culbertson simply could not agree publicly with Gordon. He could concede nothing. To do so would jeopardize relations between the company and the Sioux nation, and that would be disastrous.

"There is one other matter," said Plenty Coups.

"Yes, there is," agreed Hawkes. "The Fort Laramie Treaty clearly states that the United States is responsi-

ble for delivering the annuities to the Absaroke. They
don't have to come and get them if they don't want to.
And if they don't come and get them, that doesn't free
the government from the responsibility of getting
those goods to them."

As he spoke, the door opened and Agent Redding
walked in—a paunchy man of medium height, bald-
ing but for thick black hair around his ears and bushy
side whiskers, the style of the day, framing a heavy-
jowled face.

"The problem is," he said, having heard Hawkes,
"we've been unable to establish an agency among the
Crows. They haven't been very cooperative."

Hawkes smiled bleakly. This was hardly a helpful
attitude for an Indian agent to have. But he wasn't surprised.

"Ah, Mr. Redding," said Culbertson. "These men
have come from the Absaroke to discuss the matter of
this year's annuity."

"I'm here to make sure they get what they've been
promised," said Hawkes, leveling a steady gaze on
Redding. "I'm talking about *all* of what they've been
promised."

"And I suppose you know exactly what that is," said
Redding, cautiously noncommittal.

Hawkes nodded. "You bet I do. Fifty pounds of
corn, forty pounds of hard bread, two thousand
pounds of sugar, a thousand pounds of coffee, twenty-
five hundred pounds of flour, nine thousand yards of
cloth, various quantities of buttons, thread, cooking
utensils, knives, horseshoes, lead and gunpowder, and
one hundred muskets. One hundred muskets in *work-
ing* order. Did I forget anything, Plenty Coups?"

"Yes, White Crow. Thirty silk cravats and thirty shawls."

Hawkes smiled wryly. "Oh, yeah. Mustn't forget the shawls and the cravats."

"You are well informed," said Redding. "But I can't help wonder what it is that you are implying. Why wouldn't the Crows get all of the annuity?"

"Not implying a thing," said Hawkes. "Just stating a simple fact. Telling you that I am here to see to it that every last button and coffee bean—and cravat—reaches the Absaroke."

"That is my intention as well, sir," said Redding stiffly.

"Good," replied Hawkes promptly. "Then we shouldn't have a problem."

"Gentlemen, gentlemen," said Culbertson soothingly. "We are all of like mind in this matter. So let us work together to accomplish our shared goal, shall we? Mr. Redding, Mr. Gordon here has inquired after the use of some keelboats to transport the annuity to the Crows."

Redding grimaced. "Did he, now? Well, it's my job to get those goods to the Indians, and that is what I am going to do. I intend to transport them up the river to Fort Sarpy, just like Agent Vaughn did before me. And then I will send messengers to summon the Crow chiefs. I will see to the keelboats and their crews."

"Then it seems, Mr. Gordon," said Culbertson, smiling amiably, "that you have come this long distance for nothing."

"I wouldn't say that. You see, I gave my word to Red Bear that those goods would reach his people, and I keep my word. So, Mr. Redding, I'm coming along.

Hope you don't have any objections. If so, I'd like to hear 'em now."

Redding's eyes narrowed. "You do not trust me, sir?"

"I'll trust you until I have a good reason not to. But you may as well know that there are rumors that some of the government annuities are being sold, with the profits going into private pockets."

"Outrageous accusations," snapped Redding, "not to mention untrue."

"I'm glad to hear that. So you won't mind if I tag along."

"Not at all," rasped the Indian agent. "Suit yourself."

"Well, I, for one, am perfectly satisfied with the arrangements," said Meldrum, "and I put my faith in Redding here. Reckon I'll stick around here for a spell and enjoy some more of your hospitality, Major." He finished off his sour mash.

Hawkes nodded. He didn't much mind parting company with Meldrum. "What about you, Plenty Coups?"

The Crow warrior was staring with thorough disapproval at Meldrum. "I too gave my word. I will come with you, White Crow."

"Fine," said Redding curtly. "Be prepared to leave in two days, three at the most."

"Until then," said Culbertson, "you will be my most welcome guests."

Hawkes didn't like the idea of lingering at Fort Union. Even though many years had passed since the murders of which he had been unjustly accused, he was still very much a fugitive, and Fort Union was a major frontier crossroads. Under different circumstances he would have ridden off into the seclusion and relative safety of the trackless plains, with the intent to return at the appointed time for the departure of the boats. But in this case he did not feel free to do that. He had to stay close by and keep an eye on the Crow annuity. Though he had no solid evidence to prove that Redding—and, who knew, maybe even Culbertson—were engaged in some kind of underhanded scheme to profit illegally at the expense of the Absaroke and the federal government, he had no good reason to trust these men, either. So he had to stay; he only hoped he could manage to keep a low profile.

He had no idea just how impossible that would be.

Chapter 2

Late the following morning, Plenty Coups found Hawkes sitting at the rim of the bluff beyond the walls of Fort Union. From this vantage point the mountain man could look down at the confluence of the Yellowstone and Missouri rivers, one of the great crossroads of the frontier. The riverboat had departed earlier, bound down the Big Muddy with a cargo of hides and furs that would be sold in eastern markets, the profits going into the already overflowing coffers of the American Fur Company. It was a hot and breathless day, and the sun, blazing in a sky of brass, hammered down upon his shoulders, but Hawkes had long ago become impervious to the harsh extremes of weather.

One look at the expression on the Crow warrior's face and Hawkes knew that something was wrong. His first thought was that it had something to do with the annuity destined for the Absaroke. This was stored within the outpost, and yesterday Hawkes had looked it over quite thoroughly, much to the displeasure of Agent Redding. All had appeared to be in order. Even so, Hawkes had not been able to shake the feeling that in some way their unexpected presence had thwarted a nefarious scheme in which Redding figured prominently. He just flat out didn't trust the Indian agent. Since then, Plenty Coups had taken it upon himself to stand guard over the merchandise, even though Hawkes had assured him that they would go through it again crate by crate before it was loaded onto the keelboats.

"What is it?" he asked Plenty Coups, rising to face the warrior.

"There is a man here who looks for you, White Crow."

Hawkes felt the blood run cold in his veins. He had few friends, for it had been a habit of many years to avoid contact with his own kind whenever possible. If someone was indeed looking for him, it more likely than not meant trouble.

"Who?" he asked, his voice a raspy whisper.

"A killer of buffalo. His name is Ring."

"Billy Ring," breathed Hawkes. "Damn it."

"What does this man want with you?"

"Reckon he wants to kill me, Plenty Coups."

"What will you do?"

Hawkes smiled bleakly. "Guess I'll have to give him the chance."

"I will stand with you. This man rides with many others."

"Thanks, friend, but I want you to stay clear out of this. If anything happens to me, somebody needs to be here to make sure your people get the annuity."

Plenty Coups frowned. He felt honor-bound to aid a fellow Absaroke in his time of danger, but he also had a distinct responsibility to his people. Meldrum could not be relied upon, and Redding had yet to prove he could be trusted. Thus Plenty Coups was torn—between a warrior's duty to aid another warrior in need and a man's obligation to his tribe and his family.

Making the tough decision, a grim Plenty Coups nodded to Hawkes, who turned to make his way to Fort Union's main gate alone.

He was met there by Major Culbertson.

"Billy Ring has got the word that you are here, Gordon," said the American Fur Company man.

"Yeah, I know."

"He's over at the sutler's, drinking corn whiskey like it's water and saying he is going to make damn sure you're on your way to hell before the sun sets."

"Thanks, Major."

"Hold on just a minute, Gordon. What's the reason for this bad blood between you and Ring?"

"Well, this being your place, I reckon that makes it your business."

"You're quite right. It does."

"I killed Billy Ring's brother."

"Christ," muttered Culbertson. "How did that happen?"

"Billy and his brother tried to bushwhack me and a friend some years back. I shot Charley Ring in self-defense."

"You might should have done the same to this one."

"So I was told at the time. But Billy didn't put up a fight."

"He seems to want to now. I suggest you head on upriver. A day or two out, you make camp and let the keelboats catch up with you."

"Is that what you would do, Major? Run?"

Culbertson grimaced. "That's right. I would—to avoid having to kill a man, or being killed myself."

Hawkes shook his head derisively. "No, you wouldn't."

"Damn it, Gordon, I don't want this kind of trouble in my post."

"Sometimes you just can't duck trouble. It has a way of catching up to you, no matter how hard you try to get away from it. I don't need to spend the rest of my days looking over my shoulder to see if Billy Ring is there. Sorry, Major."

He turned away from Culbertson and started through the gate, half expecting the American Fur Company man to try and stop him. But Culbertson let him go.

Billy Ring was still in the sutler's store, and he was still drinking hard. It was here that a man could buy just about anything he needed, from foofaraw to catch the eye of an Indian woman, to powder, shot, percussion caps, skinning knives, beaver and bear traps, blankets and skillets, tobacco and whiskey—even though Culbertson forbade the sale of liquor to Indians—and even a few store-bought clothes from back East. There were shelves and counters stocked with a variety of merchandise on three sides, and a long trestle table down the middle of the room that could seat twenty men, with a cold stove standing nearby. When Hawkes walked in, he counted eleven men in the store—a company employee, a clerk scribbling in a ledger, and the rest either seated at the table, like Ring, or gathered round it. By their smell and appearance Hawkes could tell that all but a few of them were buffalo runners, so he assumed that they were members of Billy Ring's crew.

"We had a spot of trouble with Injuns, it's true," Ring was telling a buckskin-clad man that Hawkes recognized as another of Culbertson's AFC men. "But we made short work of them savages, didn't we, boys?"

There was loud, gruff affirmation from the rest of the buffalo runners, and one of them laughed, and tossed several scalps bound together with a rawhide strip on the table.

"Those be Dakota scalps," remarked the company man.

"So what if they are?" asked Ring, leaning forward with a truculent scowl. "They attacked us. What was we supposed to do? Let them hang our topknots on their lodgepoles?"

"We don't want to start anything with the Sioux nation, that's all."

"Then why don't you have a talk with your Dakota friends and tell 'em not to mess with Billy Ring and his crew no more?"

It was then that the company man glanced across the store and saw Hawkes standing in the doorway. Billy Ring followed his gaze even as he lifted a whiskey jug to his lips. When he recognized Hawkes the buffalo hunter froze, the jug suspended halfway to its destination. Ring hadn't much changed during the years that had passed since their last confrontation. He was a big, stocky man, rawboned and long-haired, with a matted beard and a crooked eye and tobacco-stained teeth. He looked every bit as mean as Hawkes remembered.

"I hear you're looking for me," said Hawkes.

All eyes were glued on him as a heavy silence descended on the sutler's store. He stood there, framed against the bright summer light, his Plains rifle cradled in one arm, a thumb hooked in his belt so that his right hand brushed against the butt of the percussion pistol he carried.

Billy Ring's eyes brimmed with hate as they fastened on Hawkes.

"You got a lot of hard bark on you, Gordon, coming in here like this. Or are you just weary of life?"

"I'm just weary of you, Ring, and your big mouth."

"You should have kilt me when you had the choice, hoss," sneered the buffalo runner. "You should've buried me right next to my little brother."

"You didn't give me a reason like he did."

"You're a fool. You had a reason. You had to know I would never rest until you were dead."

"Look here," said the company man who sat across the table from Ring. "The major don't want no—"

"Shut the hell up," growled Ring. "This is none of your business."

Hawkes kept an eye on Billy Ring's crew. They were easing away from the table, spreading out to his left and right, and it wasn't because they wanted to get out of the line of fire. They were ready to start shooting at Ring's order. A couple of them had their long guns in hand. All the others were armed with at least a pistol and a knife. Hawkes smiled coldly.

"You going to let your boys do your dirty work for you, Ring?" he asked.

"Stand back," Ring snapped at his crew. "The pleasure of spilling this man's blood is gonna be all mine. It was my brother he kilt. Vengeance is mine."

"I say you and I go outside and settle this matter," said Hawkes. "I see you still use that big English .704."

"I'll fight you any way you want, Gordon. Long guns, pistols, knives, bare hands—it don't matter none at all to me. One way or the other, I'm gonna be cuttin' out yore heart in a few minutes."

"Long guns, then, at a hundred paces. We both start unloaded. If your first shot doesn't hit the mark you can reload and try again, assuming you're still above snakes."

Billy Ring grinned. "You are a fool, Gordon. I make my livin' with long shots. I can put a ball through either one of your eyes at five times a hunnerd yards. Problem is, I don't want you to die that fast. I want you to suffer a good long time."

"All right, then. Here's your chance. Come on, there's been enough talk."

Hawkes turned his back on the room and walked out into the bright sunlight.

Billy Ring shot to his feet. Only then did he feel the effects of the prodigious amount of whiskey he had consumed during the last hour. The floor seemed to tilt precariously under his feet and the room began to spin. Swaying, he steadied himself against the table and laughed.

"Damn. I must be gettin' old, boys. Cain't hold my whiskey like I used to."

"He knows what he's doing, Billy," said a hunter with the swarthy, black-haired look of a half-breed. "You get out in that sun all likkered up like you are and you won't be shooting too straight."

"The hell you say," snarled Ring. "I'll take him. You'll see."

"But what if you don't?" asked the breed. "What if you're the one who goes down? What do you want us to do then?"

"What do you think?" sneered Ring. "Are you as

stupid as you look? Kill the bastard! I want his company when I spit in the devil's eye."

Taking up his long gun, powder horn, and shot pouch from the table, Ring started for the door.

"That Plains rifle he carries is a percussion piece," warned another of the buffalo runners. "I reckon he uses cartridges, too."

"Stop frettin' over me like goddamn mother hens!" roared Billy Ring. "I can get off three shots in less than a minute. You all seen what I can do. So quit worryin' like a passel of women."

With that he stepped outside. The sun hit him like an axe handle between the eyes, and he reeled slightly, caught himself, and looked around. His eyes narrowed into painful slits against the merciless midday glare, until he chanced to spot Hawkes standing there watching him, a faint, contemptuous smile on his lips. The smirk served only to infuriate the buffalo hunter.

"Get a move on, Ring," said Hawkes. "I've got better things to do."

"You son of a bitch," muttered Ring. It got under his skin that Hawkes treated him like a minor annoyance that could be dealt with in short order.

Hawkes saw Culbertson standing in the doorway of his office across the wagon yard. "We'll do this outside the fort," he told Ring. "You might hit an innocent bystander."

Thunderstruck, Ring stared at Hawkes. He told himself that this man, his brother's killer, was just trying to goad him, that his calm and confident facade was just that—a mask Hawkes used to conceal his fear. But try as he might, Billy Ring could detect not a bit of evidence that Hawkes was at all worried about losing his life. This was a completely new experience for Billy

Ring. He had never before tangled with a man who wasn't scared of him. He knew the value of intimidation, and knew how to use it, too. But for some reason this bastard didn't appear to be worried in the slightest degree. And that in itself was worrisome. For the first time in his life, Billy Ring began to have doubts about his ability to prevail in a scrape.

Once again turning his back on Ring, Hawkes headed for the fort's main gate. Billy Ring briefly considered putting a bullet in the man's back, but he decided against that course of action, glancing about at all the people who were watching the confrontation from what they hoped was a safe distance. It hadn't taken very long for word to spread. There was going to be a killing. But it had to be a fair fight. Back-shooting would not be tolerated. There wasn't much law to speak of on the frontier, and very few ironclad rules of conduct, but the rules that did exist had to be abided by. So Billy Ring shouldered his big English buffalo gun and shuffled after Hawkes, weaving slightly as he did.

Hawkes emerged from Fort Union and turned toward the bluff. Billy Ring followed twenty paces behind him, a crowd of onlookers in his wake, including Major Culbertson and Robert Meldrum and the rest of Ring's seedy-looking crew of buffalo runners. Reaching the crest of the bluff, Hawkes lifted his Plains rifle to his shoulder and discharged it, aiming at the eastern sky, then turned to face the buffalo hunter. Again Ring glanced at the audience and cursed his luck. Had there been no witnesses, he would have killed Hawkes on the spot and to hell with those burdensome notions of fair play about not gunning down an unarmed man. Ring wasn't hampered by conscience. But he knew

Culbertson well enough to realize that he would be wearing a rope around his neck if he did anything underhanded. So he too aimed his buffalo gun skyward and fired.

"You stay here," Hawkes told him. "I'll take one hundred paces in that direction, along the edge of the bluff. When I stop and turn, you can commence to loading. That suit you?"

"Let's just get on with it."

With a businesslike nod, Hawkes walked away along the rim of the bluff, carrying the Plains rifle down at his side so that Ring could keep an eye on both of his hands. As he walked, counting paces softly under his breath, thoughts of Eliza and his children intruded, and with those thoughts came the tendrils of fear wrapping themselves around his heart—fear that if something went wrong he might never see his family again. And along with the fear came doubt about whether what he was doing was the smart thing. But he forced those thoughts out of his mind, banishing the fear and ignoring the doubt. Smart or not, right or wrong, this was the only thing he could do. He had to deal with Billy Ring on his own terms. It was certainly better like this than to wait for Ring to ambush him and put a bullet in him that way. This was really his only option.

Sixty paces. Eighty. He wondered if Billy Ring would keep his nerve. Hawkes was betting he would, that he didn't have any choice, not with all these witnesses. A backshooter was a dirty coward in anyone's book, and those who lived in the wild country had no use for cowards. If Ring fired before he turned around, then Ring would also die before the day was out.

Ninety paces. One hundred.

As he turned, Hawkes dug a linen-wrapped cartridge out of his shot pouch, tore it open with his teeth,
poured the powder down the barrel, then dropped the
ball in, followed by the linen as a patch. A hundred
yards away, Billy Ring was feverishly loading his buffalo gun. Hawkes tamped the load down with his ramrod, watching Ring doing precisely the same thing at
the same instant. Then Hawkes took a percussion cap
from his pouch as Ring primed his English .704.

A split second before Hawkes could bring his Plains
rifle to bear, Ring raised his own long gun to shoulder
and in the next instant squeezed the trigger.

Hawkes felt the searing burn of the bullet as it
grazed his ribs. Gasping, he steadied himself, drawing
a bead on Billy Ring's heart.

For his part, the buffalo hunter lowered his rifle and
stared in slack-jawed disbelief at Hawkes. He couldn't
believe his eyes. The son of a bitch was still standing.
The impossible had happened. He had missed his
shot. A split second later, the consequences of that failure struck him. Ring's first instinct was to run. Instead,
he stood his ground, tossing his long gun aside and
holding his arms out away from his sides, blinking
rapidly to clear his blurred vision. He wanted to see
death when it came.

"Come on!" he roared, glowering hatefully at
Hawkes. "Take your shot, you bastard! What are you
waiting for?"

Hawkes hesitated, impressed in spite of himself by
Ring's raw courage.

Billy Ring started to growl like a riled grizzly. The
way he saw things, Hawkes was just tormenting him,
lingering over the shot in an attempt to make him suffer, or maybe even hoping his nerves would break and

he would turn tail. Instead, Ring started walking toward his adversary.

"Shoot, damn you! Shoot!"

Still Hawkes hesitated. Until a few seconds ago he had been sure in his mind that Ring needed to die, that the threat to him and his family posed by the vengeful buffalo runner was just too great and needed to be removed once and for all. But now he just wasn't too sure he could do the deed.

Seething at being toyed with, Ring drew his pistol. "You better kill me now, God damn you!" he yelled.

Hawkes drew a bead and squeezed the trigger. The Plains rifle kicked sharply against his shoulder and he sidestepped immediately out of the powder smoke to see that Billy Ring was on the ground.

Culbertson and several members of Ring's crew rushed to the fallen man, followed by many of the spectators. Hawkes took the precaution of reloading his Hawken, with a sour taste in his mouth that made him slightly queasy. He looked bleakly at Plenty Coups as the Crow warrior joined him. Plenty Coups glanced at the stain of blood on Hawkes's buckskin hunting shirt and correctly judged that the wound was minor.

"Why did you not kill him?" asked the Absaroke.

"I couldn't."

Racking the Plains rifle across one shoulder, Hawkes headed for the crowd, which parted to let him pass. Culbertson was down on one knee alongside Ring, and one of Ring's fellow hunters, the breed, was applying a tourniquet to the fallen man's arm. Ring himself was out cold. Seeing Hawkes, Culbertson stood to confront him.

"He won't be using that arm again," remarked the

American Fur Company man. "I'd be surprised if he doesn't lose it altogether. I'd venture to say that Mr. Ring's buffalo-killing days are over. He'll have to find a new line of work."

Hawkes peered at the other buffalo runners. "Anyone else here have a quarrel with me? If so, let's settle it now."

"You should have killed him," said the breed. "Your biggest mistake was leaving him alive back when you done in his brother. Now you've gone and made the same mistake twice."

"I reckon we'll see about that," replied Hawkes, and with one last look at Billy Ring, he turned and pushed through the crowd to walk away. Indeed, he prayed it would be the last time he ever set eyes on the man. He knew in his gut that the buffalo runner was right, that he might well live just long enough to regret sparing Billy Ring's life a second time. He could easily have drilled Ring right through the heart. But the man's ferocious courage in the face of certain death had so impressed him that he had not been able to take his life. Blood had been spilled, but the problem remained unsolved. Maybe Ring would give up his vendetta—but Hawkes was inclined to doubt it. More likely, Ring would thirst for revenge now more than ever, for Hawkes had not only taken his kid brother's life but also the use of an arm, and hence his livelihood. There was going to be hell to pay. That much was guaranteed.

Chapter 3

Agent Redding waited until dusk to make his visit to the encampment of the Dakota Sioux, hoping to escape notice by anyone at Fort Union. It wasn't that as a representative of the United States Indian Bureau, he had no business among the Sioux. But the fact remained that he wasn't here on official government business. Quite the contrary. And now that the mountain man called Henry Gordon was here, keeping one suspicious eye on the Crow annuity and the other on him, Redding felt the need to take a few extra precautions. He cursed his luck, casting a wary glance back at Fort Union as he crossed the open ground between the American Fur Company outpost and the Sioux lodges. How was it, he wondered, that this rumor regarding his nefarious designs on the Indian annuities in his charge had come to spread, at least enough to trigger Gordon's suspicions? Apparently he was in the unhappy predicament of having to pay for the underhanded schemes of those who had been caught before him. Redding was a man who justified his own criminality with the argument that everyone else did the same kind of thing.

Now he had to try to explain the situation to the Dakota Sioux. Redding felt like Daniel about to be cast into the lions' den—though he lacked the sublime faith in the Almighty's protection that had given Daniel the courage he needed to face death. As he neared the Sioux encampment, a pair of Dakota warriors appeared as if from nowhere and blocked his path. Redding tried his best to mask the fear that wracked his body as he gazed at the fierce-looking men.

As the Dakotas were the largest and most warlike of all the Plains tribes, Redding made sure he had learned all he could about them. He knew, for instance, that there were seven divisions, the largest of these being the Teton, and there were seven Teton bands—the Brule, the Hunkpapa, the Miniconjou, the Oglala, the Oahenonpa, the Sans Arc, and the Sihasapa. This village he entered now was Oglala, and the two men who blocked his path both looked to be members of the Strong Heart society. Oglala males belonged to either civil, police, dream, or war societies, with the bravest of the brave reserved for the Strong Heart clan. These were fearless warriors who had proven themselves on numerous occasions in battle. Redding had heard about Napoleon Bonaparte's Old Guard, an elite group of veteran soldiers who acted not only as the emperor's bodyguard, but as the last line of defense in battle, or as shock troops in the final assault. It was Redding's impression that the Strong Hearts served much the same function among the Dakota.

Both of these men wore their war shirts, fringed and heavily decorated with ornate quill- and beadwork. The shirts had been dyed, the upper portion bright blue and the lower yellow. Their hide leggings were adorned with beaded bands, and their moccasins bore quilled tips and beaded edges. They were fully armed with knife and tomahawk and curved, sinew-backed bows carried by straps on their backs along with quivers filled with grooved arrows that had long trademetal heads. Both carried trade rifles.

"I have come to see Long Horse," said Redding, using sign.

The Strong Hearts looked at each other. Then one stepped closer to Redding. The Indian agent tried to conceal his nervousness. It would profit them nothing to harm him. In fact, the Sioux had good reason to want him alive and healthy, assuming that he had indeed persuaded them that it was in their best interests to deal with him. But you just never could be absolutely sure with the Dakota. They were nothing if not unpredictable. And they despised cowardice. So Redding forced himself to stand his ground and unflinchingly return the steely gaze of the Sioux warrior who approached him. The Strong Heart reached out and plucked the pistol from Redding's belt. He then nodded curtly toward the encampment.

With one warrior leading the way and the other following along close behind him, Redding entered the Oglala village. Men, women, and children stopped what they were doing to watch him pass by the light of their cook fires. The Indian agent began to have second thoughts about the wisdom of making this call on Long Horse. He was not the bearer of good news, and he could not rely on Long Horse's equanimity.

He was escorted into a skin lodge located near the center of the encampment. The buffalo-hide lodge covering was ornately decorated with bird and animal figures, elegant sunbursts and renditions of war bonnets. Having been here on several previous occasions, Redding knew this was Long Horse's lodge. A boy of about ten summers sat cross-legged outside the lodge. One of the Strong Hearts spoke briefly to the boy, who rose and disappeared inside. A moment later he emerged, holding the flap open and nodding at the Indian agent with a shy smile. Redding smiled back tentatively. He was fairly certain it was the only Sioux smile he would see tonight.

Bending down, Redding entered the lodge. Long Horse and two women, one old and wrinkled, the other young and plump and pretty, sat around a small cook fire. A rising plume of gray smoke escaped through a smoke hole at the top of the lodge. With her gnarled hands, the old woman was forming bread cakes made from roots and berries that were then cooked on flat stones encircling the fire. The younger woman was nursing an infant. Redding tried not to stare at her milk-swollen breasts.

Long Horse gazed earnestly at Redding for a moment, then curtly spoke to the women, who rose and silently departed the skin lodge. The Oglala chief gestured for the Indian agent to sit down. Redding did so, across the cook fire from Long Horse. The firelight cast the Oglala's rugged, high-cheekboned face in sharp relief and danced in his obsidian eyes.

"Why do you come to me, Redding?" he asked.

The Indian agent thanked the Lord above that Long Horse spoke English. He was going to have to talk himself out of a pretty tight spot here and was glad he didn't have to sign to do so. As a boy, Long Horse had been educated back East in the white man's schools, under the auspices of a missionary, and due in no small measure to the fact that he was the son of a prominent chief. That was back in the days when the Sioux had lived in what was now known as Minnesota and Wisconsin. Long Horse's father had tried to live in peace with the whites. But the Sioux had gradually been forced westward, pushed out of their homeland by an irresistible tide of white settlers. This, coupled with the death of his father—who fell victim to one of the white man's diseases—had hardened Long Horse's heart against Redding's race.

"I have brought you something, my good friend," said Redding, taking several twists of tobacco from the pocket of his coat and handing them to Long Horse. "I know how fond you are of tobacco."

Long Horse looked at the tobacco for a moment. "Soon," he said, "you will bring me much more than this, won't you, Redding?"

The Indian agent cleared his throat. "That's what I have come to talk to you about."

"Is something wrong?"

Redding had an uneasy feeling that Long Horse already knew the answer.

"Well, yes, as a matter of fact, there is," he said. "We do have a *slight* problem."

"You promised us guns and powder and lead," said Long Horse. "In return we would give you many horses and many skins. You are not going back on your word now, are you, Redding?"

"I cannot take the guns and the other things from the annuity that the government has sent for the Crows."

Long Horse shrugged. "I do not care where you get them. Just get them."

"You don't understand. That is the only possible source, at least for the time being. Now, I'm not saying I won't carry out my end of the bargain, my friend.

But, well, it's just going to take a little longer than I thought at first."

"I want them now, as you promised. The white man has the luxury of time. My people do not."

Redding grimaced. "I didn't expect the Crows to send men here to make sure they got everything that was coming to them. How was I supposed to know this would happen?"

"How many men did the Crows send?"

"Three."

"Then just kill them."

Redding stared at the Oglala chief, then laughed nervously. "You can't be serious. I—I can't do that."

"Then I will kill them myself."

"Now look here. One is a Crow warrior, one is an employee of the American Fur Company, and the other is a white trapper. What are you trying to do, start a war?"

"I want what was promised to my people."

"It's simply impossible at the moment. Tomorrow the last of the Crow supplies will be loaded aboard the keelboats and then we're bound for Fort Sarpy. When I get back I'll think of some way to get the guns for you. You have my word on that."

Long Horse did not seem too reassured. He tossed the twists of tobacco into the fire. The smoke between the two men thickened. The tobacco's pungent aroma filled the skin lodge.

"I am curious," said the Oglala chief, "how you planned to explain the missing guns to the Absaroke, and to your own people."

"I intended to fill the gun crates with wood, the boxes of lead with large stones, and the casks of powder with river sand. Then, on the way upriver, there would be a mishap, and many of the goods would be lost—including, of course, all the guns and the powder and the lead. Because, you see, apart from two other men—men I needed to assist me and who can be counted on to keep their mouths shut as long as they're paid well—no one was ever to know about this."

Long Horse nodded. "You white men are very clever."

Somehow Redding knew this was not meant as a compliment. "My friend," he said, "I'm smart enough to know not to cross you—and clever enough to devise some other means to find the guns I promised you. All I ask from you is a little patience."

"Patience," sneered Long Horse. "My father counseled patience. He told his people not to strike back against the white settlers who were cutting down the forests and scarring the earth with their plows. He said, 'Be patient, as the White Father has promised us that we will be allowed to stay on our land.'" The Oglala chief smiled, but there was no warmth in his eyes. "'Allowed to stay on our land.' How do you like that, Redding?"

Redding shook his head, trying to convey sympathy for Long Horse's point of view and disgust for the concept that the United States would dare dictate to the Indian tribes where they could live. The problem was that, like most whites, he really didn't care. Why should a few thousand Indians be permitted to stand in the way of progress? The United States had a great destiny, ordained by God and guaranteed by the stalwart courage and tireless enterprise of her intrepid citizens. The needs of a relative handful of primitive redskins would never be a priority. Redding saw his task as Indian agent in terms of placating the tribes, keeping them as peaceful as possible while persuading them, whenever he could, that resistance would be futile. There were plenty of Indians who could be bought off with a few cheap trade goods. But Long Horse would not be won over with trinkets and empty words. He was not naïve, nor was he a fool. He knew perfectly well what was happening to his people, and that made him extremely dangerous.

"So you see," continued the Oglala chief curtly, "I know all about patience and the promises of the white man. I do not put my faith in either."

Redding swallowed the lump in his throat, realizing just how perilous his situation was at that moment. Long Horse did not fear the repercussions that might follow on the heels of the killing of an Indian agent. *The only reason I am still alive,* Redding mused, *is because he still thinks I could be of more use to him alive than dead.*

"Well, I had best be getting back," said Redding. "When I return from delivering the Crow annuity, we will talk again."

"I will not be here," replied Long Horse. "You may go."

Redding nodded. Rising, he left the chief's skin lodge. The two Strong Hearts were waiting to escort him out of the Oglala village. Only then was his pistol returned to him. Redding tried not to look like he was in too big of a hurry as he put the Sioux encampment behind him. It was completely dark now, the last shred of daylight having leaked out of the western sky, and the indigo dome of heaven was filled with stars. A cool, dry wind washed over the plains. As he bent his steps toward Fort Union, the Indian agent wondered if he had succeeded in buying himself a reprieve. Had he left Fort Union without providing the Oglalas with some explanation why he was unable to produce the guns and powder, Long Horse would have hunted him down and killed him. There was no doubt in Redding's mind about that now. But what could be the reason for Long Horse's leaving Fort Union before his return? Had the Oglala chief given up on getting the guns after all? Or was he plotting some mischief? Redding decided the latter was more likely the case.

Redding relaxed a little as he passed through the outpost's gate. He felt marginally safer now. But he knew he would not feel completely secure until he had fulfilled his end of the bargain struck with Long Horse. He'd made a deal with the devil, and the devil always got his due.

Chapter 4

The two keelboats provided by Major Culbertson, compliments of the American Fur Company, were sturdy river craft ideally suited for the task at hand—namely, transporting goods by way of a western river that, like so many of its counterparts, was notorious for its treacherous shoals and sandbars. Sixty feet long and ten feet wide, each craft could safely carry thirty tons. Each had a crew of eleven men—one to handle the long steering oar at the stern and the rest to perform the arduous task of poling the keelboat, or, if necessary, to man the stout cordelles to go ashore and haul the craft upstream, a technique called bushwhacking.

The crews, paid by Redding in government scrip, were a tough and hardy lot of mixed heritage—Spanish, Russian, French Canadian, and more than a few half-breeds. Keelboat men worked hard and played hard as well. Generally they took a fierce pride in their profession. They were brawlers and braggarts, loud and profane and sometimes vicious. But they usually got the job done. All in all, Gordon Hawkes was impressed by their ability to labor tirelessly from dawn to dusk. Then, after a huge meal, they would sit around and tell tall tales, play cards or thimblerig, or dance atop the keelboat's low-slung cabin to the music provided by fiddle and Jew's harp.

Running upriver to Fort Sarpy was a journey of at least ten days' duration. But arrival at the outpost would not mark the end of the task that Hawkes had taken upon himself. Redding would still have to bring the Absaroke chiefs in so that the annuity could be fairly and fully distributed. By his reckoning, Hawkes figured he was still a good month away from the day when he could put all this behind him and head for home. He was mighty homesick already. He missed Grace and Cameron and longed to wrap his arms around his wife. Of course, he was sure Cam was taking care of things quite adequately in his absence. His son was twenty-one years of age, a full-grown man, and wise in the ways of the wilderness. Hawkes had left his family in Red Bear's village with the understanding that within a fortnight they would be returning to their mountain home north of the Uinta Range.

Only one thing had given Hawkes cause for concern in leaving his family with the Absarokes. And that was his hunch that Cameron still had feelings for Walks in the Sun, and that her family—especially her brother, Raven—still harbored a grudge against Cam for what had happened six years ago.

It had helped some that four summers back, Walks had submitted to her father's fervent wish that she become the woman of a warrior named Yellow Legs, who lived among the River Crow and who had loved her so passionately that he was evidently willing to overlook the fact that she had lain with Cameron. Cameron had never spoken of his feelings regarding this development. The hurt ran deep, too deep to talk

about. Hawkes had assumed that in time Cameron's
heart would mend and that eventually he would give
it to another woman. But it did not seem as though either had happened yet. As for hunches, Hawkes had
another—that Walks still had strong feelings for his
son as well, and did not love her husband with the
same passion that Yellow Legs demonstrated for her.
There was, then, at least a possibility that the final
chapter of that story had not yet been written. And
Hawkes did not want to be absent if and when that
chapter began.

He and Plenty Coups did not travel on the keelboat. Instead they rode alongside the river, sometimes scouting ahead, taking upon themselves the
responsibility of hunting for the keelboaters, providing fresh meat for every night's cook fires. Hawkes
preferred this arrangement for several reasons. He
didn't think that being confined to those cramped
craft, knocking shins and elbows with the keelboat
men, was his cup of tea. And he could cover a lot
more ground on horseback in his search for game. On
the third day out of Fort Laramie, when he learned
that there was a large party of Indians in the vicinity,
he was doubly glad that he had the mobility provided by the gray mountain mustang he rode.

It was Plenty Coups who saw the tracks first, and
he led Hawkes back to the sign. They followed it for
a while and came to a place where the Indians had
paused and dismounted. Plenty Coups studied the
imprints of moccasins on the ground and told
Hawkes that they belonged to Dakota warriors. They
were heading roughly southeast, parallel to the river,
in the same direction as the keelboats were traveling.
Hawkes and the Absaroke warrior agreed that there

were about fifty warriors in the party. That there was
no sign of women or children along indicated that
these braves were bent on making some kind of mischief.

When Hawkes reported these findings to Redding,
the Indian agent thought immediately of Long Horse,
and alarm shot through him. But he remained out-
wardly impassive, shrugging indifferently at the
news.

"I am sure it is of no concern to us," he told
Hawkes.

"No? Well, I can tell you one thing. This isn't Sioux
country. So whatever those Indians are doing, it
spells trouble for somebody. The Dakota aren't
known for making social calls on their neighbors."

"What would you have me do?" asked Redding
dryly. "Go after them and inform them that they must
return to Sioux territory at once?"

"Well, you are representing the United States government, I thought," replied Hawkes with just as
much sarcasm as Redding had employed. "Who
knows, maybe they would listen to you."

"At the moment, my job is to get this annuity delivered to your friends, the Crows. I do not have time
to worry about a handful of Sioux."

"You should always worry about Sioux, even a
handful," said Hawkes, and left it at that.

In fact, Redding was very worried. If the tracks that
Hawkes and Plenty Coups had found indeed belonged to Long Horse and his Oglala braves, then it
was quite possible that the Dakota chief had decided
to take the guns and powder he felt were owed to
him by force. Problem was, Redding couldn't tell

Hawkes that, since to do so would more than likely expose his scheme to steal from the Crow annuity.

Hawkes was also thinking about the Sioux in the Indian encampment he had seen near Fort Union. He thought it was very possible that the warriors who had made the tracks came from that band and, like Redding, he wondered if they were after the goods on the keelboats. As his job was to get the annuity to the Absaroke, the Sioux war party was of grave concern to him. The Dakota were the predators of the High Plains, and this merchandise could have easily excited their avarice. He doubted that they would even think twice about killing an agent of the United States government and attacking keelboats that belonged to the American Fur Company. They feared nothing, least of all possible reprisals from the company or the government.

Hawkes and Plenty Coups returned to the sign of the Sioux, following it for the remainder of the day. They called it quits at dark, made a cold camp, slept a few hours, then rose with the three-quarter moon, which provided enough light for trackers as adept as they were to continue. Hawkes concurred with Plenty Coups when the River Crow said that the Sioux were less than six hours ahead of them. But the Dakota were traveling swiftly, and it soon became apparent that they, too, were continuing on their way well into the night.

Early the following morning the tracks veered suddenly toward the river. Hawkes was saddle sore, his belly was empty, and his eyes felt gritty from lack of sleep, but he forgot about all these things when he saw that the war party was bound for the river. He and Plenty Coups pressed their tired mounts onward and in an hour's time reached the Yellowstone. The trail led them upriver along the bank for several miles. And then suddenly there was less sign to be read. Hawkes knew immediately that part of the war party, about half of them by the looks of it, had crossed over to the other side. He muttered a curse.

"That's it, then," he told Plenty Coups. "They must be after the boats. They wouldn't split up like this for any other reason that I can see."

He peered upriver. He was quite certain that somewhere up ahead the Sioux would prepare their ambush. But he just wasn't sure what to do about it. Should the keelboats turn back? The Sioux outnumbered them two to one. But if they did go back to Fort Union, would the Absaroke ever get this year's annuity? Would Redding make the effort to try to deliver the goods again? Would he, Gordon Hawkes, ever get home to see his family again?

He turned to Plenty Coups.

"You ride back and tell Redding I want him to hold up for a spell. But don't tell him what we know. Not unless I don't get back by daybreak tomorrow."

"What if he will not stop?"

"Then tell him everything, but only if there is no other way."

"And what will you do, White Crow?"

"I'm going after the Dakota. I've got to find out how they plan to ambush the boats. If we know that, then maybe we can think of some way to mess up their plans and still get those goods to Fort Sarpy."

Plenty Coups clearly did not like the idea of Hawkes going on alone. "I will go with you," he said. "When we know about the Sioux, then I will go back and tell Agent Redding."

"Nope. That won't work. If something happens to both of us, that fool Indian agent would just keep on coming and walk straight into a trap. You have to go back."

"You go back, then. You can make him stop better than I can."

Hawkes grinned tautly. "You River Crow are sure hard to get along with. This was my idea, so I get to go on and have the fun. You have to go back to the boats. Sorry, but that's just the way it's going to be."

Plenty Coups nodded gravely. "I will do as you say. The Absaroke will forever honor your name, White Crow."

"Thanks," said Hawkes wryly. "But don't count me out just yet. Now get going."

He watched Plenty Coups until the Crow warrior had ridden out of sight, then turned his mountain mustang around and headed upriver. He held the horse to a walk and kept his Hawken Plains rifle near at hand, laid across the saddle in front of him.

It was really just a question of whether he saw the Dakota before they saw him. He was lucky because he did manage to see them first, just as he was about to break from the cover of a stand of willows. He spotted a sandbar that squeezed the river into a deep, fast-running channel just below a sharp bend. There were trees on both banks along here, and within them he saw the Sioux who had crossed to the other side. Dismounting, Hawkes tethered his horse and, rifle in hand, moved forward with caution. From his side of the river came an easily recognizable sound—the sharp, percussive sound of wood being chopped in the stillness of the warm afternoon. He needed to know what the Indians were up to, and that meant

getting closer still. Sliding soundlessly through the
trees, he found a vantage point from which he could
see five braves applying their tomahawks to the base
of a tree near the water's edge. The others stood
nearby, pointing at the river on the opposite side, dis-
cussing the ambush in groups of three or four or five,
while several more watched the ponies, who were
held back beyond the trees.

In a glance Hawkes saw what the scheme was all
about. The Sioux would cut the tree but not fell it—
not until the keelboats were committed to the channel. In all likelihood Redding's crews would be
bushwhacking the craft through the channel, and that
meant that most of the men would be ashore, heaving
on the stout cordelles. Focused on their task, they
would be easy prey for the Sioux, who would be lurking deeper in the woods, waiting until the white men
had blundered into their trap. The cutting on the tree
would be artfully concealed with brush, and once the
boats were past that point, the attack would commence. Several warriors would rush to the tree, brandishing their hatchets. A few more strokes of the
tomahawks and the tree would topple into the channel, blocking any escape should the men remaining
on the keelboats think to cut the cordelles in the hope
that the current would sweep them back down the
river and out of danger. More Dakota would fall
upon the bushwhackers, and those Indians concealed
on the opposite bank would rush forward across the
sandbar and attack the keelboats.

It was a fine plan, Hawkes had to admit. Whoever
led these Sioux warriors had picked the perfect site
and devised a bold and innovative scheme that
seemed certain to succeed. But he saw immediately

that there was one flaw. The Dakota had divided their force. If Hawkes could persuade the keelboaters to fight with him, he could bring them ashore down-river, slip up on the warriors on this side, and with the element of surprise and some good fortune to boot, rout them. The Sioux on the other side would not be able to cross the deep channel to come to the aid of their brethren. Hawkes thought it likely that they would withdraw once it became clear to them that their white adversaries had prevailed on this side of the river. It was risky, but Hawkes figured it was worth the chance. At least better than turning back without so much as trying to get through. If all did not go as planned, there was still a good chance that the keelboats could escape down the river.

After spending a few more minutes watching the Sioux and committing the lay of the land to memory, Hawkes turned to retrace his steps.

His horse was only a few dozen yards away when two Dakota warriors appeared, seemingly out of nowhere, and launched themselves at him, one from the left, the other from the right. Their shrill war cry chilled the blood in his veins, as it was intended to. For one fleeting moment, Hawkes had time to wonder why they hadn't killed him at a distance with a rifle shot or an arrow. Then he stopped thinking and reacted, firing the Plains rifle from hip level at almost point-blank range into the chest of one of the Sioux. The impact of the ball hurled the Indian backward, and Hawkes knew he was dead before he hit the ground. Whirling, Hawkes sensed that the second warrior was nearly upon him and used the empty rifle like a club, swinging it as hard as he could. But the Dakota was ready for him, ducking under the rifle's arc and driving his body into Hawkes, who was already off balance. The mountain man fell, and the Sioux came down on top of him, punching the air out of his lungs. Hawkes caught a glimpse of the warrior raising his tomahawk, and he could do nothing to stop the tomahawk flashing down. The world went black.

Chapter 5

It was a long, exhausting climb back to consciousness and before he could muster up the strength to open his eyes Hawkes heard Indian voices. He believed at first that he was in Red Bear's village in the Wind River Valley and that he would awake to find himself in a skin lodge and open his eyes to see his beloved Eliza's smile, the smile that warmed him like the morning sun after a cool mountain night, a smile every bit as bright as the sun. He would rise to find that Gracie had gone off to be with the Absaroke maidens who were her friends and that Cameron was already gone too, on a solitary excursion, as he was often inclined to do.

But then Hawkes realized that the language was not familiar to him. These were not his friends, the Absarokes. And hard on the heels of that realization came the sobering memory of the attack by the two Dakota warriors. Suddenly wide awake, his heart racing wildly, Hawkes forced himself to lie perfectly still, seeking to quell the panic that threatened to spread through him like venom, forcing himself to think, to reason. One question was foremost in his mind: *Why was he still alive?* And would they kill him once they knew he was conscious? His head hurt horribly, a relentless pounding that spread through his skull and down the back of his neck. He could feel that he was bound hand and foot. Fear became his worst enemy in those terrifying moments as the full scope of his predicament became apparent to him, and he had to fight fiercely to keep himself composed. *If you're going to die,* he told himself savagely, *die like a man and not like a whimpering dog.* Dying was the last thing a person got to do in life, and for that very reason it seemed doubly important to do it well.

He was sure it was still daylight—he could feel the warmth of the sun on his back. He lay on the ground on his left side, and he could hear the whisper of the wind in the trees and, very faintly, the distinctive murmur of the river. Somewhere behind him came the soft whicker of a horse. But he heard no more human sounds. And something else was missing. What the hell was it? A moment later he realized what it was: there were no birds. That seemed odd, especially in a riverside woodland at this time of year.

Opening one eye just enough to see, he spotted two of the Dakotas, painted for war and crouched about twenty paces away. They were looking into the woods, toward the river and away from him. By the slant of the sunlight he could tell that it was late in the afternoon. The Sioux were still in place to spring their trap, then. Hawkes derived some satisfaction in knowing that they would not get the chance. He would not be making it back to the keelboats by morning, and he was confident that Redding would realize he had fallen prey to the Sioux and would turn back for Fort Union.

So at least the Crow annuity would be saved. Now all he had to worry about was his own skin.

But why was he still alive? The only answer that made any sense at all was that the Dakota had some notion of using him as bait to lure the keelboaters to their destruction. If that was the plan, they were doomed to be disappointed. With the exception of Plenty Coups there wasn't a soul in the expedition who would risk his neck to save him. Of course, the Sioux had no way of knowing that. It would be a point of honor among Sioux warriors to do all in their power to free one of their own who was in the hands of an enemy. For once, Hawkes was glad his own kind did not measure up to the Indian in terms of honor. He didn't want other men to lose their lives in an attempt to save his. *I got myself into this,* he thought. *And it's up to me to get myself out.*

Occasionally one of the Sioux warriors glanced back at him, but Hawkes hadn't moved an inch. The Indian could not tell, looking into the late sun, that one of the prisoner's eyes was just barely open. The other Dakota paid him no attention whatsoever. Hawkes wondered how far away the horses were, how many braves were watching over them, and if those horse guards could see him where he lay. He could learn nothing about any of that unless he looked behind him, and this he was not prepared to do. He was in no hurry to find out what the Sioux had in store for him.

A quarter of an hour later—it seemed much longer than that to Hawkes—one of the two warriors spoke briefly to the other, rose, and walked past the prisoner, heading in the direction of the horses. Hawkes decided that now was the time to act. The odds against him were so steep that he didn't bother even trying to calculate them. There was no doubt in his mind that the Sioux would kill him, probably sooner rather than later. Even if he didn't have a prayer, he had to at least try to get away. And to get away he had to free himself from the rawhide thongs that bit into his flesh at wrists and ankles. He needed a knife. And the only knife he could see, since, of course, his captors had relieved him of his own weapons, was the one his guard carried.

Heart hammering against his rib cage, Hawkes let out a low moan and rolled slowly over on his back, then lay quite still again.

The Dakota warrior heard him and shot to his feet. Standing there a moment, he watched Hawkes and then stepped closer, wanting to find out if the mountain man was conscious or not. One eye narrowed to a slit, Hawkes watched the Indian draw cautiously closer. *Come on, just a little bit more. Just a little closer.* The warrior obliged, nudging Hawkes in the ribs with one moccasin-clad foot. Hawkes whipsawed his body around, striking the warrior behind the knees with his legs. The Sioux sprawled backward and before he could recover, Hawkes had raised his legs and brought his heels down as hard as he could into the man's face. The impact slammed the brave's skull against the ground and he was out cold, blood leaking from a smashed nose and split lips.

Sitting up, Hawkes threw a look behind him, back into the woods where the horses were being held, the direction in which the second guard had gone. He could see nothing. Luck was still with him. Lying on his side, he rolled over against the body of the unconscious warrior and fumbled for the sheathed knife at the Dakota's side. Once he had it in hand, he slid his arms under his hips, squirmed onto his back, brought his knees up tightly against his chest, and strained to

slide his arms up to the back of his knees. Expelling all
the air out of his lungs, he straightened his legs, winc-
ing as he pulled his arms up over his heels, back
arched and rolling up on his shoulders. Then, with his
arms finally in front of him, he sat up and quickly, savagely, applied the blade to the rawhide that bound his
ankles.

As the thongs parted beneath the blade's sharp ca-
ress, a shout of alarm jerked his head around, and
Hawkes saw the other guard running toward him
through the trees. He didn't waste time trying to free
his hands, but got to his feet and stumbled forward.
The rawhide thongs had been soaked before being
used to bind him and had tightened as they dried.
They had cut off the circulation to his feet, so there was
no hope of making a run for it at the moment. Adjusting to this reality, Hawkes turned to face the onslaught
of the Dakota warrior, putting his back against a tree
and grasping the knife in his bound hands. The Sioux
rushed straight at him wielding a tomahawk, and it
was clear that his intentions were to kill. An errant
thought entered Gordon's mind—they weren't going
to use their rifles unless they had to, for fear that the
keelboats were close enough to hear a gunshot. The
tomahawk swept downward and Hawkes ducked as
the blade bit deeply into the tree trunk. The mountain
man lurched forward, thrusting with the knife, but the
Dakota warrior was agile and danced out of harm's
way. Hawkes stumbled and fell to one knee, cursing.
His feet were on fire; it felt as though a thousand nee-
dles were pricking his skin. Drawing his own knife,
the Dakota lunged. Hawkes twisted his body, taking
the impact and driving his knife up into the warrior's
belly even as the Indian's blade plunged into his

shoulder. Snarling at the pain, Hawkes twisted the knife and with all his strength eviscerated his foe, feeling hot blood gushing over his hands as the man's weight bore him to the ground.

Heaving the dying brave's body off to one side, Hawkes struggled to his knees and looked up in time to see the butt of a rifle an instant before it struck—and once again the world blacked out.

He came to this time very suddenly—someone was striking him in the face, time after time after time. Hitting him hard, the blows snapping his head back sharply. He was tied to a tree, standing, but his legs were not bound, and he opened his eyes to see a warrior drawing his arm back in preparation for delivering another blow. But before that blow could come, Hawkes kicked the man as hard as he could between the legs. The Dakota doubled over and Hawkes kicked him again, this time in the face, and the Indian sprawled backward. He bounced immediately to his feet, growling in rage, and drew a knife.

"Come on," rasped Hawkes, contemptuously. "You bastards keep trying to kill me. Get the job done. How hard can it be to kill one man?"

The Dakota began to move in for the kill—but then another Indian appeared and pushed him roughly aside. The second man barked a curt order. By his tone and demeanor as much as by the war bonnet he wore, this one was clearly a chief. The first warrior backed away with a murderous glance in the mountain man's direction.

"I am Long Horse," said the chief, and his splendid English startled Hawkes. "You are my prisoner, and it is up to me to decide when and how you die."

Hawkes took a quick look around. Night had fallen.

Several fires blazed in the woods, and around each were gathered a dozen or more Sioux warriors, clearly celebrating something. Disoriented, Hawkes couldn't be sure if these were the woods by the river, the site of the intended ambush. Had the trap been sprung? Had the ambush been called off?

"You want to know why you still live," said Long Horse, scrutinizing Hawkes speculatively. "The ones who first attacked you could have killed you from a distance. But a Dakota warrior earns great honor by killing his enemy at close range—and even greater honor by counting coup on a brave enemy without killing him. You are a brave man. You have more courage than any white man I have met. For that reason only, you are still alive.

"But," continued Long Horse, with a cold smile, "the same cannot be said for your friends."

He turned to speak to three Dakota warriors who stood around a small fire, and one threw a deerskin pouch to the chief. Opening the pouch, Long Horse took out several fresh scalps. Hawkes could tell at a glance that they had been taken from white men, and a sudden nausea swept over him, for then he knew why the Sioux were celebrating. He knew, too, why all the warriors had blackened their faces with ash from the fires—signifying that their burning desire to kill their enemies had been fulfilled. The fires within them had been put out. They had spilled blood and were now content.

Hawkes took one look at the scalps, then fastened a cold and hostile gaze upon Long Horse.

"The Sioux are thieves and cowards," he said.

Anger flashed in the eyes of the Dakota chief. But Long Horse drew a tight rein on his temper. He barked another order, and two warriors at the fire moved quickly off into the darkness.

"You will change your mind," predicted Long Horse smugly.

"Don't bet on it," replied Hawkes, silently cursing Agent Redding for a fool. Obviously the Indian agent had refused to heed Plenty Coups's warning and the keelboats had proceeded upriver, straight into the Sioux trap. Everything was now lost. The Crow annuity, the lives of brave men—and his own life. Hawkes had no doubt that Long Horse would kill him. He would probably not live to see tomorrow's dawn. It was quite likely that some hideous torture lay in store for him.

The two Dakota warriors returned, shoving Plenty Coups forward between them. The Absaroke was bound, his arms behind him. There was blood on his face and he had been stripped down to his breechcloth. He had been badly beaten, yet he still managed to hold his head high. The Sioux braves gave him over to Long Horse, and the Dakota chief shoved him closer to Hawkes, then grabbed the Absaroke's hair and pulled his head back, laying the blade of a knife to his throat.

"As you will see," sneered Long Horse, "it is the enemy of the Dakota who become cowards."

Hawkes realized with a sickening certainty that the Sioux chief was going to slit Plenty Coups's throat. Plenty Coups knew it too—Hawkes could see it in his eyes.

"Your name will be forever honored around the council fires of your people," said Hawkes to his Crow friend.

"Beg," said Long Horse, looking at Hawkes. "Beg for your friend's life and I will let him live."

Hawkes was sure it wouldn't do any good—but he could not refuse.

"I . . ."

"No!" roared Plenty Coups, turning his head and spitting in the Dakota chief's face.

Enraged, Long Horse drove the knife into the Absaroke's throat and with savage relish cut him deeply from ear to ear, then let him fall. As the Crow warrior's body thrashed for a few horrible seconds at his feet, Hawkes kept his eyes fastened on Long Horse. Gloating, the Dakota chief watched his victim's final moment of agony with relish. Only when Plenty Coups was dead did he look up to meet the mountain man's gaze. Then he stepped over the corpse and laid the bloody blade against Hawkes's neck.

"Had you begged, I would have killed him just the same—and then I would have killed you. The Dakota do not tolerate weakness."

"You better go ahead and kill me now," said Hawkes, "because for however much longer I live, I will have one goal—and that's to see you die."

Long Horse laughed and took the knife away from the mountain man's throat. "No, you will live. But only for as long as I wish."

As Long Horse turned away, Hawkes looked down at the body of Plenty Coups. A cold anger spread through him, an overwhelming desire for vengeance. The ghost of the dead Absaroke warrior cried out for it. Hawkes let his rage consume him. He knew he would need the fire it stoked within him in order to survive the ordeal that lay ahead.

Chapter 6

In the next five days the captive walked more than 250 miles, led by a mounted Sioux warrior who held the other end of a braided rawhide rope that was tied tightly around Hawkes's neck. His hands were always kept bound behind his back.

The Dakota raiders traveled swiftly. They had taken only the guns, powder, and shot from the keelboats. Apart from a few other souvenirs, the rest of the Crow annuity had been left aboard the keelboats and put to the torch, along with the bodies of most of the rivermen who had lost their lives in the ambush.

The knife wound in Hawkes's shoulder began to fester, and the fever that accompanied the infection very nearly spelled the mountain man's doom. By the third day it was all he could do just to stay on his feet and stumble along behind the warhorse of his Dakota captor. When he fell, the warrior did not stop, and Hawkes had to struggle to his feet or meet his end strangling on the end of the rope. For the entire five days they did not feed him, and only when they came to a stream did he get any water. They forded two major rivers, and even then Hawkes remained on the rope. One crossing was made at a fairly shallow spot, but there was deep water at the other end and he came close to being drowned.

The Sioux often taunted him on the trail, and in the night camps he was frequently spat on and kicked as he lay on the ground, bound hand and foot. On a couple of occasions a warrior urinated on him. Hawkes was too exhausted, too feverish, even to notice. But somehow he found the strength to survive and the will to live.

They traveled roughly northeast, and on the second day a line of ominous gray-black clouds advanced from the northwest, releasing a cold, hard rain driven by a fierce, bone-chilling wind. The Sioux war party pressed on, giving Fort Union a wide berth as they made haste for Dakota territory. Hawkes could spare no attention to the details of their passage. He could focus only on the ground in front of him, and on the grueling task of taking one more step, and then another, day after day.

At the end of the fourth day they reached the Oglala village, located on the banks of a serpentine creek that wound through a series of steep sandstone banks. Sentries posted atop high ground spotted them, and every skin lodge was emptied as the entire band gathered to greet the returning warriors. Hawkes didn't know it then, but Long Horse had sent the women and children here from Fort Union when he and his braves embarked in pursuit of the keelboats. There were about three hundred inhabitants in the village, the majority of them women and children.

Exclamations of joy heralded the arrival of Long Horse and his triumphant warriors, with an occasional outpouring of grief from the families of the handful of men who had lost their lives in the ambush. The

Oglalas gazed in wonder at Long Horse's white captive. Many stepped closer to get a better look at the mountain man's face. But Hawkes saw no anger reflected in their expressions. No one cursed him or spat on him. He figured that kind of abuse would come his way later, for he assumed that he had been kept alive only so that Long Horse could show him off to his people. Now that he had been used as an illustration of the Dakota chief's prowess in battle, it would be time for him to die. And it would not be a quick death, either. He would be tortured, and if he endured it for a while, more honor would be bestowed upon Long Horse for capturing such a brave foe.

After being paraded through the village for all to see, Hawkes was taken to a skin lodge near the center of the village and cast inside. The lodge was empty, the ground covered with skins. Too weak and exhausted even to contemplate what would happen next, he lay where he had landed and fell immediately into a deep sleep.

When he awoke there was a warm fire blazing in the lodge, and a young Sioux woman was kneeling beside it, watching him with limpid brown eyes. She was very pretty, her long black hair capturing the fire's glow.

"I am Pretty Shield," she said shyly, "daughter of Jumping Bull."

Hawkes struggled to sit up. His hands were still bound behind him, the rawhide rope still tight around his neck.

"You speak English," he said.

"That is why I am here."

Hawkes looked around. He could see a piece of the night sky through the smoke hole above his head, a handful of glittering stars, and thoughts of Eliza and his children intruded on his mind. He felt so heartsick that he wanted to cry out in his grief.

"You are very brave," said Pretty Shield.

He looked at her again and saw genuine compassion for him.

"You're . . . very kind," he replied, with a weak smile. "What happens to me now?"

"That is not for me to say." She stood up.

"Are you leaving?"

She smiled. His voice made it plain that he didn't want her to go.

"I will be back."

"Thanks for the fire."

She nodded and, with one last lingering look at him, left the skin lodge. As she raised the flap to pass outside, he saw two Strong Heart warriors standing guard. Alone with his thoughts, Hawkes gazed pensively into the fire and prepared himself for death. Soon enough, word of the ambush and massacre would reach Fort Union, and then the Crow villages—and then Eliza and Cameron and Grace would hear of it and assume the worst. He tried to console himself with the knowledge that he had been blessed with twenty wonderful years of love and happiness. That was more than many people ever experienced. More than he had any right to expect. Eliza was strong at heart. She would survive. And she had the children, his flesh and blood, his legacy. In them he would live on.

Hawkes heard voices outside, and soon a Sioux warrior entered the lodge, followed by Pretty Shield. Hawkes guessed that this man was in his middle years, a bit past his prime, but his presence was a forceful one. He walked with a decided limp, his right leg stiffened from some injury long ago. His broad face was deeply lined, his mouth wide and thin-lipped, his eyes still as keen as a hawk's. There was no animosity that the mountain man could see in those eyes, but no sympathy either.

"This is my father, Jumping Bull," said Pretty Shield. "He does not speak your language, so I will . . ." She hesitated, searching for the right word.

"Translate."

"Yes." She smiled shyly at him.

Jumping Bull sat cross-legged on the other side of the fire from Hawkes as Pretty Shield knelt beside him. The Oglala warrior gazed speculatively at the mountain man, and Hawkes met his gaze unflinchingly. Finally Jumping Bull spoke with slow, measured words.

"My father says he can see why Long Horse let you live," said Pretty Shield. "You are brave. A brave man masters his fear. And you are proud. You think you are going to die, but you will not beg for mercy."

"I am not so much afraid as I grieve for my family."

Pretty Shield translated his words for her father's benefit. Jumping Bull responded.

"My father wishes to know more about your family."

"My wife was the daughter of missionaries. The Flatheads murdered them. We have been together for many years. We have a son and a daughter."

Pretty Shield told her father these things. This time Jumping Bull spoke for some time.

"My father says that soon there will be a council, and your fate will then be decided. It is your right to be at this council. If you wish to be, my father will see that it is done."

"I do want to be there," said Hawkes.

Jumping Bull nodded, rose with some difficulty because of his stiff leg, and spoke again to his daughter before leaving the skin lodge.

"My father says that I can bring you some food," she told Hawkes.

"Well, I could sure eat," allowed Hawkes. "Thank you."

Pretty Shield followed her father out, and returned a little while later with a bowl of pemmican. She knelt beside him, dipping her fingers in the pemmican and feeding him, not taking her eyes off of him until he had sucked the last of the food from her fingers. Then she set the empty bowl aside and reached out and touched his beard, marveling at the hair on his face. Blushing, she stood up quickly.

"The council will begin soon. We will come for you. You should sleep now."

After she had gone he lay down again close by the fire. Its warmth conspired with his full belly and he quickly dozed off.

He didn't sleep long, however. A Strong Heart guard was soon shaking him awake, roughly hauling him to his feet and hustling him out of the warm skin lodge into the cold night. Nearby, dozens of men were gathered around a large fire, Long Horse and Jumping Bull among them. A place had been saved for him next to the latter, and he sat there with the Strong Hearts looming over him, their eyes fastened on the lone white man in their midst. Finally Long Horse rose to address the others.

"This man is known as White Crow. He is a great warrior among the Absaroke as well as among his own kind. As you can see, he is nothing compared to the Dakota. How else to explain his presence here as our prisoner? I have spoken of this many times before—

we have nothing to fear from the Absaroke, or any other tribe. This man is proof that I speak the truth.

"The white man drove us from our homeland, and now he is trying to tell us where we can go and where we must not go. I say it is time to stop listening to the white man's words. They cannot be trusted. We are a strong people. We can take what we want, even from the white man. And why should we not do this? He has taken much from us."

Hawkes looked around for Pretty Shield, but there was no sign of her, and he was sorry for that. He couldn't understand Long Horse's words and would have liked a translation. And he had to admit that he would have liked to see at least one friendly face.

Jumping Bull was the next one to rise and address the council, struggling with his bad leg.

"And what will happen to this man?" he asked, gesturing at Hawkes. "Now that you have made your point by bringing him here alive, what will become of him."

Long Horse glanced at Hawkes and shrugged, exhibiting profound indifference.

"It is of no concern to me. His fate rests in the hands of the council."

A very old man sitting opposite the fire from Hawkes took a long look at the faces of the men who sat in the circle. "Is there anyone among us who wishes to speak on behalf of the white man? Will anyone argue that his life should be spared?"

"We should let him speak before his fate is decided," said Jumping Bull. "He has that right."

The old man fastened rheumy eyes on Hawkes. "You may speak to this council if you wish," he said in halting English. "I will tell the others what you say."

Hawkes glanced at Jumping Bear, who nodded encouragement. Standing, the mountain man pointed with his chin at Long Horse.

"This man is a coward," he declared.

The old Dakota stared at him a moment, startled, then translated for the others. Hawkes was pleased to see that his declaration caused a stir among the council members. Long Horse just stood there, glaring malevolently at him, his body frozen in cold fury.

"He killed a brave man—my friend, Plenty Coups," continued Hawkes. "But there was no honor in it for him. He killed a man whose hands were tied behind his back. He cut my friend's throat. He is weak and afraid." He kept his eyes fastened on Long Horse. "You are afraid of me. I know this to be true, or you would cut me loose and fight me, man to man."

As the old man finished translating these words into the Sioux tongue, the circle of men fell deathly silent. All attention was riveted on Long Horse, who made a furious gesture as he barked at one of the Strong Hearts to cut Hawkes free. The Strong Heart stepped forward, knife brandished, to do Long Horse's bidding, but Jumping Bull suddenly intervened.

"If Long Horse does not care to make a claim on this man's life, then I do," said Jumping Bull.

"Why do you do this?" asked the old chief.

"Because he is a brave man. He is worthy to become one of us. Until such time as he is ready to accept our ways, he will be my slave. Such things have been done before by the Dakota."

The old man glanced at Long Horse, then conferred briefly with the men who sat on either side of him. Each of them in turn spoke to the next man in the circle. As this went on, Hawkes tried to make sense of

what was happening. He had not understood Jumping
Bull's words. All he knew was that Pretty Shield's
father had prevented him from having his way. He
had intentionally goaded Long Horse into agreeing to
fight him. While he had realized that the Dakota war
chief would in all likelihood prevail, he would at least
have had a chance to avenge the murder of Plenty
Coups. Failing that, he would have died like a man.

Finally, after the council members had conferred, the
old one spoke again.

"If what Long Horse says about this white man is
true, then what Jumping Bull says is also true. He is
brave and would be acceptable. We have seen with our
own eyes this courage, for has he not challenged the
greatest of our fighters? Does Long Horse have anything more to say in this matter?"

Long Horse stared impassively at Jumping Bull for
a moment, his expression perfectly unreadable.

"No," he said at last.

"Then it will be as Jumping Bull says," said the old
man.

The Strong Hearts returned Hawkes to the skin
lodge. A short while later Jumping Bull arrived, accompanied once more by his daughter. Again they sat
around the fire, and Pretty Shield translated her
father's words into English, and the mountain man's
into the Sioux tongue.

"My father says he hopes you will forgive him,"
said Pretty Shield. "You wanted to die like a warrior,
with a weapon in your hand fighting your enemy, and
he stopped this from happening. He knows why you
did this." She paused, looking at Hawkes in a way that
made it clear to him that she understood as well. "Because you thought death was your fate and you

wanted to choose the manner in which you died. But you will live instead, White Crow."

She listened intently for a while as her father continued to speak. When he had stopped, she turned her attention back to Hawkes.

"My father also says he is sorry that life is all he can give you, and not the freedom to return to your loved ones. He says you must give up any hope of seeing them ever again. If you try to run away, the Strong Hearts will kill you and there will be nothing that he can do to stop them. You will live among us for the rest of your life. My father hopes that one day you will accept the Dakota way of life and become a true warrior of the Oglala. He says . . ."

Pretty Shields looked down at her hands and for the first time, Jumping Bull took his eyes off Hawkes to glance querulously at his daughter. He spoke softly to her, and she nodded and raised her eyes to meet those of the mountain man.

"He says when that day comes his heart will be gladdened. As will yours, for then you will take a woman and she will bear you children and you will have another family, and the pain in your heart will be eased. Until that day comes, you will be my father's slave."

Hawkes had listened with growing horror to this talk of never seeing Eliza and his children again. He didn't care for the idea of having a Sioux family replace them one day, but he had decided to hold his tongue. However, he bristled at the word "slave."

"I will never be anyone's slave," he rasped. "Better that I should be burned alive."

Pretty Shield said nothing.

"Tell him what I just said," snapped Hawkes furiously. "Tell him!"

She spoke quietly to her father, then translated Jumping Bull's reply. "You will be asked to do nothing that your pride will not allow you to do," she said. "The choice is yours. Life, or death. Accept life among us or death at the hands of the Strong Hearts who wait outside."

Hawkes stared at her. Pretty Shield's eyes were begging him to choose life—and he made up his mind on the spot. So long as he was above snakes there would always be a chance that one day he would be reunited with his loved ones. No matter what, then, he had to stay alive. So he swallowed his pride.

"I will do as your father says."

Pretty Shield's eyes danced with joy.

Chapter 7

"We have not yet recovered all of the bodies, I'm afraid," said Major Culbertson gravely, pacing back and forth, hands clasped tightly behind his back, his brow furrowed. "I imagine the missing fell into the river, or were cast into it, and washed downstream. My men have combed both banks for a good three miles down from the site of the ambush..." He paused, turned on his heel, and gazed sympathetically at Eliza, who sat fiercely composed in a chair in his Fort Union office. "Do you sincerely wish to know *all* the details, Mrs. Gordon?"

"That's why I am here, Major," she replied quietly.

Culbertson sighed, nodded, and spared Cameron a glance. Then he promptly resumed his restless pacing. "My suspicion is that the remains we have not found will never be found. Quite likely the bodies fell prey to scavengers once the river gave them up. No survivors—and, I regret to say, no sign whatsoever of your husband, Henry Gordon."

Cameron watched his mother. More than three weeks ago news of the ambush had reached them in Red Bear's village, where they had been eagerly awaiting the return of his father. In all that time he had not seen her shed a single tear, though once or twice, in the night, he had heard her sobbing quietly. His heart was filled as never before with love and admiration for her. She was so strong—stronger emotionally than even he. Many times in the past difficult days he had wept hot tears of bitter grief. Never, of course, in anyone's presence. Especially not hers. If she had the fortitude to bear up under the strain—and he knew she did it mostly for his sake and for Gracie's—how could he do any less?

"I believe my father is still alive," Cameron told Culbertson. "And until I see his body I will continue to believe that."

The major tried to master his incredulity. It was clear that the American Fur Company man was convinced otherwise—and that he pitied Cameron for clinging so desperately to an irrational hope.

"So it was the Sioux who did this," said Eliza. "You have no doubts on that score, do you, Major?"

Culbertson drew a long breath. He craved a good stout drink, but it was bad manners to imbibe in the presence of a lady—especially since this particular lady was the daughter of missionaries. He was aware of her history. Her parents had been massacred by Flathead Indians who resented their attempts to convert some of the members of the tribe to Christianity. The murderers had probably been convinced that the missionary couple were corrupting the souls of susceptible friends and family members, seducing them away from faith in traditional gods. Now the poor woman had lost her husband of many years and found again that Indians were responsible.

"No, ma'am," he replied. "They were Dakota, all right. In fact, I'm fairly sure they belonged to the Oglala band. They were encamped here at the fort when the keelboats departed. The next morning they were gone—the women and children heading north into Sioux country while fifty warriors rode south."

"Camped here?" asked Cameron. "You actually trade with those Sioux devils?"

Culbertson smiled bleakly. "Young man, you have grown up among the Absaroke, and I understand your prejudice against the Dakota—a prejudice justifiably compounded by what has happened to your father. But my job is not to take sides in tribal conflicts. I am here to do business with any and all. I must confess that the Dakota are excellent clients. And besides, they are too powerful for even the American Fur Company to square off against."

"So what you're saying is that they go unpunished?" asked Eliza quietly.

Feeling distinctly uncomfortable under the woman's direct and, he imagined, accusatory gaze, Culbertson looked at the toes of his English boots.

"Even if there was something I could do, Mrs. Gordon, my hands are tied."

"And what about the army?" asked Cameron. "What will the United States Army do about this?"

"I am afraid I have no idea. But if I were you, I would not expect the government to launch a reprisal against the Dakota, young man. The last thing Washington wants right now is a full-scale war to break out on the High Plains. Then all the good that was accomplished eight years ago at the Fort Laramie peace council would be undone. Hundreds of innocent lives—no, make that thousands—would be in jeopardy. The Oregon Trail would become a path to certain destruction for untold numbers of immigrants."

Cameron grimaced. "I want to see where the ambush took place."

Culbertson shook his head, smiling tolerantly. "Now, son, what end would that serve but to cause you more grief? I assure you that had there been anything to find there, my men would have discovered it."

"All I need to know is how far down the Yellowstone I need to go."

Expecting to enlist the aid of his mother in dissuading Cameron from undertaking such a foolhardy quest, Culbertson turned back to Eliza. "I am quite certain that you will agree with me, Mrs. Gordon, that no purpose could—"

"My son is a grown man. I am not about to stand in his way if he feels strongly that this is something he has to do."

"I don't need a guide," said Cameron. "I'm not asking for anything. We came here with two Absaroke warriors. They will ride with me. There are no finer trackers in the world. No offense intended, Major, but your men might have overlooked something. He Smiles Twice and Broken Bow will not overlook anything."

"Cam is too modest, really," said Eliza, pride shining in her eyes. "He is an accomplished tracker in his own right. He had a very good teacher."

Even such an indirect reference to his father made Cameron's eyes burn with pent-up tears, but he held on to his composure.

"About two days' travel by horse upriver," said Culbertson, conceding defeat. "I can show you exactly where the ambush occurred on a map, if you will kindly step over here."

He moved to a table in a corner of the room, and Cameron joined him there as Culbertson selected a chart, unrolled it, and pinned one corner down with a Spanish stiletto that was lying on the table for that purpose. Holding down the other side of the map with his hand, Culbertson studied it for a moment and then put his finger on the spot.

"Right here," he said. "The river narrows at a large sandbar. Trees on both sides make for excellent cover. A big bend in the river lies just beyond."

Cameron nodded. "While you're at it, where is the nearest Oglala village?"

Culbertson stared at him incredulously, as though he was sure he must have misunderstood Cameron's words.

"I'm sure you know where," said Cameron, with a faint smile. "After all, you have agents among all the tribes, don't you?"

"Not among the Dakota, no."

"Are you saying that you don't know where they can be found? I would have figured that was part of your job."

Culbertson glanced at the map, then back at Cameron. "And if I did know, and told you—what exactly would you have in mind? Why do you want that information?"

"Whether you tell me or someone else does, I'll find out."

Culbertson sighed. "I am not certain. But last winter they settled along here." He pointed at a spot on the map. "Porcupine Creek."

Cameron studied the map for a long moment, committing it to memory. "Not too far," he murmured.

"I want to know what your plans are, young man," said Culbertson sternly.

"If the Sioux have my father," said Cameron coolly, "then I intend to get him back. It's that simple."

"I am very sorry, but your father is no longer alive." Culbertson turned to Eliza. "Mrs. Gordon, please try to reason with your son. I know you do not want to lose him as well. What he is considering amounts to suicide. Surely you can see that!"

Cameron couldn't help but wonder whether Major Culbertson was genuinely concerned about his welfare or really just worried about the American Fur Company's profit margins. The major wanted to keep the peace, apparently at any cost. He had no desire to avenge the massacre perpetrated by the Oglala Sioux warriors. It wasn't enough that the Crows had been robbed of their annuity, or that men had lost their lives, or that the Sioux were able to violate the terms of the Fort Laramie Treaty seemingly at their whim.

"I'm not all that sure that I have lost my husband yet, Major," replied Eliza. "And I will not tell Cam that he shouldn't do everything in his power to find out whether his father is alive and where he is being held. All I can do is ask if I may impose on your hospitality until my son returns with some news."

"But of course," murmured Culbertson. "You are welcome to stay as long as you wish."

She nodded her thanks. "Cam, when are you leaving?"

"Right now," he replied. Going to her, he bent down, put an arm around her neck and kissed her cheek. "Don't worry, Ma. Remember, He Smiles Twice and Broken Bow will be with me."

"I know I shall worry. But I also know that you will come back to me. Won't you, Cam?"

"Yes, Ma. I'll come back."

He rose, nodded at Culbertson, and started to leave. But at the door he paused.

"I will be back, Ma, and I will bring Pa back with me."

As the door closed behind him, Culbertson could see that Eliza's mask of composure was on the verge of crumbling, and he turned his attention back to the map. Rolling it up, he found he could not shake the feeling that he had contributed in some way to the imminent death of the intrepid but foolhardy young man who had just left the room.

Within the hour Cameron had put bustling Fort Union behind him. With him rode two Absaroke warriors, both of them members of the Fox Clan and both good friends to his father. They had insisted on coming with him, not because the tribe had been robbed of its government annuity but because Gordon Hawkes —known to them better as White Crow—was missing. He Smiles Twice and his family had been particularly helpful and attentive since the news of the massacre had arrived at the Absaroke village in the Wind River Valley. Cameron's gratitude to these two men was almost overwhelming, and he'd been unable to find words adequate to convey it.

For three days they followed the Yellowstone. Cameron wasn't quite sure *what* he was in search of. He would be satisfied with anything that would give him justification for clinging, as he did, to the hope that his father was still alive. There was no sign to speak of—in the weeks since the ambush several storms had rolled across the High Plains, dumping heavy rains. The weather now was sunny, the days cool, the nights cold. They made good time, and on the third day out of Fort Union they reached the site of the massacre.

When he saw the sandbar and the deep, fast-moving channel and the trees where the Sioux warriors had concealed themselves, waiting for their prey to enter the trap, Cameron paused, fighting to bring conflicting emotions under control. Was this, then, the place where his father had died? Part of him did not want to go any further, and part of him wanted never to leave this spot. In spite of all his pronouncements to the contrary, Cameron knew there was a very real possibility that his father had met his end right here. Cam had come here to find some evidence and, he hoped, some answers, that would inform him one way or the other. Until he knew for certain, he could not go on with life. His whole world had come to a complete standstill.

He Smiles Twice and Broken Bow waited patiently while Cameron summoned the courage to proceed. He was ashamed of his trepidation, even though he knew that the two Absaroke warriors understood. So he did not hesitate long; steeling himself, he put his horse in motion and pressed on into the trees.

Both keelboats had been burned, and one had sunk to the bottom of the river. The charred remains of the second were wedged between the sandbar and a tree that the Sioux ambushers had felled to block the escape of the boats downriver once they had ventured into the narrow channel. According to Culbertson, the keelboat crews had been bushwhacking the heavily laden craft, which meant most of the men had been ashore, laboriously hauling the boats against the strong current. Cameron assumed they had fallen easy prey to the Sioux warriors. He could imagine the terror in their hearts as Dakota war cries split the air and painted Indians burst from the cover of the woods, falling upon them so suddenly that Cameron doubted much resistance had been put up. The ambush had no doubt been brief in duration. Then the scalping had begun, as the triumphant Dakotas took their trophies. Cameron shuddered at the thought of his father's scalp dangling from an Oglala lodgepole. Though he had never even seen a Sioux in the flesh, Cameron hated them all at that moment with a passion so fervent that he knew it would not soon fade.

The three men split up, moving slowly through the woods. The Absaroke dismounted, leading their ponies, their keen eyes sweeping the ground, missing nothing. Closer to the river, Cameron stayed in the saddle and kept his horse to a walk, steering clear of the sandy rim of treacherous cutbanks, which might give way without warning and pitch him and his mount into the cold, angry waters of the Yellowstone. He saw some debris from the battle—a man's boot, the shattered stock of a rifle, the splintered remains of a crate that had been smashed to pieces by Sioux eager to get at its contents.

At a shout, he swung his head around. It was Broken Bow. He Smiles Twice was already moving toward his fellow warrior. Cameron wheeled his horse around and galloped at breakneck speed through the trees, his heart racing, fear knotting in his throat and threatening to strangle him.

Broken Bow was pointing to something—a wampum belt that lay near the base of a tree, nearly covered with dead leaves. Cameron recognized it instantly. He leaped from the saddle, picked up the belt, and held it in his trembling hands.

"This belonged to my father," he said hoarsely. "Little Raven gave this to him many years ago, after he saved the lives of the chief's son and daughter."

He Smiles Twice nodded. "White Crow was never without it," he said.

Cameron's mind was racing. "He must have lost it in a struggle," he said, looking about him frantically. "Surely no Dakota warrior would have passed this up, if, if . . ." He could not bring himself to speak the words out loud.

"Had White Crow been dead this would have been taken from his body." He Smiles Twice nodded.

Cameron forced himself to voice his thoughts. "It's possible that he could have fought here—and been killed elsewhere."

"Many things are possible," said He Smiles Twice. "But if the Dakota missed this, it may mean that they took away something of greater value."

"The Dakota have been known to take a brave enemy captive," remarked Broken Bow.

Cameron gazed at the wampum belt clenched in his hands.

"He must still be alive," he whispered. "Somehow I am sure of it. The Oglala took him. And I have to go and find him and bring him home."

"Let us go first to Red Bear," suggested He Smiles Twice. "He will call a council, and there I will speak on your behalf. It may be that you will not have to go alone." He glanced at Broken Bow, who nodded agreement. "It may be that the Absaroke will ride with you."

Chapter 8

When Red Bear sent word to the other Absaroke bands that a council would be held to discuss a raid against the Oglala Sioux, the response was immediate. Iron Bull, Horse Catcher, and the other chiefs of the Mountain Crow came immediately to the Wind River Valley. Red Bear sent other messengers to the River Crow, but was uncertain whether there would be a response. So it came as something of a surprise to him when Big Neck of the River Crow arrived in the valley less than two weeks later, accompanied by forty of his warriors, some of whom had brought their families.

Such were the circumstances that led to Cameron seeing Walks in the Sun for the first time in years.

Following the revelation that he and Walks had been lovers, her father, Crazy Dog, had tried to convince Red Bear and others in the band that Gordon Hawkes and his family should be banished from Absaroke lands forever. There would always be some among the Crow who wanted no contact whatsoever between the tribe and the white man, and Crazy Dog was one of the most zealous members of this faction. Cameron had always suspected Crazy Dog of acting more outraged by his daughter's deflowering than he really was, in order to stir up support for his campaign to rid the Wind River band of the unwelcome presence of Cameron and his family. Red Bear harbored similar suspicions. Being a man convinced that the Absaroke needed to maintain good relations with the whites, Red Bear resented Crazy Dog's adamant opposition to this course, and he refused to listen to any talk of banishment.

The following spring, Crazy Dog's eldest daughter married a River Crow man, and Crazy Dog chose to leave Red Bear's band and join his son-in-law's group. This happened to be Big Neck's band, and two of the warriors who entered the Wind River Valley with Big Neck were Crazy Dog's son-in-law, Many Wounds, and Crazy Dog's own son, Raven—the same Raven who had attacked Cameron and his father several years ago. Many Wounds had brought his family—his two young children and their mother, Walks's oldest sister. Walks herself had come as well.

It was He Smiles Twice who informed Cameron that Walks had arrived. Eager to be off to find his father in Sioux country, Cameron had fumed impatiently as the Crow bands responded to Red Bear's summons. Winter would be here soon, and every day was precious. To pass the time, Cameron spent long hours roaming the length and breadth of the valley. He now knew the valley as well as any Absaroke. There was one particular place he liked to go—a rock outcropping several miles from the village, where he had to leave his horse below and scale a hundred-foot rock face to reach the top. There he spent many hours, gazing at the mighty snowcapped peaks that enclosed the valley. It was his place for thinking, for dealing with his doubts and his demons.

He Smiles Twice knew this, of course, and he was on his way there when he met Cameron, who was returning to the village, and told him that Walks had arrived with Big Neck.

The news hit Cameron like a hard blow. The intense anguish of losing Walks had been slow to fade, and even now thoughts of her lingered, fueling bittersweet memories. He had tried to forget her, but finally resigned himself to the fact that this was impossible to do, even though he never expected to set eyes on her again. But now the news that He Smiles Twice brought tore open the old wounds, and the anguish was as fresh as it had been so many years ago.

He Smiles Twice watched him keenly, trying to discern his reaction. Cameron knew exactly why, so he did his best to hide his true feelings behind an inscrutable mask of carefully crafted indifference.

"Thank you for bringing me this news," he said. "But it is no longer of concern to me."

Now it was his turn to try to read the Absaroke warrior. He wanted to know if He Smiles Twice could be so easily fooled.

"My heart is glad to hear your words," replied He Smiles Twice gravely. "My mind is relieved. It will not be an easy thing to talk Big Neck and even some of the other chiefs into making war against the Dakota Nation."

"I understand. The last thing you need is bad blood being stirred up."

He Smiles Twice smiled. "You are very much like your father. You have great passions, but you know how to curb them, and when."

"My father is my one and only concern," said Cameron. "I know I need help to bring him home. I won't do anything that might rob me of the aid of the Absarokes."

"That is a good thing, because Raven has returned with his sister."

Through a considerable exercise of will, Cameron remained impassive. He didn't blink an eye. "I will keep my word," he told He Smiles Twice. "I won't make trouble. But I cannot speak for Raven."

"You would not take the life of Walks in the Sun's brother right before her eyes, I know this."

"No, of course not." Cameron didn't bother adding, *Unless he gives me no other choice.*

They returned to the village. Before long, Cameron had the distinct impression that He Smiles Twice—either on his own or at the behest of Red Bear—was sticking close to him. The new arrivals were making camp on the other side of the river. A few skin lodges were being erected for the chief and those who had brought large families. Cameron remained on his side of the river and tried not to display too great an interest in what was going on in the River Crow encampment.

Cameron was sitting on his heels by a cook fire tended by the wife of He Smiles Twice when he saw Robert Meldrum walking through the village. He had met Meldrum once before, and now he realized that the American Fur Company man had accompanied Big Neck's band. Meldrum spotted him and sauntered over, smiling affably.

"You're Gordon's son," said Meldrum, proffering a hand. "I was hoping I would find you. Thought maybe all this had something to do with your father."

"It has everything to do with him, as far as I'm concerned."

"So you really think he's still alive."

"Until I see his body or his scalp, I always will."

Meldrum nodded. He looked around at the village and chose his next words carefully.

"You figure your father would want war to break out between the Absarokes and the Sioux, do you?"

"I'll ask him when I see him."

Meldrum chuckled. "The Sioux are a mighty strong nation. Big Neck is here to try to prevent a war. You have to look at things from where he's standing. The River Crow live closer to Sioux country. They'll be the first to get hit, and them Sioux can hit hard. But they won't go to the trouble of trying to tell a River Crow from a Mountain Crow. So if you and your friends kick up some dust with the Dakota, Big Neck's people will pay the price. See what I'm getting at here?"

"I see one thing clear," replied Cameron. "I see the Sioux deciding someday soon to roll right through Crow country like a tornado. Big Neck might not want trouble with them, but he's gonna get some, sooner or later. Might as well be on his own terms, don't you think?"

"I don't think the Crow nation should start a fight they can't possibly win."

"You sure it's the Absaroke you're worried about, Mr. Meldrum? Or is it profits? The American Fur Company prospers by its Indian trade, and war is bad for business, isn't it?"

Meldrum's smile froze on his lips. "I don't think I like what you're saying."

"I don't either," said Cameron, meeting Meldrum's cold stare without flinching, "and I hope to hell I'm wrong. But if you care about the Crows as much as you say you do, then you'll realize that the Dakota have to be stopped."

"I would hope," rasped Meldrum, "that the chiefs will realize that all you care about is your father and that you're willing to see this tribe destroyed for his sake."

With that, Meldrum turned on his heel and angrily walked away.

The council was convened that afternoon, with more than thirty men in attendance, the chiefs as well as the most distinguished warriors from five separate bands. They sat cross-legged or on their haunches in a big circle. Calumets were removed from sacred pipe bundles. The bundles included bird, mink, and squirrel skins, necklaces, bear claws, eagle feathers—all objects having been blessed by a shaman and possessing potent medicine. Opening the bundle within the council circle was meant to benefit all those present with the wisdom to make the right decisions. The twin sacred pipes were decorated with red and yellow stripes, and part of the long shaft was wrapped with hide that had been dyed black. Once the pipes were filled with tobacco and lighted, they were passed around the circle, one clockwise and the other in the opposite direction. Each man present would smoke both pipes, blowing the smoke skyward while offering a silent prayer to the Great Spirit. Next he would point the pipe stem downward, offering smoke to Mother Earth, and then to each of the four winds—north, south, east, and west—before passing it to the man next to him.

When this ceremony was concluded, Red Bear stood to address those assembled. He talked at length about the loss of the government annuity, and the suffering this would cause the people, and how if something was not done the Dakota would continue to take what rightfully belonged to the Absaroke. Soon they would come to take Crow horses, and then Crow land, and then Crow women. And they would surely not hesitate to take Crow lives. It was time to teach the Dakota that the Crow would not simply stand by and let them steal anything they wanted.

There was, of course, another matter—another reason to attack the Sioux. They had taken White Crow as their captive. It would do dishonor to the Crow nation, said Red Bear gravely, if no attempt was made to free White Crow. He was, after all, an Absaroke warrior, adopted by the tribe, and therefore due the same consideration that was the right of any member of the tribe. It made no difference that he was a white man. He was also an Absaroke. That was all that mattered.

For these reasons Red Bear proposed a raid against the Oglala Sioux village believed to be located on Porcupine Creek, a few days away from Fort Union. The bands represented here could muster several hundred warriors into the field for this purpose. That would be enough.

Iron Bull was the next to speak. He agreed completely with Red Bear. Then Horse Catcher rose and admitted that there was merit in what Red Bear had said, but he was worried because to attack the Oglala Sioux would violate the Fort Laramie Treaty. The Absaroke chiefs had made their marks on the treaty paper and had given their word that they would faithfully abide by the terms contained therein. It was true that the Dakota had violated the treaty by attacking the keelboats that carried the Crow annuity, but did that give the Crow nation leave to break its word? It seemed to Horse Catcher that it was the duty of the

White Father to send his blue-coat warriors to punish the Oglala, who had violated the treaty. Had not the White Father promised to keep one tribe from attacking another? If Red Bear's proposal was adopted, then would not the White Father feel honor-bound to send his blue-coat warriors against the Absaroke as well? As for White Crow, perhaps the Oglala would be willing to trade for his release.

He Smiles Twice rose to address the council once Horse Catcher was done. He said he spoke for the son of White Crow and wanted only to remind all those present that White Crow had done a great deal for the Absaroke. He had sacrificed much for the tribe. He had always had the best interests of the Crow nation in his heart. How many times had he left his family to go and conduct the business of the Absaroke, to represent them among his own kind? Had he not been there at Fort Laramie? Had he not gone to bring this year's annuity back from Fort Union? For the Absaroke to stand by and allow White Crow to remain in the hands of the Sioux would be disgraceful.

A war leader from Iron Bull's band spoke next. He scoffed at the notion that the White Father would do anything at all to punish the Sioux. The White Father was afraid of the Sioux Nation; if he weren't, he would have made war against the Dakota a long time ago. For many years the Dakota had been conducting raids against other tribes, violating the Fort Laramie Treaty at will. But the White Father did nothing. Why was that? Because he did not care about the other tribes. The answer was simple enough. The Crow nation was strong. It had withstood its enemies on every side for generation after generation. It had never relied on anyone else to fight its fights. The White Father would never attack the Absaroke for violating the treaty because the Sioux had done the same thing and he had not punished them. It was up to the Absaroke to punish the Sioux for what they had done.

Big Neck stood to speak. It was easy, he said, for the Mountain Crow to speak of war against the Dakota nation. If things did not go well, they could always withdraw to their mountain strongholds, leaving the River Crow to suffer the wrath of the Sioux. If the Sioux decided to retaliate for a Crow attack on one of their villages, it would not be a Mountain Crow village that was struck in retribution. It would be instead a village of the River Crow, perhaps Big Neck's own, that would be targeted by the vengeful Sioux.

It was true, he continued, that the Dakota had wronged the Crow by attacking the expedition that carried the Absaroke annuity. It was also true that in the past the Crow had always stood their ground against interlopers from other tribes. But times had changed. The Dakota were not the Shoshone or the Blackfoot. They were far more powerful than the old enemies of the Absaroke. The only hope the Crow had of resisting the Dakota was the might of the White Father's blue-coat warriors. Only with their help could the Crow survive. It was time, said Big Neck solemnly, to recognize and accept this fact, as unpleasant as the reality might be. And since this was so, it was foolhardy even to contemplate antagonizing the White Father by breaking faith with him and violating the terms of the Fort Laramie Treaty by attacking an Oglala village. Those days were long gone. It was time for the Absaroke to act sensibly and not allow pride to lead them into disaster. No River

Crow, he concluded, would ride against the Dakota nation.

Several Mountain Crow warriors leaped simultaneously to their feet when Big Neck was done, angrily denouncing the River Crow chief for daring to suggest that the Absaroke could not hold their own against the Dakota. Some of Big Neck's warriors took offense to their remarks, and for a moment it appeared as though the council might disintegrate into a bloody brawl. But older and wiser heads prevailed, and order was restored. A few more men spoke their minds, but they offered no new insights, and Cameron's attention began to wander. He glanced about him, looking for Robert Meldrum. He was sure the American Fur Company agent had been present at the outset of the council meeting, but now Meldrum was nowhere to be seen.

Finally it was time for a decision to be made. Every man seated in the council circle was allowed to say yea or nay to Red Bear's proposal that the Absaroke ride against the Oglala village at once. Almost all of the Mountain Crow voted to go. Only a few River Crow, however, defied Big Neck and also voted for retaliation. Then Red Bear got to his feet once more.

"It has been decided," he told the assembly. "When the sun rises again we will go."

A number of warriors could not refrain from uttering fiercely joyful war whoops. Visions of glory and loot and sweet vengeance danced before their eyes. Clearly satisfied with the result of the council, He Smiles Twice looked at Cameron—and was surprised to see a decided lack of excitement on the young man's face.

Cameron also wondered at his own lack of enthusiasm. He had known he would need help to find and rescue his father—and now he had it. Then why did he feel this dreadful foreboding? Why this sudden conviction, coming out of nowhere, that the raid they were about to undertake would be a disaster?

Chapter 9

When the sun rose the following day, two hundred Absaroke warriors left the Wind River village. It was an awe-inspiring sight. The entire war party passed through the village to shouts of encouragement from those who stayed behind. Their horses were painted for battle, often bearing white handprints, which signified that the rider had slain an enemy in combat. Horizontal lines stacked atop one another on the horses' withers or on the front legs served as coup marks.

Each warrior carried a shield, which was in many ways the most important accoutrement. The shield had great medicine. Meticulous care was taken in constructing it, as it was the warrior's most cherished object of war. A circular piece was cut from the hide of an elk or buffalo and staked tautly over a hole in the ground, in which hot stones were laid and covered with a thin layer of dirt. The heat from the stones toughened the hide and caused it to shrink, at which time it was lashed to a frame cut from a stout but flexible sapling. At every step in the process prayers were said, and when the shield was ready, a medicine man would paint designs and symbols on it as the shield's owner recounted his visions and exploits. A war song was sung as the shield was blessed and adorned with eagle feathers, tassels, and sometimes enemy scalps. After the departure from the village, the Crow warriors would carry their shields in painted buckskin covers. Often the cover was endowed with pendants made from hide, cloth, and feathers.

Such was the importance placed on this raid that Red Bear himself and one of the principal chiefs, Iron Bull, came along. Though by now well advanced in years, Red Bear demonstrated that he had as much stamina as a much younger man. The war party made very good time on the first day. The sun was out, the ground was dry, and the temperature mild. Each warrior had picked his most durable and reliable horse. Cameron calculated that they made better than seventy-five miles that day, traveling due east. On the morrow they would reach the south fork of the Powder River. At that point, they would turn north and follow the river for one day before crossing it and heading due east once more. Once across the river they would be beyond the boundary of the Crow territory as established by the Fort Laramie Treaty. They would enter the rolling grasslands south of the Black Hills, where the Oglala made their home. In a matter of a few short days, then, Cameron expected to find out once and for all whether his father was alive or dead.

His anticipation was mingled with regret. Some—perhaps even many—of these brave Absaroke warriors would die. Their sacrifice, of course, would be for the sake of the Crow nation, not just for his father. It was impossible to balance the motives involved and determine their influence on the decision of each individual to participate in the raid. Though no warrior was required to accompany his chief, there were certainly some who rode only out of loyalty to their leader. Others sought the excitement and glory of the warpath. Some were present because they wanted to punish the Dakota for robbing the Crow of their annuity, and they did not consider the fate of Gordon Hawkes sufficient reason to make war on the powerful Sioux nation. But Cameron knew that there were others, like He Smiles Twice and many from Red Bear's band, who rode principally for his father's sake. For this, Cameron was more grateful than he could say. At the same time, he knew his father would not want He Smiles Twice or any other Absaroke warrior to die for such a cause. Robert Meldrum's words rang in Cameron's ears. *All you care about is your father. You're willing to see the Crow nation destroyed for his sake.*

But that just wasn't true. Cameron was concerned about the fate of the Crow nation. And one member of it in particular—Walks in the Sun. Now with Big Neck's band, she stood in harm's way if Big Neck was right and the Dakota retaliated by striking at the villages of the River Crow. Those villages were the most convenient and most vulnerable targets. Cameron couldn't help but wonder if in attempting to save his father, he had somehow condemned the woman he loved to death.

Yes, loved. Even after all this time, after everything that had happened. Cameron's heart ached to see her again, if only from a distance—even though his head told him that it would be a terrible mistake, because he would not be satisfied with a mere glance from afar. But he had not dared to venture into Big Neck's encampment. There most certainly would have been trouble. It wasn't that it mattered if the River Crow resented such a brash intrusion on his part—they had never intended to participate in the raid anyway. But such an indiscretion might have given some of the Mountain Crow reason to think twice about helping Cameron in his crusade. As much as he had longed for a look at Walks, he hadn't dared, for his father's sake.

Instead, he had hoped against all reason that Walks would find some way to come to him. He had realized what foolishness this was—he hadn't been sure if she even knew he was in Red Bear's village, and even if she had known, he had no reason to think that she wanted to see him. Just because his love for her had not been diminished by the years of separation didn't mean she still loved him, or even thought of him anymore. Naturally, Cameron preferred to think that her feelings were still just as strong as his were. And had she wanted to see him, perhaps she had not dared to try. The end result was long, anxious hours of torment for Cameron, such exquisite torture that he had actually been relieved when the time came for him to accompany the war party out of the Wind River Valley. He wondered despairingly if he would ever get over Walks in the Sun. His sense of it was that he never would. Only death could release him from his misery.

On the second day, after the war party reached the south fork of the Powder River and turned north along its western bank, one of the scouts Red Bear had dispatched in all directions arrived on a winded pony to deliver urgent news. The party was halted while the scout conferred with Red Bear and the other leaders. Cameron had to stand by like all the rest, waiting and wondering, until much later, when He Smiles Twice searched him out. Cameron could tell by the expression on the Fox Clan warrior's face that the news was something he could probably do without.

"The White Father's blue jackets are coming after us," said He Smiles Twice.

"After us? How could they know? How far away are they?"

"A half day's ride to the southeast."

"Coming from Fort Laramie, then," mused Cameron, his mind racing. Then he shook his head. "But there just isn't any way that word of the council's decision to attack the Oglala could have reached Laramie this soon. What has Red Bear decided to do?"

He Smile Twice shrugged. "He and the other chiefs must talk."

Cameron grimaced. In his opinion, such was the weakness of the Indian style of decision making. Red Bear could not impose his will on the chiefs and warriors of the other bands. In fact, he could not even force the warriors of his own band to follow him against their better judgment. An Indian leader had to rely on personal reputation and his powers of persuasion to get others to accede to his wishes. That often meant time-consuming discussions. But Cameron was convinced that time was running out.

"We can't just stand around here all day while another council is held," he told He Smiles Twice. "We must press on."

The Fox Clan warrior nodded sympathetically. "You are right, my young friend. But this will not happen. You have yet to learn patience. But you must—you know our ways."

"I know," said Cameron, disgruntled. He muttered a curse under his breath.

The Crow warriors waited for hours. Standing or sitting alone, or gathered in small groups, they all kept their horses near at hand, ready to mount and ride at a

moment's notice. Cameron sat where he could watch
the chief's conference, reins in hand, his horse crop-
ping at the short, curly buffalo grass. Though he could
not hear the words the chiefs were speaking, he could
tell nonetheless that there was much disagreement
among them. The sun began to slide down the western
sky; the shadows of men and horses lengthened.
Cameron's uneasiness increased with every passing
moment.

Finally the impromptu council ended. The various
leaders gathered their followers to convey to them the
decision that had been reached. This, too, took some
time, as every warrior had the right to speak his mind.
He Smiles Twice again sought Cameron out.

"It has been decided that we will wait here until the
blue jackets come," said the Crow warrior.

"Wait here?" Cameron was stunned. "That—that
doesn't make any sense! Those soldiers are coming to
stop us, not help us. Surely Red Bear knows this is so."

"We are still on Crow land. But when we cross this
river we will be breaking the promises we made at
Fort Laramie. So when the blue jackets catch up to us
they must find us here, not on the other side of the
river."

Cameron shook his head. "You know there can't be
that many soldiers. There aren't that many garrisoned
at Fort Laramie to begin with. If we stood up to them
they would back down. They wouldn't do anything."

"We have come to fight the Dakota, not the White
Father's blue jackets."

Cameron gazed across the river, debating what to
do. He was of half a mind to continue on alone. Perhaps some of the Absaroke warriors would go with

him. Once the soldiers arrived, there was little chance that they would let him proceed.

"I will not try to stop you," said He Smiles Twice, reading Cameron's mind. "But I ask you not to go. You cannot fight the Sioux nation alone. What good would your death be to your father? Think on this before you act."

Cameron noticed that two to three dozen warriors were mounting their ponies and leaving the war party, returning from whence they had come. They knew— as Cameron did now, with a sinking heart—that the raid was over before it had really even begun. All Cameron could think about was the time he had wasted in the belief that the Absaroke would actually help him. Bitterly, he realized that now he would have to start all over and find assistance elsewhere. The question was, Where? He Smiles Twice was right, as usual. To go alone into Sioux country would be tantamount to suicide.

The soldiers arrived about an hour before sunset. The Absaroke had built some fires against the night chill that had descended upon the plains. When lookouts called that the blue-coat column was approaching, some of the warriors stood up to get a better look. But all had been told not to react in any way that might be construed as hostile. The dragoons had crossed the south fork somewhere farther upriver and now approached along the river bank in a column of twos. Cameron counted twenty of them, plus a man he mistook at first for an Indian scout. Only when the column drew nearer did he recognize the buckskin-clad man riding alongside the officer leading the soldiers.

It was Robert Meldrum.

The officer raised a gauntlet-clad hand and the column came to a stop. Sharply spoken orders compelled the blue-coated soldiers to break out of column formation and array themselves in a single line facing the Indian encampment. The men remained in their saddles, carbines in hand, gun stocks resting on thighs. *So much,* mused Cameron, *for hostile behavior.* The rifles could have remained in their saddle scabbards. Clearly the officer in charge was trying to convey the impression that he and his command meant business and were fully prepared for trouble.

As Red Bear, Iron Bull, and a few of the other Crow leaders approached the line of soldiers, Cameron edged closer as well. The officer, a broad-shouldered, towheaded man with a sweeping tawny moustache, dismounted and stripped off his gauntlets, holding them together in his left hand and slapping them in what Cameron took to be an imperious manner against his thigh.

"I'm here to talk to the Crow chief named Red Bear," he announced.

"I am Red Bear," said the Absaroke leader in halting English.

"Good. I am Lieutenant Thayer, Second Dragoons. It has come to the attention of the United States government that you have conspired to violate the terms of the Fort Laramie Treaty and attack the Oglala Sioux. We heard of your call for the other bands to meet in a council at your village in the Wind River Valley. I was instructed to proceed there, and was on my way when Mr. Meldrum here met up with us."

Red Bear studiously ignored the American Fur Company agent. Cameron, though, turned his attention to Meldrum—and found that the man was watching him intently. Not bothering to conceal his contempt, Cameron glowered at Meldrum, who smiled coldly before looking away.

"It was thanks to Mr. Meldrum," continued the lieutenant, "that we learned of your plans, Red Bear. You should give this man your thanks. You were about to make a grave mistake by crossing this river into Sioux country. Perhaps you don't realize how grave."

Red Bear said nothing in reply. His expression was perfectly inscrutable.

Perturbed by the chief's failure to respond, Thayer grimaced and put an edge on his words. "I presume you will not bother to deny any of this. You're just fortunate that we caught up with you in time. As it is, I must insist that you disperse at once to your various villages. If I hear of any more talk about an attack on the Sioux, you and the other ringleaders will be slapped in irons."

Cameron bristled. Throwing caution to the wind, he stepped forward.

"Who do you think you are," he snapped at Thayer, "talking to Red Bear like that? This is a chief of the Absaroke. He is a great man, yet you scold him like he was a child. Last time I checked, this was Crow land. The Crow can go anywhere they want to on their land."

Thayer reddened. He kicked at the ground, leaving a deep gouge in the dusty earth and sending a spray of dirt in Cameron's direction.

"This land also happens to be part of the United States of America, Mister. And you and your Crow friends would do well to start remembering that."

"By the way, Lieutenant," drawled Meldrum, still gazing at Cameron with hooded eyes, "this is the man I was telling you about. Cameron Gordon."

"I thought as much," rasped Thayer. He turned abruptly to one of the mounted dragoons. "Sergeant Landrum, place Mr. Gordon under close arrest."

"Sir!" The burly sergeant leaped from his horse and advanced on Cameron. He was a big, scowling man with a bulldog's face. A plug of tobacco bulged in one cheek. The big knuckles on his meaty hands bore plenty of scars. Cameron pegged him as a career army man, tough as nails and mean as hell with the hide off. Clenching his fists, Cameron stood his ground. He was primed to resist being taken into custody. How could he find his father if he was locked up for God knew how long in Fort Laramie? Sergeant Landrum looked like a brawler, and Cameron figured he had no chance against him, but that didn't mean he was going to surrender meekly.

But suddenly a number of Crow warriors moved as one. They reached Cameron as Landrum closed in. He Smiles Twice and Broken Bow were among them. It was obvious to all present that they weren't inclined to stand by and watch Cameron be arrested by a blue jacket. And as the warriors moved, some of the dragoons brought carbine to shoulder—and Cameron realized that one wrong move now, by anyone, would result in a bloodbath.

Landrum paused and surveyed the belligerent expressions on the faces of the Absaroke warriors arrayed behind Cameron. Then he glanced over his shoulder at Lieutenant Thayer. The lieutenant sized up the situation in a heartbeat.

"As you were!" he shouted at his men—and the carbines were lowered. Thayer stepped forward until he was right in front of Cameron, with Landrum behind his left shoulder. Cameron didn't see so much as a glimmer of fear in the sergeant's craggy face. He knew that at Thayer's command, Landrum would wade right into the Crows and joyfully commence the fight. And there was no lack of determination to be seen in Thayer, either. The lieutenant fastened his cold blue eyes on Cameron.

"Mr. Gordon, one way or another you are coming to Fort Laramie with me. By all accounts you are the man who instigated this damned raid."

"By Meldrum's account, you mean," said Cameron. "The Oglala Sioux have my father. One thing is certain—the army won't do anything about that. Which means I have to."

"You have no proof that your father is a captive of the Sioux."

"I'll bring you proof."

"No, sir," snapped Thayer. "You're not going anywhere—except back to Fort Laramie in my custody. What happens now is completely up to you. Any bloodshed here will be on your hands."

Cameron looked at Thayer, at the dragoons behind the lieutenant, and then at the Absaroke warriors who stood with him. He realized that no one here was going to break down. No one was bluffing. Thayer was right—it was up to him whether there would be any killing today.

"Okay," he said. "You win."

He Smiles Twice stepped up beside him. "His skin is white," he told Thayer gravely, "but he is Absaroke. Remember this."

"I don't care what he is," replied Thayer. "He is my prisoner. I'm taking him to Fort Laramie. Soon enough, a decision will be made as to what will be done with him."

Red Bear spoke to He Smiles Twice, in English for the lieutenant's benefit, telling the Fox Clan warrior to go with Broken Bow and follow the blue jackets to Fort Laramie. He wanted to make certain, he said, that White Crow's son met with no harm on the way.

Within minutes Cameron had shackles on his wrists and was riding at the tail end of the column, guarded by Sergeant Landrum and another dragoon. As they headed south, Cameron glanced back at the Absaroke encampment, his heart heavy. Thayer had issued a stern warning to Red Bear, advising against crossing the river. It was the lieutenant's intention to camp a short distance upriver and dispatch scouts in the morning to make certain that the Crows had headed for home. Cameron was pretty sure the Absarokes would comply. Few of them cared to wage war against the United States.

He Smiles Twice and Broken Bow trailed along behind the dragoons. Their presence was a comfort to Cameron, even though he realized there was nothing they could do to help him. His fate now rested in the hands of the army, and he doubted the army would treat him mercifully. He had let his father and his mother down, and he despised himself for having done so.

Chapter 10

In the weeks following his arrival in the Oglala village, Gordon Hawkes recovered swiftly from his ordeal at the hands of Long Horse and his war party. Thanks in large part to the salves and poultices provided by Pretty Shield, his body quickly healed. Though technically he was Jumping Bull's slave, his responsibilities while recuperating were nonexistent. He ate around Jumping Bull's fire and slept in Jumping Bull's lodge. The warrior's wife, who was called Looking Glass, did not take to him initially and protested his presence at every opportunity. Yet as time went on she became reconciled to the fact that he was here to stay. Pretty Shield had a lot to do with that. She was the only child of Jumping Bull and Looking Glass—the only one left alive. One son had died in battle against the Arikara. Another son and Pretty Shield's younger sister had recently perished as well, falling victim to a virulent white man's disease. As a consequence, Jumping Bull and his wife cherished Pretty Shield to such an extent that they let her have her way in nearly every instance. It was obvious that Pretty Shield was fond of the white man in their midst, and while they could not understand why she felt so, the fact that his presence made their daughter happy was reason enough for Jumping Bull and Looking Glass to practice tolerance where he was concerned.

Hawkes familiarized himself with the Oglala village. He was allowed to wander at will, but Jumping Bull advised against it, at least for now. There were some men in the village who did not care at all for the presence of a white man, even one who was a slave, and it was possible that one of them might decide to kill him. The killer would be forced to recompense Jumping Bull for the loss of his property. But that would be the only penalty. Such an act, however, would not be carried out in the presence of Jumping Bull or his family. So Hawkes was safest closer to home.

For this reason Hawkes usually accompanied Pretty Shield when she left the skin lodge. It seemed to him that while most in the Oglala village were willing to tolerate him, few would go so far as to associate freely with him. Some even avoided Pretty Shield, as though her association with Hawkes had contaminated her. A number of her friends acted decidedly cool toward her. When he became aware of this, Hawkes suggested that he no longer walk with her. But she would not hear of it. Being spurned by members of her band did hurt, she couldn't deny that. And yet she refused to distance herself from him. She would take him with her when she went to gather wood and water, but she would not let him help until he had fully recovered from his wounds.

He was amazed and grateful for her devotion to him, and he enjoyed her company. As time went on, he realized that he was becoming increasingly dependent on her. She alone made his captivity bearable. Even so, her fondness for him—which everyone with eyes could plainly see—was cause for concern. He didn't want her to be hurt. She obviously believed he would live out the rest of his days among the Oglala. He was just as firm in his conviction that someday, somehow, he would be reunited with his family.

No one tried to stop him when he left the village with Pretty Shield to collect water and wood, but he noticed that on every occasion a Strong Heart warrior followed at a distance, keeping an eye on him. According to Jumping Bull, they would do nothing unless he attempted to flee or ventured out of sight of the village. Initially Hawkes thought it might be possible that sooner or later his watchers would grow careless, that one of these days he would look over his shoulder and not see an Oglala warrior shadowing him. When that happened he would be ready to make a break for freedom—even though he wasn't sure how far he would get unless he stole a Sioux pony. That in itself was problematic—the horse herd remained under constant guard. And whether he was mounted or on foot, there was not much cover out there in those treeless, rolling grasslands. He could not expect to elude them in this kind of terrain.

In spite of all this, Hawkes was determined to try. Better to die than reconcile himself to life as a captive, forever separated from his loved ones.

Weeks passed, and his frustration grew, because the Oglala didn't make that one mistake he was hoping for. A Strong Heart never failed to follow him and Pretty Shield when they left the village. Desperation started spreading like a cancer within him. The days were getting colder. Violent winds carried angry storms blasting across the plains. These northers were followed by day after day of bitter cold. The first snow would come at any time. The first blizzard could not be far behind. When winter came, his chances of getting home would be greatly reduced. Hawkes knew that time was running out. If he didn't get away from the Sioux in the next couple of weeks he might have to wait until spring, and he simply could not bear the thought of Eliza and his children going so long thinking he was dead.

So he kept an eye open for an opportunity, and when part of the Oglala horse herd was moved to graze closer to the village right across the creek from the Sioux skin lodges, he decided to make his move. His excursions with Pretty Shield usually took him in that direction. When Pretty Shield headed for the creek upstream from the village he went along, convinced that the time had finally come. As usual, a Strong Heart armed to the teeth with rifle and bow followed them out of the village. Hawkes knew that if he broke for the horses, the warrior would bring him down with a bullet or an arrow in his back before he could make it to the other side of the creek. And he would be just as dead if he tried to rush the Strong Heart. The trick was to get the Oglala to move in closer.

Mind racing, he walked along the bank of the creek with Pretty Shield. She enjoyed these times alone with him, even though quite often few words passed between them. These days he carried the water bags, two on either end of a stout pole that rested on his shoulders and the bags were filled. And while he tried to focus on the problem at hand, he could not help gazing off at the western horizon wondering, as he always did, how many miles separated him from Eliza and Cameron and Grace.

"One day," said Pretty Shield, "you will stop look-

ing for the mountains that you cannot see from here."
She did not look at him—she didn't have to because
she was always aware of him, aware of everything that
he did. And she did not care to see the wistful expression on his face either.

"That will never happen," he replied. "You should
know that by now." He glanced at her, regretting the
harshness of his tone.

"I wish I could help you forget."

Hawkes was taken aback. He had known for some
time now that Pretty Shield had feelings for him. But
never before had she said anything in such a forthright
manner. It stopped him in his tracks.

"Pretty," he said softly, and she stopped and turned
to look at him, but only for an instant before looking
shyly away.

"Pretty, if I weren't married and in love with my
wife I would stay with you. I would want to. Forever."

Stunned, she searched his face. "Do you mean what
you are saying?"

"Every word of it."

"Will you never forget her?"

"It just doesn't work that way, Pretty."

"I do not know how love works. I have never been
in love, until now."

He put a hand on her shoulder and leaned over and
kissed her cheek. It was a good-bye kiss. "But, you
know, I don't think I'll forget you either. You saved my
life, Pretty. You gave me hope when I didn't have any."

Smiling, Pretty Shield blushed. "Give me the water
bags."

As she filled them, one after another, Hawkes glanced
back at the Strong Heart, who stood about thirty yards
away, watching him. The horse herd was maybe a

hundred and fifty yards away, on the opposite side of the creek. Hundreds of ponies and only one guard that he could see—on the far side of the cavallard, six or seven hundred yards away. The horses were well spread out, grazing peacefully. There was no one around except the herd guard and the Strong Heart. *I may never get a better chance,* thought Hawkes. He tried not to think about the odds. That would be too discouraging.

After Pretty Shield had filled each water bag, she turned to drape its rawhide strap over the long pole that Hawkes had laid across his shoulders. When all four bags were filled, they began to retrace their steps. Pretty Shield was smiling broadly, not speaking. Hawkes knew his words had touched her heart, and he felt a little guilty. Not because he had misled her in any way—he had spoken the truth. But because of what he was about to do. Win or lose, escape or die, he was going to break her heart. There was just no help for it.

He took a dozen steps—then gasping sharply, he stumbled and fell. He hit the ground hard, spilling the water bags, and lay facedown, eyes closed, as still as death, his right hand resting on the long pole that lay beside him.

With a cry of alarm, Pretty Shield dropped to her knees beside him. he felt her hands on his face, his shoulders, his back.

"Gordon! Gordon!" She kept calling out his name, panic rising in her voice. Then, standing over him, she looked around in desperation for someone who would help. Seeing the Strong Heart warrior, she urgently called out to him.

The Strong Heart hesitated for an instant, then jogged toward her.

When the warrior was within a few feet of where he lay, Hawkes gripped the long pole firmly and swung it with all his might, striking the Oglala in the legs. The stout but flexible sapling pole hit at knee level and dropped the Strong Heart. Hawkes pounced on him, driving a fist into the man's face, and then another, and another. Blood spewed from the Oglala's nose and he blacked out.

Grabbing the warrior's rifle, shot pouch, and knife, Hawkes glanced toward the village. So far, so good. He got to his feet and turned. The look on Pretty Shield's face gave him pause. She was startled, but not afraid. Not of him, anyway. There was a profound sadness deepening in her dark, moist eyes.

"I'll never forget you," he said, surprised by the sorrow in his own heart as he realized that this was the last time he would be with her.

Then he ran, plunging into the creek. Though not wide, it was fairly deep, and the water came up to his chest as he waded across. On the other side he paused to look back once more. Pretty Shield was still standing there watching him, and of course she was not raising an alarm. He had known in his heart that she would not.

He turned and ran for the horses. Some started and galloped away as he approached. But a few stood their ground. He headed for the nearest one, slowing to a walk as he drew closer, whispering gently to steady the pony's nerves. The animal watched him warily but did not bolt as he reached out to run a hand along its powerful neck, then moved to grasp a fistful of mane. The pony's skin quivered beneath his touch. Hawkes looked for the horse guard. There he was, riding hard toward him. At that instant he heard shouts coming from the village. He vaulted onto the back of the pony. The horse snorted and sidestepped, and for a moment Hawkes thought it was going to try to throw him off. He kicked it into a gallop and headed north along the creek, away from the village. He looked back once more. Men were running toward the creek from the village, toward where the Strong Heart lay bloodied and unconscious and where Pretty Shield stood, still watching him.

He checked the herd guard again. The Indian was whipping his pony into a stretched-out gallop, scattering the cavallard in his effort to intercept Hawkes. Guiding the horse with his knees, the Oglala brought his rifle to his shoulder. Hawkes bent lower, urging his own mount to greater exertion, counting on distance and the fact that it was difficult to hit a moving target from horseback to save him. He heard the sharp crack of the herd guard's rifle above the thunder of unshod hooves on the cold, hard ground, and for an instant he thought the man had missed—until the pony beneath him stumbled, shuddered violently, and went down, catapulting him through the air. Hawkes landed badly on his head and shoulder and was out cold before his limp body had stopped rolling.

When he came to, he was lying on the ground, flat on his back. He tried to focus on the circle of Oglalas who stood around him. He could tell by the sounds that reached his ears—many voices, a baby's cry, dogs barking—that he had been carried back to the village. Among those who loomed over him were Long Horse and Jumping Bull. It was Long Horse who leaned down, grabbed him by the front of his hunting shirt and jerked him roughly to his feet. Long Horse put his face close to the mountain man's, his hooded black eyes glittering with hate.

"Now," said Long Horse, "now you will die."

"Offer still holds," said Hawkes. "Fight me man to man if you've got the guts."

"No. You will die at the stake. The women and children will be the ones to kill you. You are a coward, and that is how cowards should be killed."

Long Horse shoved him, and Hawkes staggered backward, still groggy from the fall, into the steely clutches of a pair of warriors. Turning to Jumping Bull, Long Horse smiled coldly.

Jumping Bull gave Hawkes a long, impassive look. "He knew he would die if he tried to escape. That is what he wants. He does not wish to live as a captive of the Oglala Sioux. In his place I would not want to, either. Kill him, Long Horse. It is what you have wanted to do anyway."

So this is it, thought Hawkes, and a surprising calm swept over him.

Then he heard Pretty Shield, her voice sharp and imperious and cutting through the angry mutterings of the Oglala men.

"No!" she cried out, elbowing through the circle of warriors to stand beside her father. "He will *not* die."

"Daughter!" snapped Jumping Bull. "You have no right to speak. This is none of your concern."

"Yes it is! You cannot take his life."

"He made the decision himself."

Pretty Shield looked at Hawkes—it was a steadfast, determined look.

"He would not have tried to escape if he had known that I carried his child," she said.

"Pretty Shield!" rasped Jumping Bull, stunned. He searched for words, and finding none, simply gaped at Hawkes.

Long Horse turned on the mountain man. "Can this be true? Only a coward would lie about such a thing to save his life."

"I . . ."

"It is true," said Pretty Shield. "And now you cannot kill him."

Long Horse grabbed Hawkes by the hair and wrenched his head around. "*You* tell me. I want to hear the truth from you."

Hawkes knew, of course, that it was not true. He had never been with Pretty Shield. If in fact she carried a child, which he very much doubted, it could not be his. She was risking everything for him, giving him one last chance to live. She was putting it all on the line—her reputation, her family's good name, her self-respect—everything.

"It could be true," he told Long Horse, looking into Long Horse's hate-brimming eyes without flinching.

With a guttural snarl of disgust, Long Horse let go of him and turned away.

Pretty Shield smiled and stepped closer to Hawkes. "Will you stay with me now?" she asked softly.

"Yes, I will," lied Hawkes.

Long Horse made a curt, angry gesture, and the warriors who were holding Hawkes released him.

Chapter 11

Fort Laramie had been built as a private trading post and bought by the United States government in 1849. Astride the Oregon Trail, its garrison was charged with the protection of the thousands of immigrants who braved the westward passage to the new land of hopes and dreams beyond the mountains. Elements of the Second Dragoons had been posted there under the command of Colonel William Lovell, a West Point graduate and a veteran of fifteen years of dedicated if uninspired service, including participation in the Mexican War, fighting with "Old Rough and Ready" Zach Taylor at Buena Vista.

It was to Fort Laramie that Lieutenant Thayer brought Cameron Hawkes, who was promptly locked in a dark, cold six-by-eight-foot cell. The walls were made of stone hauled in from the nearby mountains. There was a door of rusting strap iron and a single small window that only a very thin child could have squeezed through, located high on one wall, well beyond Cameron's reach. As it faced north, the window allowed no sunlight into the cell. The floor was packed earth, worn smooth over the years and as hard as the hewn stone of the walls. A low, narrow wooden bunk with a thin horsehair mattress and a single gray army-

issue wool blanket was the only furniture the cell contained.

Twice a day, once in the morning and once in the late
afternoon, a soldier brought Cameron some food, and
once a day an empty wooden bucket was brought in to
replace the one in which Cameron had relieved himself during the previous twenty-four hours. The fare
consisted of hard biscuits, beans, and salt pork. Accus-
tomed as he was to fresh venison or buffalo meat,
Cameron found these rations hard to stomach, and he
didn't even bother trying at first. Sinking into the
depths of a black depression, he could not muster up
an appetite. But on the third day of his captivity he
was taken out of the cell, shackled hand and foot, and
delivered to the commandant's office, flanked by a
pair of guards. On the way across the parade ground,
he saw Broken Bow standing and watching from a distance. The Absaroke warrior made sign language,
placing his right hand over his heart and moving it up
to the shoulder and then back down, several times. It
was the sign for "mother." Cameron understood that
the stout warrior was telling him that He Smiles Twice
was on his way to Fort Union to bring the news of his
incarceration to Eliza Hawkes.

Colonel Lovell sat behind a kneehole desk, rigid in
his chair, clad in a double-breasted frock coat of dark-
blue wool. His shoulder straps bore the badges of silver eagle rank. An orange sash encircled his waist
beneath a wide black leather belt. His salt-and-pep-
per beard and moustache were neatly trimmed. His
bushy brows were knit in a perpetual scowl over
muddy brown eyes as he looked up at Cameron, who
was brought to a standstill in front of the desk. Lovell
looked him over with cold contempt and then tapped

the paper before him on the desk with a blunt fore-finger.

"This is the report that I am sending to my superior," said Lovell. "I am charging you with inciting the Crow tribe to war against the Dakota nation. Do you have anything to say in your defense?"

"It was not the whole Crow tribe. Just some of the Mountain Crow."

Lovell glowered. "You don't seem to fully comprehend the gravity of your situation, sir."

Cameron looked around. "I didn't realize I was on trial today. Didn't know I had to have a defense ready. But since you ask, I'll tell you what I was doing. I was trying to find my father, who was probably captured by the Oglala. And that's what the Absaroke were doing, too—in addition to wanting to make the Sioux pay for stealing the annuity that rightfully belonged to them."

"Yes, so you say," replied Lovell, his words heavy with skepticism.

Cameron smiled coldly. "You know it was the Sioux that ambushed those keelboats on the Yellowstone. How is it that you aren't leveling any charges against them? Why don't I see Oglala bushwhackers in your brig?"

Lovell bristled. "I was extending you a courtesy by affording you the opportunity to answer these charges that have been made against you. I would have included your response in my report without commentary. But I can see now that I was wasting my time."

"Yeah," said Cameron. "You sure were."

"Take him back to his cell," Lovell told the guards. "It's going to be a long, cold winter, my young friend.

I hope your accommodations suit you, for I predict you will be my guest for quite a long time."

"I reckon keeping me locked up shouldn't be too big a hill for the army. A lot easier than forcing the Sioux nation to abide by the treaty that was signed right here some years back."

Lovell got to his feet, his body rigid with anger. "The United States Army will keep the peace on the frontier. That's precisely why you are now a prisoner here. Because you represent a danger to that peace."

"Am I more dangerous than the Oglala Sioux? Go tell that to the families of that Indian agent named Redding, and all those other men who were slaughtered on the Yellowstone."

"Get him out of here!" barked Lovell.

As he retraced his steps across the parade ground, shivering as a cold north wind cut right through him, Cameron searched for Broken Bow. The Absaroke warrior stood exactly where he had been standing before. Cameron extended both hands, palm down, and then brought them out and down in Broken Bow's direction. He followed this sign with another, putting the first and second fingers of his right hand to his lips.

"Hey," growled one of the guards, "what the blazes are you up to, boy?"

"Oh, nothing," said Cameron, and walked on, looking straight, gladdened by the knowledge that Broken Bow was nearby and that He Smiles Twice had gone to get his mother—glad also that he had at least been able to say, *Thank you, brother.*

Cameron languished in the brig for what seemed like an endless procession of identical days, with nothing to occupy his time but grim thoughts. At every turn he was confronted by his own failure. He had failed his mother, for she had relied on him to find her beloved husband. And he had failed his father, who had counted on him to be there to take care of the womenfolk if anything were to happen. Now Cameron could only wonder who would look after his mother and his little sister. The Absaroke? He wasn't sure his mother would cotton to the idea of spending an indeterminate number of months with the Crows. Would she remain instead at Fort Union for the winter? The American Fur Company entrepôt could be a pretty rough-and-tumble place at times. And Cameron had failed himself, as well. When the time had come for him to do a man-size job, he had come up short. Had he been the one captured by the Oglala, his father would not have permitted anyone or anything to prevent him from staging a successful rescue. Cameron had to wrestle with the knowledge that he wasn't half the man his father was, and that he might never even come close.

He was sleeping when his mother arrived, and at first he thought her voice was just a dream—until he heard her ask to be let into the cell with her son. Then Cameron's eyes snapped open, and he bolted upright to see her standing on the other side of the cell door, wearing the long gray woolen frock that his father had traded plews to get for her four winters ago at Fort Bridger. It was a very plain garment, but she loved it just for that reason.

"Ma!" He rushed to the door, gripping the strap iron. She smiled at him and put her hands on his. "I'm so sorry, Ma. I . . ."

"Hush, Cam." She turned to the guard who stood beside her. "Are you going to let me inside or not?"

"No, ma'am. Its against regulations."

"Let me go in there with my son," she said sternly.

"No, ma'am. Just can't do it. You—you could have a weapon of some kind concealed under that there frock, for all I know."

"The only weapon I have or will ever need," she said, brandishing her Bible, "is this."

"I'd have to have special orders to let you in there, ma'am, and that's all there is to it."

"I see," said Eliza. "Then take me to see your commanding officer at once, please."

"Ma, it's okay," said Cameron. "Colonel Lovell is a pretty stubborn man."

"And I can be pretty stubborn, too, when I put my mind to it. Besides, I have a letter addressed to the colonel." She turned back to the guard. "Well?"

The guard grimaced. He knew when he was beaten. "Follow me, lady."

"I'll be right back, Cam." She patted his hand. "Don't worry about a thing. You will be out of there soon enough."

Cameron didn't tell her that he had grave doubts on that score. He had been relieved to know that He Smiles Twice had gone to Fort Union to bring his mother to Laramie, but at the same time there was a part of him that keenly regretted her presence here. He didn't like it that she had to see him like this.

To his surprise, she was back in a matter of minutes—and this time the guard unlocked the cell door and let her enter, closing and locking the door behind her. The soldier stood there as though he intended to monitor the reunion between mother and son, but after a long embrace with Cameron, Eliza fastened her steely gaze on the man.

"I would like some privacy," she told him sternly.

"So would you mind terribly? Or do I have to go back and speak to your commanding officer again?"

The soldier cleared his throat, looking very uncomfortable. "I'll be down at the other end," he said. "When you want out, ma'am, all you got to do is holler for me."

"Thank you."

The guard nodded and moved away. Eliza smiled warmly at Cameron. "How are they treating you, darling?"

"As well as can be expected, I guess." Cameron felt he had a lot to complain about—the poor fare and the fact that he never got to leave the cell. He had hoped for at least an occasional visit to the parade ground so he could stretch his legs with a short walk under guard. But he didn't think it was fitting to complain.

"You don't look well, Cam," she said, touching his cheek, checking for fever. "You're pale and gaunt."

"I'm fine, really."

She sat on the bunk, patting the mattress beside her, and he sat down too, elbows on his knees, hands clasped tightly, gazing at the floor.

"I'm sorry, Ma," he said, his voice husky with strong emotion. "I'm sorry I let you down."

"What? Do you mean to tell me that you've quit? That you've given up trying to find your father?"

"Well, no, of course not, but . . ."

"But nothing. You're not a quitter, Cam. I know you'll find him."

"I can't do much in this cell, can I?"

"You will be free of this place quite soon."

"I doubt that. They're going to charge me with inciting the Absarokes to war."

"I know. Those charges have already been made. But they will be dropped. Trust me."

"How can you say that?" He gazed at her, amazed by her assured demeanor. "Colonel Lovell seems to think I'll be his guest here for a very long time."

"The colonel will change his mind. Or perhaps I should say he'll have his mind changed for him."

Cameron shook his head. "But how? I don't follow."

"I just gave the colonel a letter from Major Culbertson."

"Culbertson? What's he got to do with all this?"

"The major sent a letter to his superiors back East. The American Fur Company has considerable influence in the halls of government in Washington. A lot of pressure will be put on the president and on General Winfield Scott, commander of the United States Army. I doubt those charges against you will remain on the books for long."

"But—but why would Culbertson do that for me? The way I see it, he should be glad I'm locked up. The American Fur Company doesn't want troublemakers threatening the peace any more than the government does."

"Because Culbertson, and the company he represents, want to have good relations with the Crow as well as with other tribes. So he wants to get the credit for getting you released. You see, Cam, it made quite an impression on Culbertson that you were able to get so many of the Absaroke to ride with you. That tells him you have a lot of influence with the tribe."

"I think I see. But to be honest, I didn't have much of anything to do with the decision by Red Bear and the others to attack the Oglala."

"Be that as it may, the very fact that the army wants

you charged with inciting a war gives Culbertson good reason to think you must have influence, and a lot of it."

Cameron nodded. "Interesting games people like the major play, don't you think?"

Eliza smiled, a little wistfully. "That's the way the white man's world works, Cam."

"But what does he think I'm going to do once I do get out of here? Isn't he afraid I'll just stir up more trouble?"

"I assured him that *I* would keep you out of trouble."

"So that's the deal you struck with Culbertson."

"That's it, in order to be certain that he wrote the letter."

"But what about Pa? Do you really want me to stop looking for him?"

She took his hand in both of hers and squeezed it. "Absolutely not. I never wanted you to, and never expected you to."

"So you—you lied to the major."

"I did. God forgive me, but I had to. I would lie, cheat, steal, to get you out of here—and to get my husband back."

"You'll have him back. I swear it."

"I know." Her eyes were bright with love and admiration, and wet with tears. She smiled bravely.

"Winter is coming soon," he said, his mind racing as he contemplated being free once more to continue his quest. "Reckon it will take some time for Culbertson's letter to work its magic."

"I'll stay right here with you, darling," she promised.

"No, Ma. You must go and find me a few good men.

Men who will ride with me into Sioux country. I will go alone if I have to, but we both know I'll have a better chance of coming out with Pa if I have some help. Broken Bow and He Smiles Twice will help you. I'll need men and supplies so that when I *do* get out of here, I can head straight for the Oglala village."

Eliza nodded. "I'll do the best I can. But . . . but where should I start?"

"You could start with Jim Bridger. He knows everyone. I'm sure he will help. He and Pa go back a long ways. And Ma—I don't care what kind of men they are. I don't care why they would agree to ride with me. Whether it's out of friendship for Pa or for a good fight or a chance to take Sioux scalps, or any other reason. I don't care. Long as they'll go. Long as they'll die, if need be. Then I'll take them."

Eliza stood and placed her Bible on the bunk. "Perhaps this will make the hours shorter for you while you're here."

Cameron rose and wrapped his arms around her, and they held each other for a good long while, until finally she broke away and called for the guard. But before the soldier could arrive she turned back to her son with determination etched in her face and said, "You'll have everything you need ready and waiting for you, Cameron. You can count on me."

"I do, Ma," he said. "I do."

Chapter 12

Gordon Hawkes had a simple choice. Marry Pretty Shield or die.

To save his life she had manufactured the fiction of his child in her belly, and once Hawkes had gone along with the story, Jumping Bull had expected them to take the next step—marriage. Pretty Shield's father would have preferred that she wed a warrior who brought with him the prospect of fame and prosperity, someone who was able to provide Jumping Bull with ponies and buffalo robes and other gifts on the occasion of asking for Pretty Shield's hand.

The white slave, of course, had nothing of the sort to offer. He did not even have a hunting knife to his name. He had no more possessions than a camp dog. Yet Jumping Bull had no choice but to give his blessing to the marriage of Pretty Shield and the mountain man. In fact, he had to at least pretend to be pleased and optimistic about the match. He let it be known that he had high hopes for Hawkes one day becoming a Dakota warrior renowned for his great deeds of valor. To do otherwise would be to shame himself, his wife, and Pretty Shield. And to refuse to allow the marriage would immediately condemn Pretty Shield to a life of dishonor. It was bad enough that she had debased herself by lying with a white man, and a slave at that. Some of the people in the village shunned her for it. But to allow her to give birth to a half-breed child without a man to call her own was unthinkable.

So Jumping Bull gave his blessing, and Hawkes was married to Pretty Shield in a simple ceremony inside her father's skin lodge, witnessed only by her parents, the old chief, who had decided Hawkes's fate at the council, and a shaman. As the medicine man chanted a song meant to bring happiness and success and longevity to the union, Hawkes and Pretty Shield stood facing one another and allowed Jumping Bull to slice open their thumbs. The thumbs were then bound together and their blood mingled. "Now you will live as one flesh forever," said Jumping Bull. And that was that. Hawkes had expected there to be more of it. He had witnessed a good many Indian rituals in his day—complicated and time-consuming ceremonies to celebrate a young maiden's coming of age, the successful culmination of a young man's vision quest, or entreaties to the Great Spirit to smile upon some endeavor such as a buffalo hunt or a horse raid. But within only about a minute, he was married to Pretty Shield.

She was a beautiful bride, he couldn't deny that—made even more beautiful by the glow of sheer happiness that emanated from her. Her large brown eyes were filled with joy and love for him. It shamed him even to think of it, but she was prettier than Mokamea, the Crow maiden who had so beguiled him those long years ago when he had first come west. And Pretty Shield was even more sensuous than Eliza. Hawkes could not deny that he wanted her, but his desire fed flames of guilt. And it didn't do much to ease his conscience to know that his feelings for Pretty Shield—gratitude, desire, friendship—did not match up to the deep and abiding love for Eliza that he kept locked away in his heart. Indeed, he was betraying not only Eliza but Pretty Shield as well. He was doing this for only one reason—to stay alive.

Of course, Pretty Shield understood this and was willing to live with it. She kept telling herself that eventually, his longing to return to his old way of life and to the woman he truly loved would fade. For now she would be content with having him. The rest would come in time. And one day he would stop gazing westward in that wistful way, the way that hurt her so much that it was all she could do to pretend that she was not saddened. Then he would love her the way he loved the other woman, the way Pretty Shield loved him. She kept telling herself that all of this would come to pass, even though quite often she knew she was deluding herself. Because she knew what kind of man he was. A good man. A loyal man. A brave and stubborn man. The very attributes that made her love him were also the reasons she knew in her heart that her dreams would never be fully realized. Being the kind of man that he was, Gordon Hawkes would never stop gazing to the west.

Their life together was by no means unpleasant. A skin lodge was erected for them. Jumping Bull provided the hides used to construct the covering, as Hawkes was in no position to do so for himself and his new bride. Looking Glass and her friends helped Pretty Shield sew the hides together, while Jumping Bull and Hawkes gathered the poles, traveling for half a day to a stand of timber where Porcupine Creek converged with a larger stream. They harvested fifteen young trees and trimmed the trunks smooth. Three were larger than the rest, but all were straight and strong, roughly eighteen to twenty feet in length. They were lashed together into two bundles and hauled back to camp behind the horses.

Hawkes was a little surprised that no Strong Heart accompanied them and that Jumping Bull was willing to risk going out alone with him. He figured Pretty Shield's father to be a smart man and a good judge of character, and as such he must suspect that in spite of everything that had happened—in spite of Gordon's marriage to his daughter and the implicit commitment that his action entailed—that Hawkes still wanted to escape. And what better opportunity than this? Hawkes was far from the village for the first time since his arrival. He had a good horse under him. He had access to weapons, if he chose to try to take Jumping Bull's. It might well be his only opportunity in a good while. And yet Hawkes did not take advantage of it. For his part, Jumping Bull never appeared the least bit concerned. The idea didn't even seem to cross his mind. That puzzled Hawkes.

But then, when they got back to the village, Hawkes learned the truth. Jumping Bull came to his fire that night, and with Pretty Shield acting as interpreter, solved the mystery.

"My father wants to know why you returned with him," translated Pretty Shield. "He is surprised that you are still here."

"That's a good question," admitted Hawkes. "I'm not really sure I know the answer."

She told Jumping Bull what he had said, but did not take her eyes off Hawkes.

"My father says he thinks you are not speaking the truth."

"Well," said Hawkes, "I guess you could say it's on account of you, Pretty Shield. And in a way, because of your father, too."

"I do not—we do not understand." She was about to say more when Jumping Bull spoke again. This time she looked with sharp surprise at her father, then looked away in a vain attempt to conceal her shock and sadness.

"What is it?" asked Hawkes. "What did he say? Tell me, Pretty."

"He says he had hoped you would run away today. He says he would not have tried to stop you."

"Oh, I see." Hawkes felt bad for her. Now she knew her father had wanted to be rid of him. Wanted it so much that he had been willing to risk his reputation. Had Hawkes escaped, Jumping Bull would have been scorned. "So that's it. He took me out there hoping I would make for the tall timber. I'll be damned."

"That is what my father wanted," said Pretty Shield, and try as she might, she could not disguise the bitter disappointment that filled her.

Anger surged through Hawkes—anger directed at Jumping Bull for causing Pretty Shield such pain. But he kept his anger in check.

"Do not be upset with your father," he told her with a gentle smile. "He only wants what is best for you. He thinks it would be better for you if I was gone."

"But you are not gone," said Pretty Shield. "Why is that?"

He thought it over. It was because he owed her so much. She had given him the will to carry on. She had tended his wounds and been a light in the terrible darkness of those first days of captivity. And she had risked everything to save his life—even after he had tried to leave her and escape. He had this vague thought that another, better chance would present itself in time. The Strong Hearts would no longer be watching him. Apparently the Oglalas could not readily conceive of a man so bereft of honor that he would abandon his wife, especially one who was going to bear him a child. So they were letting down their guard. Soon he would leave. But a few more days, perhaps even a week, maybe even a fortnight—he could stay that long and by staying, keep Pretty Shield's dreams alive a little while longer. In the end he would hurt her; there didn't appear to be any way around that. He just wanted to postpone the inevitable result as long as possible.

Naturally he couldn't tell her any of this. So all he could think to say was, "Because I want to stay with you, Pretty Shield." And he hated himself for saying it as the hope and happiness lit up her eyes again. Jumping Bull asked her what Hawkes had said, and triumphantly she told him. He looked at Hawkes in some astonishment, and then resignation. With a grave nod of the head he rose and left the fire.

Their skin lodge was soon completed, the tripod poles tied together at the top and anchored with a stout rawhide tie pegged to the ground. Then the slighter poles were stacked against the tripod and lashed securely together at the top. The outer cover of hides sewn together with sinew was lifted with hoisting poles and unwrapped around the frame, then pegged down at the bottom. As with the skin lodges of most Plains tribes, the entrance faced eastward. A door flap, also of buffalo hide, covered the entrance, and two exterior poles were inserted into loops at the top of the lodge covering. Adjusting these poles could make the smoke hole at the top of the tipi larger or smaller as the need arose; when it rained or snowed, the smoke flaps could be shut completely. The interior of the lodge had a diameter of about fifteen feet at its base, but someone of Gordon's height could only stand up straight in the center.

That day Hawkes found a sorrel pony and a bow and quiver of arrows outside the lodge. Pretty Shield explained that it was up to him to provide for their food. His father could be expected to give them some of his winter stores, but they could not rely solely on his largesse. That suited Hawkes. He didn't want to feel beholden to Jumping Bull, and he preferred to fend for himself. He left the village immediately. No one followed him. The sense of freedom was exhilarating. Then thoughts of Pretty Shield intruded—and he didn't feel quite so unencumbered as before. He turned the agile pony right around and rode back to the skin lodge. She was standing outside, watching for him. He sat astride the shaggy sorrel pony, looking down at her, and then said, "I'll be back." As she smiled, relieved and trusting, he whipped the horse around and left the village again.

Hawkes was an accomplished hunter and adept at using a bow and arrow, having learned during his first sojourn among the Absaroke, twenty years earlier. Since then, he had often resorted to the bow in order to conserve his powder and shot. Pronghorn and deer were the most available game, and he soon adapted to the tricks of hunting on the open grasslands. He never returned to the Oglala village empty-handed.

For Pretty Shield's sake, he shaved the beard from

his face, scraping the hair off with a sharpened knife. She made new buckskin leggings for him, as well as a new hunting shirt and moccasins. Then she started to work on a buffalo coat to keep him warm during the winter. Except for when he was away hunting, they spent all of their time together. And gradually some of the Oglalas began to accept his presence among them. Jumping Bull and Looking Glass became reconciled to the fact that he was married to their daughter. Pretty Shield's friends continued to associate with her, and sometimes several young Oglalas, male and female, would sit around the lodge fire and visit for a while. For the most part they were civil to Hawkes, if reserved. He began to pick up the basics of the Sioux language.

The days passed uneventfully into weeks. The first snow came like a thief in the night, and the new day dawned on a world dressed in pristine white. Hawkes figured it had snowed long ago up in the high country. Before long, Eliza and the kids would be pretty well snowed in in the cabin nestled in a remote valley north of the Uinta Range. He missed them every waking moment. At night when he lay down to sleep, he longed for the warmth of Eliza's slender body.

He and Pretty Shield slept on opposite sides of the fire lodge. Hawkes could tell she did not care for the sleeping arrangements. He would catch her looking at him in a way that made it clear she wanted to share his blankets. But not once did she broach the subject. He tried to subdue the desire he had for her—a desire that nonetheless seemed to grow stronger with each passing day. The subject could not be avoided forever, however, and one night, as they sat alone around the lodge fire, while she tutored him in the Sioux tongue, he asked the question that had been nagging at him for quite some time.

"You're not with child, Pretty, and before long everyone is going to know it. I'm sure your mother has asked you about it, and a few of your friends."

Pretty Shield would not meet his gaze, looking instead into the fire.

"What will happen when the truth becomes known?" he asked. "What will they do when they learn you lied?"

"I did what I had to do. I wish I was carrying your child. Then, when you are gone, I would still have a part of you with me."

"My God, Pretty," groaned Hawkes.

"I am sorry. I know you do not love me."

He shook his head. "But I could. Very easily."

She stood up. "It is time to sleep."

"No."

She stared at him, her lips parted slightly, her eyes very bright.

"Come lie with me," he said, and when she did not move or respond, he added, "God help me, I want you, Pretty."

She smiled as she had never smiled before and in one smooth, graceful motion lifted her deerskin dress up over her head. He gazed in wonder at her trim body, desire bursting into a raging fire within him. As she knelt near, he reached out to touch her, his hand traveling up one arm, across a shoulder, and down over one dark-tipped breast. Pretty Shield closed her eyes, tilted her head back, and moaned softly, such was the pleasure his touch gave her. Then Hawkes slipped his hand behind her neck and pulled her down to him, crushing her lips with his in a feverish kiss, and she slid her hands underneath his hunting shirt, lifting it so that when she lay on top of him, he could feel her firm breasts against his skin. Hawkes rolled her over and stripped off his shirt and, looking down at her, was consumed by the love in her eyes, so pure and unconditional, and her arms and legs embraced him as he lowered himself into the warmth of that love.

Chapter 13

When Lieutenant Thayer was summoned to the headquarters building at Fort Laramie he had no idea why Colonel William Lovell wanted to see him—until he chanced to look across the parade ground as he trudged through the thick blanket of snow on the ground. He saw something that made him pull up short. The two Absaroke warriors he knew as He Smiles Twice and Broken Bow, along with the woman he knew as Eliza Gordon, mother of the young man who had been held for the better part of two months in the Fort Laramie brig, were sitting their horses on the far side of the parade ground, outside the building in which Cameron had been incarcerated. They had a fourth horse, saddled and ready for a rider, and a pack mule.

It was immediately obvious to Thayer what was happening. The woman and the two Crow warriors were about to leave the fort with a fourth person, and the lieutenant would have bet a year's pay that that person would be none other than the young trouble-maker he had arrested on the banks of the Powder River. He had steered clear of a confrontation with Eliza Gordon. Barracks scuttlebutt had it that she had put pressure on the colonel to release her son. Apparently, whatever she had done had worked. Thayer was shocked and perturbed. Lengthening his stride, he made haste to the headquarters building and a moment later was in Lovell's presence.

"Colonel, is Cameron Gordon being released?"

Lovell scowled at Thayer. "Do you have a problem with that, Lieutenant?"

"Yes, sir, I do. And I would have thought you would, too."

"I'm following orders," said Lovell, sitting back in his chair and brandishing a dispatch. "Orders from none other than General Winfield Scott himself."

"General Scott! But . . . but how can that be?"

"Politics, Lieutenant. Politics. That boy's mother prevailed on Major Culbertson, who made the case to his superiors, who pulled some strings in Washington, and this—this is the result." With a flick of the wrist he tossed the dispatch on the desk. In disbelief, Thayer picked it up and read it.

" 'You are hereby directed to release one Cameron Gordon forthwith. No charges will be . . .' " Thayer shook his head. "It doesn't make sense. Don't they realize how things are out here? Cameron Gordon is the most dangerous man on the frontier right now. Any little thing could start a war. Is that what Washington wants? How are we supposed to keep the peace if we let people like him stir up trouble?"

"Well, that's our problem, isn't it, Lieutenant?"

Disgusted, Thayer let the dispatch fall from his fingers and went to the window to look out across the parade ground. Eliza Gordon and the two Absarokes were still across the way, still waiting.

"We can only hope," continued Lovell, "that two months in a cell have served to cool his ardor."

"Not a chance, sir. Not him. I'll wager he still plans to go into Sioux country in search of his father." Thayer turned to face Lovell. "And who can blame him? Were I in his shoes I can't say that I wouldn't do the same."

"His father is dead. All he is after is revenge. And you know what will happen if he tries to exact vengeance on the Dakotas."

"Yes, sir, I do. The Sioux will strike back. They'll turn the Oregon Trail into a river of blood."

"We will have a full-scale war on our hands," said Lovell, nodding grimly. "And now is hardly the time for that, especially with the trouble brewing back East. Mark my words, Lieutenant. In the not-too-distant future, I fear, there will be open rebellion in the southern states. All the signs point to it. We must do everything we possibly can to keep the peace out here."

"Then what do you suggest we do about Cameron Gordon?" asked Thayer.

Lovell gazed moodily at the dispatch on his desk. "Stop him somehow."

"What are you saying, Colonel?"

"I am in a delicate situation here, Lieutenant. I have been ordered to release him. But letting him go about his business is a dangerous proposition. Unacceptably dangerous, in my opinion."

Thayer looked outside again. A guard was escorting Cameron out of the building. There were no iron shackles adorning his wrists and ankles. Cameron went to his mother and put an arm around her waist as she leaned down in the saddle to hug him. In spite of himself, Thayer was moved. He had to admire Eliza Gordon. She had conducted herself well in trying times, fighting courageously and doggedly for her son's freedom. And she had won. Thayer was glad for her. But then he thought of the other mothers who would brave the Oregon Trail next year, thousands of them with their families. Eliza Gordon had her son back, but at what price? How many mothers would lose their sons, daughters, husbands—even their own lives—if Cameron Gordon stirred up a Dakota hornet's nest?

"What is it that you want me to do, Colonel?"

"Keep an eye on him. Perhaps he will go home, if only to wait out the winter. Maybe he will give up his quest altogether."

"And if he does neither?"

"Then he will have to be stopped."

Thayer tugged on his tawny moustache. He had a fairly good idea what Lovell was getting at, and why the colonel had summoned him today. Thinking it over, he didn't much care for where all this appeared to be heading.

"So I should follow him and find out what his intentions are."

"Yes," said Lovell. "I think that would be a good idea."

"Are you issuing me direct orders, sir?"

Lovell grimaced. "No, I am not, Lieutenant."

"Then I don't have to do this."

Lovell didn't like being put on the spot, and what was worse, he knew that Thayer was intentionally doing just that.

"No, you don't have to, Lieutenant. But I believe you will, because I know you fully understand the consequences if that young hothead makes trouble with the Sioux."

Once again Thayer looked out the window. Cameron and his mother and the two Absaroke warriors were crossing the parade ground now, about to depart the fort.

"I have given you a furlough, Lieutenant," said Lovell. "I trust you will spend your free time in a useful manner."

"I would like to request that Sergeant Landrum also receive a furlough, Colonel."

"Very well. I will see to that."

"Thank you, sir."

An hour later Thayer was leaving Fort Laramie too, with the burly sergeant Landrum riding along beside him. Landrum had accepted without question Thayer's terse notification that they were riding out that day. That was one of the things Thayer liked about the Sergeant. Unlike so many other noncommissioned officers and enlisted men, Landrum didn't grumble and grouse and feel like it was his God-given right to complain about everything under the sun. Landrum was no shirker, either, and he was loyal to Thayer because Thayer, as opposed to the other officers in the regiment, didn't look down his nose at him. That in itself was enough to buy Thayer the sergeant's unquestioning allegiance. It didn't matter one bit to Thayer that Landrum was a crude, uneducated brawler who didn't know how to do much of anything well, except fight and drink and terrorize new recruits.

It was a clear day, but bitterly cold. The snow lay heavily on the ground, and the sun cast no warmth. The trail was easy to follow, and before long Thayer was convinced that Cameron Gordon and his party were not headed westward to Crow country. No, they were going north instead, toward Sioux territory. It was clear, then, that the "young hothead," as Lovell had called him, was not giving up the crusade to find his father. Was it possible that Cameron's father was in fact still alive and being held by the Sioux? Did it make any difference, really? Thayer pondered that all-important question throughout the day. As for Landrum, he didn't seem to be wondering about anything except the sign they followed and the country through which they passed. It didn't appear to matter at all to Landrum why Thayer had brought him along or where they were going.

A few hours after leaving Fort Laramie, they noticed that one of the four riders they were trailing had branched off in a westerly direction. As soon as he saw this, Landrum yanked his carbine out of its saddle scabbard and gave their back trail a long, careful perusal. Thayer dismounted for a closer look at the tracks in the ice-crusted snow.

"Think it must be one of the Crows," he said. "He might have circled around to see if anyone was following. Or it's conceivable that he might be going home, for some reason."

"Crows?" echoed Landrum.

"Would you like to know who we're tracking, Sergeant, and why?" asked Thayer, with a faint smile.

"If you wanna tell me, Lieutenant, I'll listen."

Thayer told him. Landrum chewed methodically on a wad of tobacco, his eyes betraying little interest in the information the lieutenant imparted to him.

"So we're not really on furlough, Sergeant," added Thayer.

Landrum grunted, then gave a nod. "Don't worry, Lieutenant. I wasn't getting my hopes up."

"Our job is to prevent Cameron Gordon from starting a war with the Sioux nation."

"Get me close enough and I'll stop him," said Landrum, lifting the carbine.

"We're not going to resort to that kind of thing just yet, Sergeant."

Landrum shrugged his brawny shoulders. "Just give the word, sir, and I'll do the job for you."

"Problem is," said Thayer, looking off to the north in the direction that his prey was traveling, "maybe he's right and his father is still alive."

"Why is that a problem, Lieutenant?"

Thayer fit a booted foot into a stirrup and swung up into the saddle before answering. "It's one thing to go into Sioux country to try to rescue his own flesh and blood. Quite another if he's just going to wreak a personal vengeance."

Landrum chewed and thought and thought and chewed, his bushy brows furrowed. Finally he said, "Seems to me that don't really matter none. Either way, he'll have to spill Sioux blood. Then the Sioux will feel obliged to spill white blood in return. Them Injuns have an Old Testament way of looking at such things. You know, an eye for an eye, blood for blood. They ain't the kind to turn the other cheek."

"I know, Sergeant, I know."

"Me, I'd just as soon tangle with them Sioux bastards now as later."

Thayer glanced across at Landrum. He was used to the sergeant speaking in such a belligerent manner—a fight was always Landrum's first choice when it came to settling an issue, and the bloodier that fight was, the better. But this time Thayer had a hunch there was more to the sergeant's remark than the man's usual bellicosity.

"Now as later, Sergeant? Explain."

"Hell, Lieutenant, you know it's coming. We're gonna have to take on that there Sioux nation sooner or later. Us and them, we're like two bulls in the same pasture. Gonna lock horns one day, sure as rain is wet. What I can't figure out is why we're pussyfootin' around 'em these days. Why, you'd think Uncle Sam was skeered of them red sons of bitches."

"That's why you're wearing the chevrons, Sergeant, and Winfield Scott has all that gold braid to carry around," said Thayer, smiling.

"Is that why? Hmm." Landrum spat, and brown tobacco juice splattered on the pristine snow. "I'll be damned. And all along, here I was thinking it was on account he was just naturally purtier than me."

"He is, when he's got all that gold braid on."

Landrum grinned, flashing crooked yellow teeth as big as tombstones, with a few gaps here and there where a fist, a handle, or a pistol butt had robbed him of a chomper. "Well, it's no secret that I didn't get to West Point, so what do I know?"

"You know plenty. And you're right about one thing. We will tangle with the Sioux sooner or later. But the head honchos in this outfit think it needs to be later."

"Now, you know I'll pull the trigger on that Gordon feller," said Landrum, "and I won't lose much sleep over it. But was you to ask me my druthers, I'd druther draw a bead on a Dakota buck all painted up for the warpath. That would feel righter to me, since they been playing hell on the frontier for years now and we just been sitting on our butts and letting 'em do whatever the hell they pleased."

"Thanks, Sergeant, for telling me what I already know."

Landrum grinned again. "Well, shit, Lieutenant,

you're so damned much smarter than I am, how can I not?"

"Shut up," said Thayer fondly and kicked his horse into a faster gait.

The next morning they reached the place where Cameron and his companions had camped for the night. It was there that the fourth rider had rejoined them.

"Well, it's a cinch they know we're following them now," remarked Landrum.

Thayer had to agree. The fourth horseman had circled around to check the party's back trail, and it was fairly certain that he had spotted the two shadow riders. Question now was, What would they do about it? Thayer had no idea. He didn't know how Cameron's mind worked, or how desperate the young man truly was. That put him at a real disadvantage, for Thayer knew, as did every good military man, that the old adage "Know thine enemy" was one of those eternal verities. But then there was the woman to consider. She was the daughter of missionaries, a good Christian woman. Would her presence or counsel dissuade her son from resorting to violence, no matter how reckless and desperate he had become? Thayer hoped so, but he braced himself for trouble just the same.

But trouble didn't come their way, and a few days later Thayer and Landrum reached Fort Union, still only a matter of hours behind Cameron, his mother, and the two Absaroke warriors.

Even in winter the American Fur Company post was a beehive of activity. A late immigrant train, caught by the heavy snow on the Oregon Trail, was encamped near the fort, as was a large party of men that Thayer took to be buffalo hunters by their looks and equipment and, when he chanced to pass downwind of them, their smell. There was also a small contingent of the Second Dragoons camped just beyond the walls of the outpost—fifteen men commanded by Lieutenant Jonathan Coopersmith. Colonel Lovell rotated small units to Fort Union every few months so that the regiment could maintain a presence at this all-important crossroads. Coopersmith's standing orders were to patrol a three-hundred-mile section of the Oregon Trail, an order that, like so many orders in this army, was highly unrealistic. It gave Coopersmith a task that required ten times the number of men he had under his command. Such, mused Thayer, was the delightful irony of service on the frontier. The nation's hopes and aspirations—indeed, its entire future—hinged on expansion, on achieving the "manifest destiny" that the politicians and editors and other grandiloquent men back East spoke of in stirring orations and fiery newspaper pieces. Yet where was the military strength necessary to ensure that expansion? The Second Dragoons were charged with patrolling an area greater in size than all of New England. What chance would fewer than five hundred men have against a Sioux nation that could put ten thousand warriors in the field.

Coopersmith was happy to see Thayer and invited him into his tent, while Landrum joined some enlisted men and a corporal huddled in their greatcoats around an open fire of buffalo chips and wood culled from the banks of the two rivers that met at this site. Thayer accepted the offer of a dollop of sour mash whiskey in the tin cup of coffee Coopersmith presented to him.

"Don't suppose I could be so lucky that you're here to relieve me," Coopersmith said with a smirk.

"Sorry, Coop. But why are you complaining? You can

get whiskey at Fort Union, and almost anything else, for that matter. That's more than you could do at Fort Laramie, with the colonel watching your every move."

"That's very true, my friend. Lovell doesn't have much use for me, does he? No coincidence that he gave me this duty this time of year, you know."

Thayer nodded sympathetically.

"Is it my fault that I have never seen action?" asked Coopersmith. "Or that my family has enough money to buy the colonel ten times over?" He shook his head in disgust. "I tell you, I often wonder what possessed me to join the cavalry, when I could have lived quite comfortably back in Philadelphia without having to lift a finger."

"Love of country? A sense of duty?"

Coopersmith laughed out loud, and Thayer laughed right along with him. They both knew the truth. Coop had agreed to go to West Point—his father's lifelong dream—only under extreme duress. A notorious man-about-town, he had been a gambler and a womanizer and a rakehell, and a real embarrassment to his staid, upper-crust family. A question concerning the paternity of a baby born to a woman of ill repute, followed by the rumor of blackmail paid by Coopersmith's father, had prompted Coop to accede to his father's request and, even more, to do his best at the military academy. Thayer knew Coopersmith to be an intelligent and capable officer when he put his mind to it. But he had done only enough to get by, graduating near the bottom of his class. That was just his way. And it was also why Colonel Lovell did not think highly of him. The army was the colonel's life; it was all he knew, and he thought it deserved the best effort from everyone who served in it. Coop did not show the respect for the uniform that Lovell thought was only fitting and proper in a commissioned officer. So it was that Thayer had to laugh about Coop's sense of duty. The good thing about Coop was that at least he could laugh about it too.

"Well, if you're not here to relieve me," said Coop, "what the hell are you doing here?"

Thayer proceeded to tell him the whole story, starting with the attack on the keelboats carrying the Crow annuity. He reported how Cameron Gordon was convinced that his father had been taken captive by the Oglala Sioux, and how he had apprehended Cameron, taking him back to Fort Laramie in irons. He also explained the circumstances behind Cameron's release and the gist of his conversation with Colonel Lovell. When Thayer was done, Coop nodded and poured some more whiskey in their tin cups.

"You're a fool, my friend," Coop decided. "You are right in the middle of a situation that could get out of hand very quickly."

"I realize that."

"Then why in God's name did you agree to undertake this without written orders? The way it stands now, Lovell can claim he had no idea what you were up to. In making it so that he can save his neck, he's put your head on the chopping block."

Thayer smiled ruefully. "I'm well aware of this."

"I thought you wanted to make the army your career."

"Well, there are a few things more important than a career."

"You don't have to tell me that. So what can I do to help?"

"I'm sure you have made friends here. Find out as

discreetly as possible, and as quickly as you can, what Cameron Gordon has come here to do."

"That's easy enough. I should be able to handle that little chore. I'll go about it right now. You stay here. Help yourself to the whiskey. There's always more where that came from."

Thayer stretched out on Coop's cot and promptly dozed off, only to be shaken awake by his fellow officer after he returned from the fort.

"The word is out," Coop told him, "that your fellow is looking for volunteers for a raid into Sioux country."

Thayer sat up sharply, cursing under his breath. "I was afraid of that."

"I'll have him arrested right away," said Coop. "You just give the word."

Thayer drew a long breath. "No, the last thing Colonel Lovell wants is that man back in the brig at Fort Laramie."

"No, of course not. Lovell wants to see him dead. Are you to be the assassin? Or is that why you brought Sergeant Landrum along?"

Thayer ran a hand over his beard-stubbled face. Then he shot to his feet and stuck his head out the tent flap, bellowing Landrum's name. Seeming to fill the close confines of the tent with his considerable bulk, Landrum gave Coop a perfunctory salute, then turned his attention to Thayer.

"Time for me to get my carbine, Lieutenant?" he asked laconically.

"No, Sergeant, I think it's time for me to desert."

Coopersmith and Landrum just stared at him. Both men were rendered speechless. Thayer had to smile.

"Yes, that's right. That's what I said. I'm going to join up with Cameron Gordon."

"You can't be serious," said Coop.

"I've never been more in earnest. I keep thinking there must be some way to prevent a war, short of committing cold-blooded murder."

"You want that I should desert too, Lieutenant?" asked Landrum, recovering from his shock.

"And would you do that, Sergeant?"

"Reckon so, if you ordered me, sir."

Coop laughed out loud. "You're both out of your minds."

"My being here in the first place testifies to that—wouldn't you agree?" asked Thayer.

"Yes, I would. You know you're going to have to do away with that Gordon fellow. There won't be any other way. Besides, he's not going to let you ride with him. He would have to be a bigger fool than you are—and I don't honestly know if they make them any bigger."

Thayer grinned. "Thanks for the vote of confidence, Coop. But I'm going to find out for myself, if you don't mind."

Coopersmith shrugged. "You're too hardheaded for me to try to talk sense to. And who am I to do that, anyway? So what can I do to help in this insane venture?"

"Nothing," said Thayer.

"What about me, Lieutenant?" asked Landrum.

"Sorry, Sergeant, you have to stay in the army. But I want you to stick as close as you can. Close, but out of sight. And if I get into trouble, I'll be counting on you to get me out of it."

Chapter 14

While her son had languished in the Fort Laramie brig, Eliza had sent word to Jim Bridger that Cameron needed help in rescuing his father from the Sioux. She knew Bridger as her husband's closest friend. The legendary Old Gabe had a small farm down at Little Sante Fe, having leased his trading post, Fort Bridger, to the army after it had been partially destroyed by Mormon raiders during the recent troubles between the United States government and Brigham Young's Saints. Eliza had hoped that Bridger would round up a company of brave, dependable men to accompany her son on his desperate venture into Sioux country. But she was met with disappointing news when she arrived at Fort Union.

Two men, Jim Dougherty and Antoine Le Due, were waiting at the American Fur Company outpost, and Eliza and Cameron met with them in Major Culbertson's quarters. As soon as Dougherty and Le Due entered the room, Culbertson excused himself.

"I hope you understand my position, Mrs. Gordon," he said, impeccably courteous, as he always was in her presence. "I have no desire to know any of the details regarding this affair."

"I do understand, Major. You have already done

more than enough to help us, and I will be forever in your debt."

"It was the least I could do."

"We won't be here long," Eliza assured him. "I realize you want to stay in the good graces of the Sioux."

"Sadly, there is no morality in business," sighed Culbertson. "I am grateful for your, um, discretion." He nodded at Cameron. "Best of luck to you, son."

"Thanks, Major, for everything."

After Culbertson was gone, Eliza turned to Dougherty and Le Due and asked about Jim Bridger. Dougherty stepped forward and, belatedly remembering manners that were rusty from disuse, swept the blue woolen cap off his head, exposing a mass of carrot-colored hair. He wrung the cap in his big-knuckled hands as he spoke, and as Eliza listened she studied those hands. They belonged to a trapper of many years, scarred and powerful hands that knew exposure to the burning sun and the freezing water of snow-fed mountain streams. Her husband had such hands. Eliza thought about him every waking moment, and when she chanced to sleep he haunted her frequent dreams. But in the presence of Dougherty and Le Due, men cut from the same cloth as Gordon Hawkes and forged in the same frontier crucible, her thoughts became even more powerful. She liked these two men immediately, for her first impression was that they were good, brave, reliable men—just the kind her son would need in the adventure that lay ahead.

"Old Gabe sent us, ma'am," said Dougherty. "He wanted me to tell you and your son here how sorry he was he couldn't come along himself."

"Bridger isn't coming?" asked Cameron in dismay. The prospect of having the assistance of the most legendary mountain man alive had encouraged him to think that he might actually have a fair chance of succeeding in his endeavor.

"He just can't," said Dougherty. "When he got back home from scouting for General Albert Johnson in the Mormon War, he found that his wife had died giving birth to his son, William. That really tore him up inside. Got an Injun woman to take care of the baby and he went and signed on with a Captain Reynolds of the Corps of Engineers to explore the Yellowstone River region. Old Gabe was on his way out the door, bound for St. Louis to join up with Reynolds, when your message got to him, ma'am."

"I see," said Eliza, trying to mask her disappointment.

"He told me to tell you he just couldn't get out of the bargain he struck with the army to go with Captain Reynolds. He also said to tell you to try and not fret overly much about your husband. Said he figured Gordon was alive. Said he didn't think there was much of nothing out here that could kill your man iffen he didn't want it to. Old Gabe said he was sorry as the dickens that he couldn't be of more help, but that he wasn't sure how much good he could do anyhow, seeing as how he was so old and all. Claims his eyes ain't what they used to be and his trigger finger's got the trembles. He asked me and Le Due here to come in his place, and here we are, and glad to do it. Le Due, he knows Sioux country like he knows his squaw's behind." Dougherty looked suddenly stricken and blushed a rosy hue. "Excuse my language, ma'am. Too many years floating my stick with the wrong sort, I reckon." He grinned sheepishly.

"That's quite all right, Mr. Dougherty. I have lived

out here for twenty years. My ears are no longer tender."

"Is that true, that you know the country well?" Cameron asked Le Due.

"I'll have to speak for him," said Dougherty. "You see, them Dakota devils cut the tongue out of his head a few years back. They finally caught him in their territory and made him pay the price. He's right lucky a tongue is all he lost. But he knows that country, yes, he does, and you can rely on that. He knows the ways of the Sioux as well as any white man alive."

Le Due made some hand gestures that Cameron could make no sense of—they were vaguely similar in some respects to Indian sign language, but not similar enough to be of any help to him. He thought maybe it was sign that Le Due and Dougherty had worked out for themselves."

"Oh, yeah," said Dougherty when Le Due was finished. "He says to tell you he hates them Sioux more than he hates anything in this world, and he would be obliged for a chance to kill a good many of 'em so's he can collect their tongues."

"Tongues? Not scalps?"

Dougherty grinned. "Tongues for him. Me, I'll take the scalps."

Cameron glanced at his mother, wondering what her reaction would be to such brutal talk. But Eliza showed no reaction whatsoever.

"Is that why you're here, Mr. Dougherty?" she asked. "To collect some Sioux scalps?"

"Oh, no, ma'am. That there would be just like a bonus. I'm here on account of I don't cotton to the idea of one of my own being taken by them red bast—them Sioux. Now I ain't gonna lie to you. I don't know that

I ever had occasion to meet your husband, but Old Gabe, he says your man is a good one, and if Old Gabe vouches for that, hell, it's plenty good enough for me."

"Yes," said Eliza, smiling. "He is a good one."

Dougherty nodded. "Well, iffen it was me who had done been made a slave by the Sioux, I'd want my own kind to lift a hand to help me out of that bind. Who knows, maybe someday your man will be able to return the favor. We all got to stick together."

"We will owe you both a great debt," said Eliza. "Assuming you survive, that is."

Dougherty grinned again. "Shoot, ma'am, I been beating the odds and cheating that old Reaper ever since I stepped foot in this country. Besides, I ain't inclined to live to be too old. I want to die while life is still worth appreciating. And I'd rather take someone along with me when I go, even if it is a Sioux buck, so I don't have to face the devil alone."

Eliza turned to her son. "Well, Cam? You have to ride with them. What do you say?"

"I say yes."

Eliza nodded. "As do I."

Cameron stepped up to shake Dougherty's hand, and then Le Due's. "Hopefully none of us will have to die," he said.

"We be going up against the Dakota, ain't we?" inquired Dougherty.

"That's right."

"Then there'll be some killing to do. You can bet your horse on that."

Le Due made some more hand gestures, and when he was done Dougherty added, "He wants to know when you aim to leave?"

Cameron sighed. "Well, I was hoping for a few more volunteers."

Le Due signed again, and Dougherty translated. "He says the fewer the better. A smaller bunch has a better chance of getting up close enough to make a difference."

Cameron smiled ruefully. "Then it's just as well, isn't it? I expect tomorrow will be soon enough."

Again Le Due made his gestures.

"He wants to know where your pa is being held."

"I can show you where I think he is." Cameron took them both to the chart table, found the map that Culbertson had shown him months ago, and pointed to the same spot.

Dougherty studied the map and then nodded. "Four, maybe five days' hard travelin' in heavy snow. The Oglalas, I reckon."

"Yes, the Oglalas."

"How big is that village, you reckon?"

"I have no idea."

The door opened and Major Culbertson entered the room with the last man on earth Cameron wanted to see.

"This is Lieutenant Thayer," said Culbertson, looking more worried than usual. "Of the Second Dragoons."

"Thank you, Major," said Thayer. "Mr. Gordon and I are already acquainted."

"What are you doing here?" asked Cameron. "Have you come to arrest me again?"

Thayer smiled and turned to Eliza, coming to attention and then bending forward slightly at the waist to bow to her. "Mrs. Gordon. I have not had the pleasure of making your acquaintance, though. I hope you understand that I was only doing my duty when I took your son into custody."

"Has your duty brought you here today, Lieutenant?"

"No, ma'am. My conscience did that."

"Please explain."

Thayer glanced at each man in the room, then turned back to Eliza.

"I want to help you get your husband back, if he's still alive."

"He is still alive," said Cameron coldly.

"I sincerely hope that's the case."

"I was told my son was arrested to prevent an attack on the Sioux that would, it was said, start a war," said Eliza.

"That's indeed what we wanted to prevent," said Thayer. "Sioux attacks on the immigrants who travel the Oregon Trail, and on the villages of the River Crow. Those would be the most convenient targets."

"They will be, regardless," said Cameron. "Whenever the Dakota decide to attack them. Why should they abide by the Fort Laramie Treaty? They know the army isn't going to do anything to stop them."

"You're wrong. The army will act, when the time comes."

"When the times comes! Why didn't it act when the Oglalas ambushed the keelboats carrying the Crow annuity?"

"It's not quite that simple," said Thayer with a chilly smile.

"Well, it's very simple to me," replied Cameron.

"I've come to offer my services, to assist you in your endeavor. Not to argue."

"But why, Lieutenant?" asked Eliza. "Why would

you want to be a party to something that might start a war? Why has the army suddenly changed its mind?"

"The army hasn't. But I have."

"Colonel Lovell didn't send you?"

"Yes, he sent me. To keep an eye on your son."

"Where's the other man?" asked Cameron. "The one who rode with you when you followed us from Fort Laramie?"

"That would be Sergeant Landrum. You might remember him. But he doesn't know I'm here, or why."

Cameron left the map table and walked up to Thayer and stood toe to toe with the dragoon. "I don't care why you're here. But unless it's to take me back to Fort Laramie in irons, I think you should get out."

"Wait, Cam," said Eliza. "Maybe we should hear him out."

"He can't be trusted, Ma."

"Let's just hear what he has to say, shall we?"

"I don't want to start a war, Mrs. Gordon," said Thayer. "But I will help get your husband back. With luck, we can do that without anyone getting killed. How did you plan to free your father?" he asked Cameron.

"I don't know, exactly," admitted Cameron. "Just go in and get him out, I guess."

"I thought the purpose was to rescue him. You'll just get him and yourself killed with that plan."

"And you have a better idea?"

"I think I do. Want to hear it?"

Cameron glanced at his mother. "All right. I'm listening."

"It will be virtually impossible to get close to the Sioux village without being seen. The best chance is to travel at night. The moon is on the wane, so the nights will be dark. We probably won't be spotted. Of course, there's a chance someone will cross our trail, but that can't be helped. Now, if we can manage to get close enough to the village without being discovered, we find a place to lay low out of sight and do a little scouting. Try to find out how many men we're up against, and where your father is located. Then, at daybreak, your two Crow friends run off the Sioux horse herd. I assume those two will be going with you?"

"I haven't asked them," said Cameron.

"Well, assuming that they do, they would be the ones to hit the horse herd."

"Why them, Lieutenant?"

"Because the Sioux will think it's a horse-stealing raid. That way, whoever is left in the village—and I expect most of the men will be trying to save their ponies—won't be expecting the rest of us when we ride in, make straight for your father, get him, and ride out. With any luck, in all the confusion, we will be able to avoid a shooting scrape."

Cameron looked at the others—his mother, Dougherty, and Le Due, and then Culbertson, who stood just inside the door. In spite of the deep-seated animosity he had for Thayer, he had to admit to himself that the horse soldier had a good plan in mind for the rescue of his father. The question remained, though—could Thayer be trusted? Cameron just wasn't sure. If Thayer wanted to stop him, then why bother joining the rescue party?

"Sounds like it could work to me," offered Dougherty.

"What do you think, Cam?" asked Eliza.

Cameron turned back to Thayer.

"All right," he said. "You can come along. That's not

saying I trust you. But I reckon you might as well be where I can keep an eye on you."

"Fair enough," said Thayer. "Then I think it's time I bought some civilian clothes. I can't very well wear this uniform into Sioux country."

"You are putting your career at risk, Lieutenant," observed Eliza. "You're willing to do that?"

"Not for your husband alone. For all the innocent people who will come up the Oregon Trail next spring. See, I figure your son is crossing the Missouri River with or without me. With me along, there's a slightly better chance we can avoid any killing. And if nobody gets killed, it's possible the Sioux won't feel the need to seek vengeance."

Eliza nodded, and Cameron could tell she was satisfied with Thayer's explanation. He could only wish that he was as sure of the lieutenant as his mother was. But for her sake he extended his hand to Thayer, who took it with a firm grip.

"This calls for a drink," said Culbertson, heading for the decanters on the sideboard.

Dougherty grinned. He had already scouted out the liquor supply. "I was hoping somebody would say that."

When Cameron and Thayer and Dougherty and Le Due had their drinks—Eliza declined the major's offer—Culbertson raised his glass in a toast.

"To brave men, a noble cause, and a safe return for all."

Chapter 15

The next morning, as the gray light of predawn began to chase the night out of the eastern sky, they gathered in the Fort Union wagon yard. Thayer had exchanged his uniform and greatcoat for stroud trousers tucked into sturdy mule-ear boots, a flannel shirt and a knee-length mackinaw coat. Dougherty and Le Due were present and accounted for, as were He Smiles Twice and Broken Bow. Cameron had not spoken to the two Absarokes about their coming along, and had no intention of ever doing so. He would not insult them by pointing out the obvious— that there was a very real possibility that no one would be coming back from this expedition alive and that their presence in the rescue party could bring the wrath of the entire Sioux nation down upon their own people. The two warriors were well aware of what was at stake. They knew the risks, not only to themselves but to their tribe. Their presence here now showed that they had weighed it all and had come down on the side of riding with Cameron to find their blood brother, White Crow.

Eliza was there, too, of course, and Major Culbertson as well, watching the men saddle their horses and check the packs on the extra pony—cartridges, hard biscuits, pemmican, coffee, several extra rifles and pistols. It was in Cameron's mind that if all went well, this horse would carry his father home, so yesterday he had carefully examined Culbertson's company caviarde and finally selected this tall coyote dun that looked like it could run all day. The supplies were lashed down on a saddle rather than a wooden frame, and covered with wagon canvas and oilskin. When the time came, the supplies would be distributed among the members of the party, freeing the saddle for use by Gordon Hawkes. Cameron lived for that moment—the moment when he would see his father astride that coyote dun, riding for home.

When all was ready and the others had mounted up, Cameron turned to his mother and hugged her tightly. She clung to him a moment, and he was afraid she would lose her composure. But she released him before it was too late and even managed a brave smile, gazing proudly at her son for what might be the last time.

Cameron turned to Culbertson and shook the major's hand. "Thanks for everything you've done, sir. I'm still willing to pay you back, somehow, for the supplies and the horses."

"No need, young man. It's the least I can do. I am honored to be of some service. And do not be concerned about your mother and little sister. They will be well provided for here, and I am privileged to have them as my guests for as long as they choose to stay."

"Thank you, Major." Cameron took one last look at his mother. "I'll be back soon, Ma."

"God go with you, Cam."

Cameron turned to his horse, climbed into the saddle, and led the way out of Fort Union.

They had gone but a few miles when a rider caught up with them. He was a big, burly man with an unkempt beard and a crooked eye. The buckskins under his buffalo coat were blackened with years of grime. His right sleeve was empty. To Cameron's eyes he looked tough enough to give a mad-as-hell grizzly a run for its money— even with only the one arm. The man checked his winded horse alongside Cameron's and gave a yellow grin.

"Reckon you must be Gordon's boy. You're the spittin' image, I'd swear to it."

"That's me," said Cameron. "Who are you?"

"Name's Billy Ring. Your pa ever mention my name, as you can recall?"

Cameron searched his memory, then slowly shook his head. "No, I don't think so. You know my father?"

"Oh, yes, I know him well. Met him a good many years back. He was on his way to Missouri and came upon me and my crew."

"Crew?"

"Buffalo runners, lessen my nose is playing tricks on me," said Dougherty.

"That's right," said Ring, still grinning. "Anyways, we got hit by some Pawnees and got into a big scrape. Your pa stood with us. He's a good man to have on your side."

"Funny, I don't think he ever said anything about a fight with the Pawnees," said Cameron.

"Well, he's more a doer than a talker, ain't he? Anyways, I done heard what's happened, and what you're aiming to do about it. And I'd like to give you a hand."

Cameron glanced at Ring's empty sleeve, and the buffalo runner read the question in his eyes.

"True, I ain't got but the one arm anymore," he acknowledged. "Some months back I took a bullet in the right one. Tore it to pieces. Gangrene set in and had to have the damned thing chopped off. But I've already taught myself to shoot with one arm, and I ain't half bad at it, so long as the range ain't too far. You got no cause to worry. You won't be saddled with no useless cripple. I'll more than hold my own."

"This on account of my father?"

"That, and I ain't much fond of the Sioux, either. Last year they attacked me and my crew and killed some good men. Friends of mine. They've been making trouble for me and I ain't one to pass up a chance to return the favor."

Cameron glanced at Thayer. The lieutenant was sizing Billy Ring up, and it was plain that he didn't much like what he saw.

"You best keep one thing in mind, if you aim to ride with me," Cameron told Ring. "The reason we're doing this is to bring my father back, alive. It's not to see how many Dakota scalps we can take."

"Suits me."

"Let's ride, then," said Cameron, putting his horse in motion. "We're wasting time."

When they had put the Missouri about a day's ride behind them, they knew they were in Sioux country, and Cameron started feeling a lot more edgy. The world around him took on a much more sinister hue. The sky was the same as before, the wind still blew steady out of the north to turn his cheeks into blocks of ice, and the snow-covered terrain hadn't changed— but suddenly it was all endowed with a kind of creeping menace that made Cameron's skin crawl. He kept telling himself that the Dakota were just ordinary people, no meaner or crueler or stronger or smarter or deadlier than any other. But he still couldn't shake the feeling that he had just stepped through the gates of hell and would any minute find himself face to face with the devil himself.

They made camp a couple of hours before sundown in a hollow between two hills, dug a hole in the snow down to the frozen earth, and started a buffalo chip fire. Dougherty had brought along a sack full of dry buffalo chips, and Cameron was glad he had such experienced men with him—he hadn't given a moment's thought to building a fire on this trip. But after a day's ride across the frozen plains he wanted a fire worse than anything else he could think of. They melted some snow in a pot, and threw a few handfuls of coffee into the water when it began to simmer. The brew was strong and bitter, but at least it was warm going down, and Cameron felt better because of it. The buffalo chips didn't produce any smoke to speak of, and since the camp was shielded by higher ground on all sides, the wind was less severe. The wind—an almost constant presence on the High Plains—was the real killer, not the snow and ice or the low temperatures. Besides buffeting the frigid gales, the shelter of the hollow also kept their camp out of sight of prying eyes. Cameron hadn't seen a sign of another living person all day, but he had a feeling they were out there—Dakota scouts, prowling like wolves. When you had made as many enemies as the Sioux, you couldn't afford to let your guard down, not even in the dead of winter.

He Smiles Twice and Broken Bow kept watch just below the rim on the high ground, one to the north of the camp and the other to the south. Cameron took them both some coffee, and sat for a while with He

Smiles Twice, looking off to the north across the seemingly endless expanse of snow-blanketed plain. Ominous blue shadows lengthened as the sun began to slide down to the western horizon, like an old man whose strength is slowly fading after a long exertion. Of all his companions, Cameron felt closest to He Smiles Twice. He thought of the Absaroke warrior as an uncle of sorts. He Smiles Twice was not here for revenge, or to count coup, or to bring home scalp trophies. He was here for just one reason—to find his good friend White Crow and bring him home.

Broken Bow, Cameron thought, had come because White Crow was an Absaroke, and no Absaroke should be allowed to languish in captivity. Dougherty, on the other hand, was here because Jim Bridger had prevailed on him to come, and he didn't cotton to the idea of a white man, and a fellow mountain man to boot, being kept prisoner by redskins. Le Due was here to harvest Sioux tongues, since it was the Sioux who had robbed him of his. Billy Ring was here for Dakota scalps and revenge against the Sioux for making life so chancy for him and his fellow buffalo hunters. It occurred to Cameron that Billy Ring probably didn't mind the idea of a war with the Sioux nation one bit. The sooner the Sioux were defeated, the sooner Ring and his kind could go after the great northern herd of buffalo. They were already well on their way to thinning out the southern herd, so it was only natural that they would cast their eyes to the north. The major obstacle in their path was the Dakota.

As for why Lieutenant Thayer was here—Cameron still wasn't really convinced that the dragoon was being completely candid about his reasons for jeopardizing his career, not to mention his life, to participate in this venture.

They rested until an hour after sundown, Dougherty, Le Due, and Billy Ring rolled up in their blankets and lay down to catch a little sleep. Thayer sat by the fire while the two Absaroke warriors kept a tireless vigil. Restless, Cameron could not bring himself to lie down, or even stay in one place for very long.

"You need to relax," Thayer told him during one of his frequent trips to the fire. "You'll be all worn down by the time we get where we're going. And tired men make mistakes. One mistake and we could all be dead."

"Can't seem to settle down," confessed Cameron. "Nerves, I guess."

"We all get the jitters. That's natural. Ever been in a scrape?"

"Nothing to speak of. Never been in a battle. Never had to kill a man. I guess you have."

Thayer nodded pensively. "I've served down in Texas until recently. Fought Mexican raiders and Comanche war parties. Had to kill a few. This is one time when you don't want to think much about the job you have to do. Think about anything else but having to kill someone, or be killed."

"What do you think about?"

Thayer smiled. "I think about home. Back in Maryland, the Eastern Shore."

"Maryland," said Cameron. "I'm not sure I know where Maryland is. But it sounds like it must be a long ways from here."

"Yes, it is. Many miles away."

"What do you think about when you think about home?"

"Sitting on a dock at a marsh pond, fishing, watching the cranes out in the tall grass. They're fishing, too. Watching the morning sun lay a golden trail across the water. And I think about walking to and from school every day with Becky."

"Becky?"

"Childhood friend," said Thayer, seeming to snap out of his reverie.

"More than a friend, I reckon."

"Well, yes, she was. I always thought she and I would be married one day. I never once imagined spending my life with anyone else."

"You married her, then?"

"No, someone else did. While I was away at West Point. She said she would wait. But, well, sometimes the heart overrules the head. You can't control love. It's like a herd of runaway horses. You can try to turn it one way or the other and hope to take it along the direction you want it to go, but it won't always cooperate with you. One bad break and you lose the herd. Or your heart. She met someone else. Not that she was looking, mind you. But they just happened to meet. Pure chance. And they fell in love. And they . . . Well, what happened after they met isn't really important. That's the moment that I lost the herd."

Cameron could tell that these memories had a strong impact on Thayer, and so he sat on his heels by the little fire and chose to say nothing more.

After a while Thayer looked across at him. "Ever been in love?"

"Yes," said Cameron. "I still am. But she married someone else too."

"Indian girl?"

Cameron nodded. "Walks in the Sun was her name."

"Pretty name. I'm sure it suits her."

"She's an Absaroke. But I lay with her, and her folks wanted her to have nothing more to do with me. Her brother tried to kill me. I had to go away. And then she became the woman of a River Crow."

"They tell you to let go when you've lost someone," said Thayer. "To get on with your life. That's easier said than done, isn't it? The people you love become a part of your life. They take up residence in your heart, and they won't leave until the day you die. You can't just forget them, or pretend they never were. You can try to get on with your life, yes, but they'll be coming along with you and there isn't a damn thing you can do about it."

Cameron stared at Thayer in astonishment. He was surprised that he had talked so openly with the lieutenant about one of the burdens he bore. And he was just as surprised that Thayer seemed willing to share his own secret sorrow with him. The last thing he had ever expected was to feel a kind of kinship with this man. It made him uncomfortable and quite a bit confused because he still had the unwavering hunch that Thayer was his enemy, not a friend. So he stood up and left the fire and went back up to the snowy rim to sit with He Smiles Twice and watch the night stretch out across the plains.

Chapter 16

They started moving again a couple of hours after sundown. The frozen sky was full of stars, casting a pale-blue glow on the snow-covered earth. A bone-numbing cold invaded Cameron's body, and he was grateful that at least the wind had died down a little. No one spoke as they rode single file through the night. Cameron led, followed by He Smiles Twice, then Dougherty and Le Due, Thayer and Billy Ring, with Broken Bow bringing up the rear, continually checking their back trail. Charged with keeping them on course, Cameron regularly consulted the heavens, keeping the north star in front of him and a few degrees to the right, an image of Culbertson's map clearly etched in his mind's eye.

Le Due, who knew this country better than any of them, had told him through Dougherty that they would cross several creeks. One of them would be the stream on the banks of which the Oglala winter village would be found. He was confident he would know which creek, and when they reached it they would turn upstream, and within a day's time arrive at their destination. It occurred to Cameron that no one really knew for sure that the Oglala village would be where it was expected to be. Plains Indians often returned to the same site for their winter quarters, but not always. During the warmer months they were constantly on the move, often in relation to the movement of the buffalo. Relocating was not a problem for them. A village could be packed up and on the trail in a matter of hours. Culbertson had just assumed that Long Horse's Oglala band would settle for the winter along Porcupine Creek, and so had Le Due, because they had done so more than once before. Cameron prayed that they had done so this winter as well.

Seven long, torturous hours they rode, the only sounds the crunch of horses' hooves in the snow, the creak of saddle leather and the occasional whicker of a horse. The cold took its toll on man and horse alike, and the night seemed to never end, and when at last he saw the first slender threads of daylight streaking the eastern sky, Cameron was so relieved he almost shouted with joy.

They found a stand of wind-bent willows growing along a frozen creek and decided to spend the day there. A fire was quickly built, this time using deadwood instead of Dougherty's cache of buffalo chips. Some coffee was brewed, because everyone was in desperate need of it. Then the fire was extinguished before day broke, so that no telltale wisp of smoke would be seen. Cameron tried to eat some pemmican and a hard biscuit, but he had no appetite. His stomach was tied up in knots, and he was entirely too weary to think about anything except sleep. His body, tensed against the cold hour after hour, ached from top to bottom. It was agreed that they would all take turns standing watch, in two-hour shifts. Dougherty agreed to take the first watch. Cameron tied the reins around his wrist and took his blanket roll off the back of his saddle. The blankets were rolled up in an oilskin to keep them dry. He spread the oilskin out on the ground, rolled himself up in the blankets on top of it, and immediately feel asleep, his horse pawing at the snow next to him, trying to get at the grass underneath.

A gunshot woke him.

Leaping to his feet, rifle in hand, Cameron tried to make sense of the pandemonium. The others were scrambling for their weapons, or their horses, or both. Then he spotted Dougherty, running and reloading while he moved, heading deeper into the stand of willows.

"Injuns!" yelled the trapper. "Three of 'em that I saw. Think I hit one!"

He Smiles Twice and Broken Bow were mounted and on the move, galloping right through the middle of the camp and nearly running over Billy Ring. The buffalo hunter jumped out of their path and hurled a curse at them, and then the Absaroke warriors were gone, their ponies leaping the narrow, ice-coated creek.

"Le Due, Ring, you go with Dougherty!" snapped Thayer. "Cameron, mount up and come with me."

Cameron asked no questions. It just seemed perfectly natural for Thayer to take charge, and Cameron, who realized he had no idea what to do under such circumstances, bowed to experience. The lieutenant had been in action before. Remembering at the last minute to tug the cinch tight—he had loosened it for his horse's sake—Cameron vaulted into the saddle and followed in Thayer's wake as the dragoon rode hard in the opposite direction from that taken by the pair of Fox Clan warriors.

It only took Cameron a moment to figure out what was happening. Dougherty had spotted Indians deep in the woods and fired at them. He Smiles Twice and Broken Bow had crossed the creek to circle the woods to the north, and he and Thayer were engaged in a similar maneuver to the south. Meanwhile Dougherty and Le Due and Billy Ring were going in on foot to flush out the Sioux. Cameron knew they had to be Dakota scouts. And that meant they could not be allowed to leave the woods alive.

The woods extended about three hundred yards along the creek, largely on the southern bank, and a hundred yards deep in places. Once someone broke from the trees there was very little cover—Cameron doubted the Indians could slip away unseen. He and the others had camped at the eastern end of the woods, and so he surmised that the Sioux scouts had tried to get close enough for a better look by using the trees for cover, probably entering at the forest's western end.

Another gunshot rang out—followed quickly by another—and Cameron heard someone shouting; he thought it was either Billy Ring or Dougherty. Then he caught a glimpse of an Indian running through the willows, fleet as a deer, and instinctively he steered his horse in that direction, but Thayer called him back.

"We'll meet him at the other end," said the lieutenant. "With any luck we can get to their ponies before they do and that will settle things."

Cameron nodded. The lump in his throat was so big he didn't think he could utter a word. He wasn't sure if he was more scared or excited, but the adrenaline surging through his body left every nerve ending tingling.

They reached the western end of the woods and Thayer paused there a moment, peering into the trees and then shooting a glance across the creek. Cameron assumed he was looking for He Smiles Twice and Broken Bow, but the Absaroke warriors were nowhere to be seen.

"See anything?" asked the dragoon.

Cameron shook his head.

"Okay, then, let's go in. Stay in the saddle. Keep your eyes open. And keep me in sight. One of them may have stayed back with the ponies."

Cameron nodded. That was often the case—the youngest, most inexperienced member of an Indian party, be it on a scouting expedition, a hunt, or a raid, was assigned the task of watching over the horses while his companions went about their business.

They entered the woods twenty yards apart, Cameron keeping Thayer to his right and trying to make sure he didn't get too far out in front of the lieutenant. They kept their horses to a walk and their rifles at the ready. In no time at all, Cameron saw the Sioux ponies off to his left. There were four of them, all painted with medicine and coup signs. Wetting his lips, he let out a low whistle to get Thayer's attention, and when the lieutenant glanced his way he pointed toward the Indian horses. Thayer turned his horse in that direction. Cameron continued on, peering deeper into the woods, wondering where the Sioux were, and deciding not to get any closer to the ponies until Thayer had joined him. He heard nothing—no more shooting, no more shouting, no sounds of pursuer and pursued. The silence was a little unnerving. And where was the horse guard? Had he gone to the aid of his companions when he heard the gunfire? *If so*, Cameron thought, *I can get those ponies out of here and the Sioux will be done for, with no chance of escaping.*

Abruptly, the horse beneath him snorted in alarm and jumped sharply sideways, nearly pitching him out of the saddle. The Sioux horse guard had concealed himself beneath an old log and waited until Cameron was nearly on top of him before rolling out from under it, leaping to his feet, and with a shrill cry, lunging forward to grab Cameron and drag him down. Caught completely off guard, Cameron hit the ground painfully and lost his grip on his rifle. As he desperately tried to suck air back into his lungs, he glimpsed the young brave's exultant face and the knife raised over his head, posed for that fatal downward stroke that would plunge the blade into Cameron's heart.

Then Thayer's rifle spoke—and the young Dakota was flung forward by the impact of the bullet between his shoulder blades. He lay still, facedown, one leg over Cameron's heaving chest. Cameron squirmed out from underneath, repulsed by contact with a corpse. Then he looked up at Thayer, and shame burned in his cheeks.

"I'm—I'm sorry," he muttered. "I didn't see him."

"He didn't want you to," remarked Thayer. He spoke matter-of-factly. There was nothing judgmental in his words or his tone of voice. His eyes scanned the depths of the woods. "Are you hurt?"

"Just my pride." Cameron got to his feet and bent down to retrieve his rifle. "You saved my life."

"Yeah. Well, maybe one day you'll have a chance to return the favor."

"I hope so."

"I hope not. But then, I'd also hoped we wouldn't have to kill any Sioux. I guess that's always been my problem. Too damned optimistic. Go catch up your horse and let's get these ponies out of here. Don't let any of them slip away—they'll head right back to wherever they came from, and that will turn out just as bad for us as if there was a Sioux warrior riding it."

Cameron went after his horse, which had not strayed far. He was thankful that the animal did not shy away from him. At least he was spared the further ignominy of having to chase his mount through the trees with Thayer as an audience. Mounting up, he took two of the Sioux ponies and followed the lieutenant, who had the other two in tow, back out of the woods.

As they emerged, He Smiles Twice and Broken Bow appeared on the other side of the creek. The two Absarokes signaled that all was well, and Thayer appreciated the fact that he didn't have to tell them to stay where they were. The Absarokes weren't going to let any of the Sioux get across the creek.

Another gunshot rang out from deep within the woods, and then Cameron spotted a Dakota brave bursting out of the trees. Instinctively Cameron raised his rifle. The Sioux saw the two Absarokes first and stopped in his tracks. Then he turned his head and spotted Cameron and Thayer. *You should kill him,* Cameron told himself. *Do it now. Don't hesitate. Your father's life may depend on it.* But he couldn't pull the trigger. And then Billy Ring appeared at the edge of the trees. The Dakota turned to face the buffalo runner—and just stood there as Ring raised his English rifle. He began his death chant, dropping his rifle— which Cameron assumed was empty—and raised his arms skyward in an entreaty to the Great Spirit to accept him into the next world. Ring's long gun boomed and the Sioux fell dead.

With a shout of triumph, Billy Ring jogged to the spot where the fallen warrior lay. Down on one knee, he set his rifle aside, drew his skinning knife, and with several deft incisions, lifted the Dakota's topknot. Clearly this was not the first time he had taken a scalp trophy.

"My God," muttered Cameron, sickened.

Le Due and Dougherty came out of the woods. The French Canadian rushed to join Billy Ring, while Dougherty hurried over to where Thayer and Cameron sat their horses.

"We got 'em all," he said. He counted the Indian ponies. "Well, we got three of 'em anyway," he added, as his face fell.

"I took care of the fourth," said Thayer.

Cameron was watching Le Due, who, like Ring, was kneeling with knife in hand beside the Dakota that the buffalo hunter had slain.

"What is he doing?" asked Cameron. He had a pretty good idea, though.

Dougherty glanced in that direction. "Oh, he's just collectin' himself another Sioux tongue is all." Seeing the look on Cameron's face, he quelled the smile that had begun to form on his lips. "Well, think I'll get back to the camp now."

When he was gone, Thayer glanced at Cameron. "I think it was Shakespeare who said something about letting slip the dogs of war."

"What are we going to do with these ponies?"

"We have to kill them."

"I'll let Billy Ring do that," said Cameron dryly. "He seems to enjoy that kind of work."

Now that the hunt was over, He Smiles Twice and Broken Bow were crossing the frozen creek, leading their ponies over the ice. Cameron put his horse in motion and took the two Indian ponies in his charge over to where Billy Ring was standing. The buffalo hunter finished reloading his rifle before acknowledging Cameron's presence.

"You look a little green around the gills, son," said Billy Ring. "Too much excitement, I reckon."

"These ponies have to die. You do it."

"Sure. I won't waste powder and shot on 'em, though. I'll just cut—"

"Just do it." Cameron handed him the bridle ropes and turned his horse around to ride away.

He hadn't gone far before he checked his horse, whirled it back around, lifted his rifle, and fired. One of the Indian ponies dropped dead in its tracks. Billy Ring let out a shout, caught by surprise. It was all he could do to keep the other pony from bolting. Cameron reloaded, raised the rifle to shoulder again, drew a bead, and fired once more. The second pony went down. Billy Ring found himself holding the bridle ropes of two dead horses in his hands. He let go of the ropes and turned to glower resentfully at Cameron.

"What the hell was all that about?" Ring asked crossly. Cameron's actions had startled him—and Billy Ring hated to be caught off guard.

Cameron didn't answer. He wheeled his horse and started back to camp. There was no point in even trying to explain to the buffalo hunter that he hadn't wanted the Indian ponies to suffer when they died. He hadn't wanted to think of them thrashing in blood-splattered snow, their throats cut, fighting a losing battle for life. If they had to die, it was better that they die quickly. But Billy Ring wouldn't have understood, so Cameron didn't waste his time trying to explain.

Chapter 17

When he saw his father it was all Cameron could do to refrain from leaping to his feet and running right through the Oglala village so that he could touch Gordon Hawkes and make sure he wasn't imagining things.

He and Thayer had been belly down in the snow behind the rim of a low rise a quarter mile west of Porcupine Creek and the Sioux village for almost two hours. They had left the other members of the rescue party about a mile and a half to the southwest in a cold camp nestled in the bend of a horseshoe-shaped hill. Then they had ridden to within half a mile of the Indian village, left their horses, and proceeded the rest of the way on foot. They'd arrived at this vantage point before daybreak. Thayer had brought along a pair of field glasses, and they used these to get a closer look at the village. Thayer counted the skin lodges and then perused the horse herd to the north of their position and decided that there were probably less than two hundred warriors in this band. But not much less.

It had taken two days after the run-in with the four Sioux scouts to get here, and they had made fair time, traveling at night and meeting with no further mishaps. The weather had held for them. Like the day before, this new day dawned with the promise of a clear blue sky. Thayer had been happy to have good weather during the journey, but now found himself praying for some bad weather to blow through. An overcast sky and some light snow would be perfect. It would make sneaking around this close to the village a somewhat easier proposition, for one thing. And it might serve to slow down any pursuit, assuming that this scheme advanced to that point.

When the eastern sky began to lighten and the village started to awaken, Thayer handed Cameron the field glasses. Cameron scanned the village, checking each person who emerged from the skin lodges. His pulse was racing, his heart pounding as though it might break through his rib cage. Morning fires were started, and plumes of smoke rose from one end of the village to the other. The minutes crawled by, each one the purest agony for Cameron.

Thayer felt sorry for his companion. This was the moment of truth. This was the day that Cameron would find out if his prayers would be answered, or if his worst fears would be realized. If the young man's father wasn't here, then the game was up. And Cameron would have to go back and tell his mother that she was a widow. Thayer wasn't a very religious man. He believed in God, but his God was one who did not take much interest in the everyday affairs of men. But now he said a prayer, just in case.

When Cameron saw his father, Thayer reached out to lay a hand on his arm so the young man wouldn't leap to his feet shouting.

"That's him!" gasped Cameron. "He's alive! My pa is alive!"

"Are you sure?" asked Thayer, and realized what a stupid question it was. "Let me have a look."

Cameron reluctantly surrendered the field glasses and tried to direct Thayer in his attempt to get a first look at the man they had risked so much to find. Eventually he located the skin lodge that Cameron described for him. It was a rather plain one, not adorned with painted symbols as the others were. And in front of the lodge, talking to a young Sioux boy, was a tall, sandy-haired man of fair complexion, and clean-shaven. Despite his Indian garb—hunting shirt, breechcloth, leggings, and moccasins—he was clearly not an Indian. As Thayer watched, the boy ran off, and with one last look around, the man turned and disappeared inside the skin lodge.

"What is he doing now?" asked Cameron, beside himself with excitement.

"He's gone back into the lodge," said Thayer, handing the glasses back to Cameron.

"I knew it," murmured Cameron. "I knew he was still alive. No matter what anybody said."

"You were right, and I am glad of that."

"So tomorrow, then, at dawn. That's when we get him out."

Thayer nodded. His happiness for Cameron was dampened by the realization that now they were going to have to put his rescue plan into motion—and the chances of its success did not encourage any optimism on his part. And if by some miracle his plan did work, the odds were good that the Oglalas would strike back. Where and when and against whom didn't really matter. Lives would be lost. Regardless of whether or not there was a Sioux attack, Thayer could safely assume that his career was over. He wasn't sure when it

had happened, but somewhere between Colonel
Lovell's office back at Fort Laramie and here, he had
made up his mind not to stop Cameron from finding
out the truth about his father. He was glad for
Cameron that his father was alive, but he had to admit
to himself that he had hoped, in a way, that the tall,
sandy-haired man he had just seen had died in the
Sioux ambush of the keelboats on the Yellowstone
River. That would have been tragic for Cameron and
his mother. But it would probably have been better for
everyone else.

Watching through the field glasses, Cameron saw
the boy his father had been talking to earlier return to
the plain skin lodge, bringing an Indian pony with
him. Again his father emerged from the lodge, this
time with a bow case on his back. And then a young
Indian woman came out of the lodge. Cameron wondered idly who she was, thinking she was very
pretty—as pretty as Walks in the Sun, as a matter of
fact. But then there wasn't anything at all idle about
his curiosity concerning the woman because his father
put an arm around her and kissed the corner of her
mouth.

Cameron was so stunned that he couldn't even listen to what Thayer was saying to him.

"Cameron!"

"Sorry. Sorry, what did you say?"

"What's going on? What do you see?"

Cameron wasn't quite sure he wanted to see any
more. All he could think about at that moment was his
mother, waiting for her husband's return, clinging
bravely to hope, sustained by her undying love.

He handed the field glasses to Thayer.

The lieutenant located the man he knew as Henry

Gordon in time to see the mountain man vault onto the back of the pony in Indian fashion. Then a young Sioux woman came closer to the horse and, speaking to Gordon, rested her hand on his thigh. A moment later Gordon was riding out of the Oglala village.

Alone.

Thayer could hardly believe his eyes. He wasn't sure what it meant, but Gordon was *leaving the Sioux village, by himself, and with weapons*. That certainly didn't seem like something a captive would be permitted to do. So what the hell was going on?

Unless . . .

Thayer lowered the glasses and glanced at Cameron. Was it possible that this boy's father wasn't a captive of the Sioux after all? That he was here of his own free will? That he had adopted the Sioux way of life and . . . even taken an Oglala bride? What other explanation could there be? And how did one go about rescuing a man who probably did not want to be rescued?

"What do you want to do?" he asked Cameron.

"What do you mean?"

"I mean are we getting him out, or not?"

Cameron didn't look at him. "That's why I'm here. What about you?"

Thayer could tell Cameron was angry and upset, and he had every right to be. The lieutenant wanted to tell his companion how sorry he was that things had turned out this way. But he had precious little experience in expressing such sentiments, and he didn't honestly think they would do Cameron much good anyway. He just put the field glasses back to his eyes to see Gordon riding out of the village, heading north.

"Well," he said, "your father is definitely leaving, and he's definitely alone. As I am always one to look for the bright side of things, I'd have to say this is a stroke of luck for us. I say we go get him right now."

Cameron was already ahead of him. "Let's go." He slid down a ways from the rim of the low rise before standing, then began to trudge hurriedly through the deep snow. Thayer lingered a few seconds longer to bring the field glasses to his eyes and search for the plain skin lodge once more. The pretty young Sioux woman was talking to the boy who had brought the Indian pony. He could see her laugh as she put a hand on the boy's head. Then the boy turned and trotted away, and the young woman looked in the direction Gordon had taken before going back into the skin lodge.

Thayer drew a long breath, shook his head, and followed Cameron, all the while thinking that maybe he had thrown his career away and was risking his life and who knew how many other lives for a man who wasn't worth it. After all, what kind of father would take up with a Sioux woman and give up any thoughts of rejoining his wife and children? The answer was simple—a man without integrity. A man who did not warrant the kind of son Cameron had turned out to be.

Thayer and Cameron rode a wide loop around the Oglala village, crossing the creek more than a mile downstream from the encampment, keeping to the low ground as much as possible, using the rolling terrain to their advantage. They were well to the west of the creek and the village, and the Oglala horse herd was grazing to the east, so Thayer thought it was unlikely that they would run into any Sioux, with the possible exception of a solitary hunter or a scout returning home.

An hour later, several miles north of the village, they

cut Gordon's sign. Thayer took out the field glasses again, wiped the frost from the lenses, and scanned the snow-blanketed landscape to the north. A moment later he saw a black speck coming into view. It had to be Cameron's father, moving up a rise out of a low spot, about a mile and a half ahead of them.

"There he is," he told Cameron.

Cameron was already on the move, kicking his horse into a lope, which was about all the animal could manage in snow that deep. Thayer shook his head. Cameron was far too impetuous, and if he wasn't careful he would wear his mount out. The lieutenant took the precaution of checking the plains to the south, in the direction of the village. With the aid of the field glasses he could just barely make out the woodsmoke that seemed to bleach the blue out of the sky above the Oglala encampment. But that was all there was to see. He scarcely dared allow himself to believe that it could really be this easy.

As they quickly closed the distance between themselves and Hawkes, Thayer began to wonder just how close they would be able to get before Cameron's father realized that he was being followed. When they were several hundred yards away, Gordon disappeared down the far side of a slope, still apparently oblivious to their presence. But as Thayer and Cameron reached the crest of the slope, the lieutenant realized that he had underestimated his prey. Gordon was sitting his horse at the bottom of the slope about fifty yards away, an arrow set in his bow, ready to bring the weapon up and loose the arrow in one quick motion. Thayer instinctively checked his horse so sharply that the animal gave an indignant snort and all but sat down in the snow. Cameron didn't stop his mount until he was already halfway down the slope.

"Cam!" Hawkes swung a leg over his pony's neck and slid to the ground, coming up the slope with disbelieving eyes glued to his son, staring as a man dying of thirst might stare at a water hole, wondering if it was real or just a figment of his imagination. He reached out and put his hand on Cameron's knee, and Cameron placed his hand over his father's.

"Hello, Pa."

"My God," breathed Hawkes. It was all he could say. "Cameron! How . . . how is your mother? How is Grace?"

"They are both well, Pa."

Thayer urged his horse on down the slope. "Mr. Gordon, I'm Lieutenant Thayer, Second Dragoons. We're here to bring you home."

"Lieutenant? The last thing I expected was a rescue by the United States Army."

Thayer smiled thinly. "Well, to tell you the truth, it's not the army, sir. Just me. In fact, the army wouldn't like it very much if it knew I was here with your son."

"For whatever reason that you're here, I'm grateful."

"Thing is," said Thayer, "we expected to find you still a prisoner of the Oglala."

"Though it may not look like it, I am."

Thayer tried to mask his skepticism. "Well, it doesn't matter now. We don't have to come in and get you. You can just ride out with us right now. By the time the Sioux know any better we'll be miles away. A good head start will make all the difference."

Hawkes looked at Thayer, then at his son—and shook his head.

"I have to go back to the village once more before I leave," he said.

"What?" asked Thayer. "By God, if I didn't know better, I'd think you didn't want to get home."

"I've thought of nothing else since the day I was taken captive, Lieutenant. But it's not quite that simple."

"It's that Indian girl, isn't it?" asked Cameron.

Hawkes read his son's face, drew a long breath, and nodded. "Her name is Pretty Shield," he said.

"She's why you have to go back."

"That's right. She saved my life. She has to know I'm leaving. I can't just vanish. Not after everything she has done for me."

"This is lunacy," muttered Thayer, looking around and half expecting to see a horde of Oglala Sioux warriors bearing down on them. They were putting themselves in greater danger by standing here chatting.

"What is she to you, Pa?" asked Cameron.

"I'm going back," said Hawkes.

"And what are we supposed to do in the meantime?" asked Thayer, exasperated.

"Wait, if you want. Today I'll go back empty-handed. That way no one will think twice when I go hunting again tomorrow morning." His gaze lingered pensively on Cameron. "I'm glad to see you again, son. Damned glad. There were times when I wondered if I would ever set eyes on you again."

He turned toward his pony, but Cameron reached out to grab his arm and spin him around.

"What is Pretty Shield to you, Pa? I want to know and you're going to tell me."

"She's my wife, Cam."

Cameron let go of his father's arm and stumbl

back a couple of steps, as though he'd been struck. Hawkes forced himself to meet his son's gaze squarely, refusing to flinch from the disbelief and disgust he saw lurking in Cameron's eyes.

"For months I've prayed that you were still alive," said Cameron bitterly. He felt so nauseated that it was all he could do to keep from vomiting. It wasn't just that his father had been untrue to his mother. Cameron himself felt betrayed by his father. "Now I wish . . . I almost wish you weren't!"

"Cameron!" said Thayer.

"You stay out of this!" rasped Cameron fiercely, addressing the lieutenant but keeping his burning gaze fixed on Hawkes. "I don't even know you. This isn't something my pa would do. Not this!"

"Maybe you should hear the whole story, Cam. I—"

"I don't want to hear it!" shouted Cameron. "There's no excuse for what you've done. There can't be!"

Gordon's jaw hardened. "I'm going back, and that's all there is to it. If you're not here tomorrow morning, so be it. I'll make my way home one way or another."

"I don't think you'll be welcome," said Cameron. "You could have left a long time ago. But you're still here. I guess this is where you want to be."

Cameron turned his back on his father. Mounting up, he furiously kicked his spent horse up the snowy slope and out of sight down the other side.

Hawkes watched his son until Cameron was out of sight, then glanced at Thayer. "I'd be obliged to you if you would look after him, Lieutenant. Make sure he gets home to his mother safe and sound."

"Being this deep in Sioux country, I can't give you any guarantees. But I will do my best."

Hawkes nodded. "Don't come back tomorrow."

"Can't say what I'll do," admitted Thayer. "But I can say that I think you stayed here a little too long."

"Maybe so. Good luck to you, Lieutenant."

"Good luck, Mr. Gordon."

With that, Thayer followed in Cameron's tracks, disappearing over the rise and leaving Hawkes alone.

And Gordon Hawkes had never felt so alone in his life.

Chapter 18

Hawkes had no idea how to tell Pretty Shield that it was time for him to go. He spent all day in idleness, riding aimlessly across the prairie deep in thought, paying no attention to the occasional game sign he happened across. By the time he got back to the Oglala village he had still not come up with any alternative other than just coming right out and telling her the unvarnished truth. As soon as she saw his face, Pretty Shield knew something was wrong.

"It's time for me to leave," he said once they were alone in the skin lodge. "My son has come to bring me home."

"Your son? Where is he?"

Hawkes heaved a despondent sigh. "I don't know where he is, exactly. Somewhere nearby. Hopefully, though, he's on his way back home."

"You saw him."

"Yes. Today. This morning. A few miles north of here."

"But why would your son go home without you if you are what he came here for?"

Hawkes decided right then and there that no purpose would be served by telling her that Cameron felt betrayed by his father taking a Sioux bride.

"It doesn't really matter. Fact is, it's time I went away. Past time, really."

She looked away, turning her head to the side and casting her eyes downward so that he could not see the deep sadness there. This was the day she had long feared would come, even while she had continued to hope that in time his desire to return to his other world would fade. And when he had made love to her she had managed to delude herself into believing, if only for a few hours, that he had made the choice to stay with her forever. But still through it all, those awful doubts had persisted. And now her worst fears were realized. The man she loved with all her heart and soul was going away from her. He did not love her well enough to stay. But she loved him well enough to let him go, because it was clear that he would never be truly happy here with her. She knew then that she would never see him again.

"When will you go?" she asked.

"Tomorrow morning. Since my hunt today was unsuccessful, no one will think it strange that I ride out again in the morning."

Pretty Shield nodded and even attempted a brave smile. "So we have tonight."

"Pretty, it may go hard for you when I'm gone," said Hawkes, concerned.

"It does not matter," she said, and it truly didn't, not to her, not anymore. She didn't care what happened to her tomorrow or the day after or the day after that—or for the rest of her life, really, because without him, her life had no meaning anyway.

"It does to me," he said gently. "That's why—why I want you to come with me."

Stunned, she looked into his eyes, thinking that she

must have misunderstood his words. Surely he could not be so cruel as to play such a joke as this on her. But his expression showed her that he was in earnest.

"I know it's asking a lot," he said. "These are your people. And if you go with me they will never accept you back. If you go, your mother's heart will be broken, and Jumping Bull's too, I suspect."

"But what of your family? Your son? Your wife?"

"I'm going back to them, Pretty." Hawkes didn't want to tell her that there was a chance that they would not want him back.

"So I could not be with you."

"I would look out for you. But it would never be like it has been between us. You need to understand that."

"So it is because you think you owe me something that you do this."

"No, that's not it. Not all of it, anyway. I care about you, Pretty. I don't want anything to happen to you."

"Do you feel in your heart for me the same thing that you feel for your other woman?"

Hawkes grimaced. "No. Not the same thing. I'm . . ."

She put her finger to his lips to stop him.

"Even if you do not love me," she said, her voice no more than a husky whisper, "I would go with you. If only so that my eyes can rest upon your face again."

"Damn it, Pretty, why did you have to go and fall in love with me?"

She smiled softly. In spite of her own sorrow, a pain so profound, so deep, that it robbed her of breath, she felt sad to see him in such anguish.

"I had no choice. And I must go with you now because I am still in love with you, and always will be."

"Are you sure?"

"I am."

Hawkes nodded. "Then we go tomorrow morning."

She took his hand and held it between her own. "But how? I cannot ride out with you in the morning."

"No, you can't do that. Someone might suspect. I will leave first, then you go to the creek for water. Walk upstream as far as you dare. Then just wait for me. Be as close to where the creek makes that big bend as you can."

"I will be there. But it would be safer for you if you just rode away and did not come back. Maybe . . ."

"No." He smiled at her. "You want to come with me, and I want you to. We'll get away. Don't worry."

She moved closer and laid her head on his chest as he put his arms around her and held her tightly. And that night, though sleep eluded him until a couple of hours before dawn, he lay with her beneath the blankets and buffalo hides and continued to hold her while she slept.

Early the next morning he rode out again, once more heading north. Those who saw him go assumed that he was hunting again, as he had hoped they would. Several miles from the village he paused and checked his back trail. There was no sign of anyone following. Turning west, he reached the creek in short order. He dismounted and led his pony downstream, keeping to the creek bed, trying to stay concealed by the steep cutbanks on either side. Soon he could see the Oglala horse herd to the south. There would be several herd guards out this morning, and that was what worried him most of all.

About a mile from the village he left the pony hidden beside a ten-foot embankment, the lead rope tied to a large, flat stone, and proceeded on foot. Up ahead the creek made a sharp bend between steep banks. Just beyond that bend, if all had gone according to plan, Pretty Shield would be waiting for him. He could see no reason why anyone would suspect a thing. But there was always the unforeseen to account for. He knew, though, that if she did not show up he would have to go back to get her. Leaving without her was not an option now.

Reaching the bend in the creek, he crouched at the base of the cutbank, inching forward until he could see beyond the bend. It was not far from here that he had made his first escape attempt. He might have lost his life then but for Pretty Shield. This time he was confident that he would not fail. Even as he spotted Pretty Shield sitting perhaps twenty yards away and his hopes began to soar, he heard a male voice call out, and the blood froze in his veins. Pressing his back against the cutbank, he watched Pretty Shield leap to her feet. She looked at him and then pointed westward and called out to someone. Gordon's grasp of the Sioux language was still tenuous, but he knew enough of it to realize that she was responding to someone's greeting. It had to be one of the horse guards. Hawkes swore vehemently, but under his breath, because a moment later the mounted Oglala was just above his position, checking his pony at the rim of the embankment. Hawkes dared not move. The bow and arrows in the bow case on his back were practically useless to him in this situation, and the knife he carried was not going to match up well against the rifle he knew the horse guard carried.

Pretty Shield and the horse guard spoke for only a few minutes—though it seemed much longer than that to Hawkes. The Oglala asked her what she was doing, and she laughed and replied that he should know by now what a dreamer she was. She said she often sat on the creek bank and lost herself in her thoughts. The horse guard asked her where her man was, and she told him that White Crow was out hunting again. He had not found any game yesterday, she said. That was because he was a white man, said the horse guard with contempt. No, said Pretty Shield, her man was a great hunter. Hawkes was proud of her. There was not a hint of nervousness in her voice. The horse guard clearly was not interested in hearing about the hunting prowess of her husband and, wishing her well, moved on. Hawkes started breathing again.

Pretty Shield sat on her heels, glancing at Hawkes but not moving. From her position she could see the village, the herd, and the horse guards better than he could, and all he could do was wait until she deemed it safe to move, even though his anxiety grew with each passing moment. The longer they lingered, the better the chance that they would be discovered.

She did not keep him waiting too long. She suddenly rose and walked swiftly toward the bend in the creek, heading straight for him, glancing once over her shoulder—and then running the last ten yards, running right into his waiting arms, and as he held her close he could feel the rapid beating of her heart. Taking her hand, he led her back up the creek bed to the waiting pony. They continued on for another half mile before Hawkes paused to put his hands around her slender waist and lift her up onto the pony. He almost asked once more if she was certain that this was what she wanted—but the light of joy that gleamed so brightly in her eyes proved that there was no need for him to do so. So he led the pony by its rope bridle for another mile along the creek bed before mounting behind her, leaving Porcupine Creek, and heading west.

How long would it be, he wondered, before someone noticed that both he and Pretty Shield were nowhere to be found? Her absence from the village would alarm someone, and eventually it would come to someone's attention that he had not returned from his hunt, either. Surely by nightfall the village would realize that they were gone. Hawkes could only hope it took that long. If it did, then the likelihood was that the pursuit would not begin until daybreak. And he didn't doubt that there would be pursuit. Everything hinged on the distance he could put between himself and the village before the word spread.

Riding several miles in an easterly direction, Hawkes then turned his pony southward. Every now and then he checked their back trail. And, after six hours on the move, he looked back to see riders following, a cluster of distant dark shapes on the white snow. Alarm coursed through him. There was no way to outrun those horsemen. There were six of them— no, make that seven. If he stood his ground and took them on, what chance would he have?

Checking the pony, he slid to the ground, and when Pretty Shield made to do likewise, he told her to stay right where she was.

"You ride on," he said. "You can try for Fort Union. Tell the man in charge there, a man named Culbertson, who you are and about what has happened. Maybe he will help you. At least he will be able to direct you to a man named Jim Bridger. Bridger and I are old friends. He will see to it that you get settled somewhere safe and are provided for."

"I am not leaving you."

"You can't stay. But you have one other choice. You can ride back to the village. Tell them that I forced you to come with me and that you managed to get away. But you can't just stay here. Those warriors might not bother listening to what you have to say."

She looked at the distant riders, then at Hawkes—and then she dismounted.

"If you die, then my life is over," she said. "So I will stay and die with you."

"Damn it, Pretty, get back on that horse and get the hell out of here, *now*."

"I will not."

Exasperated, Hawkes cast a quick look around. There was no cover to be found anywhere, no good place for a defensive stand. He was caught squarely out in the open with no place to run and nowhere to hide. How was it that the Sioux had discovered so quickly that he and Pretty Shield had made a break for freedom? Not that it really mattered now. They had gambled and lost.

He handed Pretty Shield his knife. There were no words to say. Opening his bow case, he strung his bow and slung the quiver of arrows over his shoulder. The riders were much closer now. With Pretty Shield standing beside him, he watched them coming on. Then she slipped her arm in his and Hawkes knew then that he did not dare start a fight with those horsemen. He would have to give up without a struggle and take his medicine and hope that Pretty Shield came to no harm. Her chances for survival would be better that way, than if she got caught in the line of fire. As for himself, he was finished either way.

But when the riders were two hundred yards away, he realized that they weren't Oglala Sioux at all. In fact, only two of them were Indians, and those two were Absarokes. He could tell first by the markings on their horses, long before he saw the riders well enough to recognize them. When they got a bit closer he saw that the two riders in the lead were Lieutenant Thayer and Cameron. Relief surged through Hawkes, and with a shout of joy he threw down the bow, swept Pretty Shield up in his arms, and whirled her around.

"We're gonna make it, Pretty! By God, we're gonna make it!"

She wrapped her arms around his neck and hugged his so tightly that he could hardly breathe. He lost his balance and fell backward into the snow with her on top of him. They were still lying there laughing when Cameron and the others arrived.

"Cam!" said Hawkes. "Son, you don't know how happy I am to see you!"

Cameron was staring at Pretty Shield and he didn't look happy at all. "I couldn't go back without you. I made Ma a promise."

Sensing Cameron's mood, Pretty Shield got to her feet and demurely brushed the snow off her long doe-skin dress and shook it out of her hair. She then just stood there very quietly, her eyes alert and taking everything in.

Weak with relief, Hawkes also got up and looked at Thayer, and at He Smiles Twice and Broken Bow, and then took a closer look at the other three men in the party, the ones he didn't know—except he quickly realized he did know one of them . . .

"You!" he gasped.

Billy Ring was grinning at him like a wolf. "Yep. It's me, hoss. Your ol' friend."

"What the hell are you doing here?"

"Well, now, it's simple. I didn't want them Sioux bastards to have the pleasure of killing you, Gordon, seein' as how I wanted to do that myself."

Cameron gaped at Billy Ring. "You said you were his friend."

"So I stretched the truth. It's a family tradition, you might say."

Cameron turned to his father. "What's going on here?"

"Guess maybe I should have told you, Cam. Just didn't see any good coming out of it. I killed his brother some years ago, back when I was traveling to Independence."

"Yeah, and your pa cost me an arm, too," said Billy Ring. "In fact, he's just made my life miserable all around. Only thing that will make me feel better is to see him cold stone dead."

"I doubt that will happen," remarked Thayer.

Billy Ring glanced over at the lieutenant and saw the pistol that Thayer held, the butt resting on his saddlehorn, the barrel aimed at his chest.

The buffalo hunter chuckled. "I ain't that big of a fool," he said. "Not my intention to do him in right now. I'll just bide my time and wait for my chance."

"Way I see it," said Dougherty, "there's three things we can do with this feller. We can leave him, kill him, or take him along with us."

"Drop that long gun, Ring," advised Thayer.

Ring let his sheathed rifle fall into the snow.

"Pistol, too, if you don't mind."

The buffalo hunter pulled the pistol out of his belt and tossed it to Dougherty.

"Now you boys ain't about to leave me out here in Sioux country. Why, you know they would catch me certain, and then they'd skin me alive and hang my topknot from a scalp pole."

"Well, Ring," said Thayer, "I didn't come all this way to get this man away from the Sioux just to stand by and let you kill him." The lieutenant looked at each of the others. "So what do you men say? What are we going to do with this one?"

"I don't care to take him along with us," said Dougherty. "But then I don't cotton to the idea of leaving any white man to face his death at the hands of the Dakota, either. So I reckon we should just kill him." He read Le Due's expressive hand gestures and then added, "My partner ain't nearly so merciful as me. He votes to leave him."

Thayer turned to Cameron. "And you?"

Cameron shook his head. "He can't be trusted. But I don't hold with cold-blooded murder, which is what it would be if we shot him now or left him for the Sioux to finish off. I guess I don't really like any of the choices."

Thayer looked at He Smiles Twice and Broken Bow. "Do you men have a preference?"

He Smiles Twice glanced at his fellow Fox Clan warrior, then shook his head.

"Well," said Thayer, "I say we take him with us. Tie him up and drag him back to Fort Union. After that I don't care what happens. So it looks like it is up to you," he told Hawkes. "Got one vote for each option."

"Best vote to kill me, you son of a bitch," said Billy Ring. "You done had two chances. Here's your third—and it's gonna be your last. You're just the luckiest bastard I've ever run across, but your luck is bound to run out sooner or later, and you don't want me around when it does."

Hawkes smiled thinly. "I don't want you around, period. But my problem is that I'm not like you, Ring." He turned to Thayer. "I'm with you. We have to bring him with us."

"Dougherty," said Thayer, "tie him up."

Dougherty shook out a rawhide hobble and pulled his horse alongside Ring's. Putting the buffalo runner's one arm behind his back, he lashed Ring's wrist to his broad leather belt. Then he took up the reins to Ring's horse and grinned at his captive.

"Now don't you go falling off," he said. "Might be that I wouldn't notice and would just keep right on going."

Ring leered at him. "Well, hell, that's exactly what I'd do."

Hawkes helped Pretty Shield to mount the Indian pony, and He Smiles Twice brought up the extra horse for the mountain man. Once in the saddle, Hawkes looked at the others and nodded.

"Let's get moving," he said.

"I agree," said Dougherty. "This here country is the devil's playground, and his children may be along any minute. No offense meant, Miss," he added, with a sheepish look in Pretty Shield's direction. She smiled back at him to show that no offense had been taken.

They got under way, Hawkes in the lead and Pretty Shield riding alongside him. Thayer and Cameron followed, stirrup to stirrup. The lieutenant spared Cameron a sidelong glance and noticed that the young man's eyes were fastened on Pretty Shield's back. Thayer could only imagine what was going through Cameron's mind. He Smiles Twice and Broken Bow rode behind them, and Le Due and Dougherty came next, the latter leading Billy Ring's horse. The buffalo runner looked over his shoulder every now and then. There was nothing to see back there—except their tracks in the snow. But Ring had instincts honed by nearly twenty years on the frontier, and he could feel the Sioux coming. They were back there somewhere, and they would show up soon enough.

"Hell," he muttered to himself. "We're all dead men, anyway."

Chapter 19

They rode due south and for an entire day and a half made good time, with the weather holding and no sign of pursuit. Hawkes calculated that another two days at the most would get them to the Missouri River and Fort Union. He was beginning to think that he was actually going to make his escape, and that the long ordeal of his captivity was over. Of course, he recognized that this didn't mean his troubles were over. He still had Billy Ring to worry about. And then there was his wife, and the situation with Pretty Shield.

From Cameron he learned that Eliza was waiting at Fort Union. His heart ached to see her again, to hear her voice, to hold her in his arms once more. But would he get that chance? He had no intention of doing anything but telling Eliza the truth. And though they had been together for the better part of two decades, he couldn't predict how she would react to the news. She would be deeply hurt, for certain. She would feel betrayed. Question was, Would she forgive? He wouldn't ask her to try and understand. How could he? He wasn't really sure he understood it either. He would ask her forgiveness, though, and if it was not forthcoming he would go his own way, respecting her decision and making it as easy as possible

for her and the children. Hawkes was pretty sure that
Cameron, at least, would not be sorry to see him go.
During those two days on the trail Cameron spared
him not a single word, and when Hawkes caught his
son looking his way he saw nothing in his eyes but resentment.

It was not until they paused to rest their horses
around noon on the third day out of the Oglala village
that they saw the Sioux.

Dougherty was the one who spotted them first. The
trapper just happened to glance to the north—they all
checked their back trail an untold number of times
each day—and he saw a dark mass of riders in the distance, like molasses spilling over a white tablecloth.
He stared slack-jawed for a moment, with mounting
horror, at the vision.

"Good God Almighty," he breathed. "It's the whole
damn Sioux nation!"

The others stopped what they were doing and followed his gaze.

"Here come the little devils at last," remarked Billy
Ring. He sounded more amused than alarmed, and
Hawkes had to wonder if the buffalo runner really
cared whether he lived or died.

"Must be a thousand of 'em," said Dougherty.
"Ain't never seen the likes in all my days out here."

"You will never get another chance to," said Billy
Ring. "So have yourself a good long look."

Dougherty shot an unfriendly look in the buffalo
runner's direction. He knew what Ring meant.

"More like eighty to a hundred, I reckon," said
Hawkes.

"That's more than enough to get the job done," said
Dougherty.

Thayer brandished his field glasses and took a closer look at the Sioux. They were about a mile away, and though he couldn't see all that much, he decided that Hawkes's estimate was pretty accurate.

"All right, then," he said, lowering the glasses and looking at the others. "Gentlemen, I suggest we run for our lives."

Hawkes turned to see Pretty Shield at her pony. Cameron was close enough to help her up onto the horse, but instead he just moved past her to his own mount. Hawkes gave her a boost, mounted up himself, and they were off and running.

In an hour's time, the Sioux pursuers had gained a little ground on them, and Hawkes was beginning to wonder if they could keep their lead intact until night-fall. There was a possibility that the Sioux would stop, at least for a while, if only to rest their horses and wait for moonrise. Question was, Could he and his companions keep going long enough? Would their tired mounts outlast those of the Oglalas?

And then suddenly, they were presented with another problem—a river. It was wide and fast-running, the current full of ice and debris.

"What river is this?" asked Cameron, confused. "We didn't cross this."

"We're well to the east of our route up from Fort Union," said Thayer, grimly eyeing the water, that seemed to him to seal their doom.

Le Due was signing. Dougherty read his partner's hands and then said, "He thinks this here is the Muddy River. If we follow it downstream it will bring us to the Missouri."

"It's running west," said Cameron.

"It'll bend to the south."

Hawkes glanced over his shoulder. The contours of the plains concealed the Sioux from his view for the moment, but they were there, drawing closer with each passing second. He shifted his gaze back to the river and looked downstream—it was then that he saw the trees about a quarter mile away. Without a word he kicked his weary horse into a gallop and headed in that direction. The others followed.

As he drew closer to the trees Hawkes saw the island for the first time. About eighty yards long and thirty feet wide at its broadest point, it had trees and scrub and a lot of detritus deposited on its banks by the river, which split and surged around it. On the upstream point was a sandy, open expanse. The island was thirty yards from this bank and less than that from the other, but it was quickly apparent to Hawkes's experienced eye that the main current passed to the far side of the island, racing through a narrow chute. No doubt it was very deep there, and more shallow on this side of the island. But most important, a tree had fallen from this bank to form a natural bridge at the downstream end of the island. More debris had gathered in the bare, partly submerged branches of the tree. The swollen river angrily dashed itself against the partial barrier.

Hawkes checked his horse as he reached the trees, scanning the island carefully. Then he turned his mount so that he could face his companions.

"We're not going to outrun them," he said. "That's clear. I say we cross over to that island and make our stand. It's our only chance. If they catch us out in the open, we're done for."

"We're done for no matter what," said Billy Ring.

"Shuddup," growled Dougherty crossly, " 'fore I introduce the butt of this here rifle to the teeth in your head."

"We may not be done for," said Hawkes. "There's a chance that if we make the cost of killing us too steep they'll have a change of heart."

"How big is that chance?" asked Cameron.

"Pretty small," admitted Hawkes.

"Damned small, I'd say," said Thayer. "This is the Sioux we're dealing with, remember."

Hawkes had to agree. And he didn't bother adding that their chances were made smaller still because it was almost certainly Long Horse who was leading that Oglala war party. And Long Horse would not be easily deterred. It wasn't just his pride but also his unbridled hatred for the white man, that made him such a formidable foe. And even more than that was his disregard for human life. Many a war chief would break off an engagement if his losses were too high—as bad as admitting defeat was for his reputation, far worse would be answering to the grieving families of the dead, who would demand to know what prize was so great that it was worth so many lives. But these were not concerns that would affect Long Horse in any form or fashion. Hawkes was sure of this. Long Horse was a cruel and bloodthirsty adversary who would not flinch if some of the blood that was spilled came from Oglala veins.

"That's true," said Hawkes, concurring with Thayer's assessment. "Small enough for me to wish you had never come after me, Cam," he added, looking into his son's eyes.

"Well, if we're going to die, let's die game," said Cameron. "And make sure our deaths cost them dearly."

Hawkes turned to the others. "Those of you who don't like the idea of staying had best get moving right now."

The others exchanged glances.

"If you're staying, I'm staying," said Billy Ring, leering at Hawkes.

"Reckon we all are," said Dougherty.

Hawkes steered his horse alongside that of He Smiles Twice.

"You should ride on," he told his friend, using the Absaroke tongue. "It could be that they will all stop here to deal with us. At worst, a lot fewer will come after you."

He Smiles Twice shook his head. "I will stay."

"For once, don't be stubborn. The Sioux don't yet know that you and Broken Bow are Absaroke. It would be better for our people if they never knew."

"Our trouble with the Dakota will come whether we stay with you or not."

"I will not leave a fellow Absaroke to die," said Broken Bow.

"And I," said He Smiles Twice, "will not leave my friend."

Hawkes nodded and said no more. There was no point. He did not have to tell He Smiles Twice and Broken Bow what their steadfastness meant to him, nor did he have to express how grateful he was to have such true friends.

"Let's get across," he said in English. "We're running out of time."

"I don't know about trying to swim the horses cross," said Thayer.

"What do we need them for?" asked Billy Ring. "It 't like we're going anywhere."

"We might need one or two for food, if we end up having to stay a while," said Hawkes. Having had ample time to judge which of the mounts were the strongest and hence most likely to make it across the river, he said, "Cameron, you and the lieutenant keep your horses. Everyone else, cut 'em loose."

They dismounted, stripping saddles and bridles off their ponies and sending them on their way. The horses wandered into the trees while Dougherty, Le Due, and Hawkes gathered up everything they thought might be of some use—shot, powder, food, blankets, and the long length of stout rope that had initially been used to strap provisions to the horse Hawkes had been riding.

"You know," said Cameron, watching Hawkes's pony drift away. "That was an American Fur Company horse."

Hawkes looked up from his work. "Well, the company can afford to lose one head of stock."

"I owe the major for it, and a lot more besides."

"Major Culbertson?"

Cameron nodded. "He's been a lot of help. If it weren't for him I'd still be in a cold, damp cell back at Fort Laramie."

"A cell?" Hawkes glanced querulously at his son as he shouldered shot pouches, possibles bags, and the rope. "What are you talking about?"

"The one I put him in," said Thayer.

"You can tell me about it later," said Hawkes. "Right now let's get over to that island."

Cameron nodded and turned his horse toward the river, but Thayer cut him off. "No," said the lieutenant, "it'll be better to go in a little upriver from the island.

As Hawkes watched his son go upriver, it was a

could do to refrain from calling him back and ordering him off that horse. Trying to cross a fast-running, swollen river full of debris in the dead of winter was a perilous proposition, and Hawkes very much wanted to take his son's place. But he couldn't, because to do so would be to humiliate Cameron in the presence of the others. He had done enough damage already.

Sick with worry for his son's welfare, Hawkes forced himself to turn away. Curtly instructing the others to follow him, he headed for the natural bridge provided by the fallen tree. He had every intention of crossing first, so that he could test the log and make sure it would hold a man's weight, but Broken Bow beat him to it. The Absaroke warrior, agile and surefooted, hurried across. Reaching the island, he gestured for the others to come. He Smiles Twice went next, followed by Le Due. Then Dougherty nodded at Billy Ring. "You next."

"Untie me," said the buffalo runner. "If I fall in I don't have a prayer tied up like this."

"Get going, or I'll throw you into the damned river right now." He prodded Billy Ring in the spine with the barrel of his rifle. "Now get a move on, you son of a bitch."

Hawkes waited until Billy Ring and Dougherty had made it across. They were big men, and there was no way to know how much weight the fallen tree would support. A time or two it seemed as though the buffalo runner would lose his balance and topple into the river. And Hawkes wondered if maybe Dougherty was thinking about giving Ring a nudge with the rifle barrel to help matters along. Dougherty had developed a strong dislike for Billy Ring. Hawkes couldn't blame him. If by some miracle both he and Ring survived this ordeal, the problem between them would have to be resolved, once and for all. Having a conscience, mused Hawkes, was a real burden sometimes. He almost wished he could be more like Ring—a man who would not think twice about cutting a defenseless man's throat if there was something to be gained by the act.

Billy Ring reached the island safely, with Dougherty right behind him. Hawkes turned to Pretty Shield and held out his hand.

"Don't be afraid," he told her. "I won't let anything happen to you."

"I am not afraid as long as I am with you," she replied, smiling calmly and putting her hand in his.

Hawkes led the way across the fallen tree. There were branches and some debris to navigate through, and the battering of the river made the trunk vibrate beneath his moccasined feet. Laden with pouches and possibles bags, a bowcase on his back, and the rifle Cameron had brought for him in one hand, Hawkes focused on keeping his balance. Moving slowly, he constantly looked back to make certain that Pretty was doing all right.

As soon as they reached the island, He Smiles Twice and Broken Bow began to attack the trunk of the fallen tree with their hatchets. Obviously, if they had used the tree to reach the island the Sioux could do the same. Hawkes watched them briefly, and quickly concluded that there would not be enough time to cut the tree loose from its moorings on the island. He knew the Oglala war party would appear within a matter of minutes.

He also had a more immediate concern—his son's welfare. He turned his attention upriver to see

Thayer and Cameron were urging their hesitant horses into the river. Thayer's horse balked, and the lieutenant used rein leather to flay the animal into obedience. But Cameron's pony plunged bravely right in. Hawkes forgot to breathe as he watched his son. Cameron clung with both hands to the saddlehorn, swimming alongside his horse. The powerful current was sweeping them down to the island. Shrugging everything off his shoulders, Hawkes tossed his rifle to Le Due and told Dougherty to give him the rope. With the coil in hand, he ran to the upriver end of the island. When Cameron was about fifty yards upstream from the island's sandy point, Hawkes shouted at him to let go of the saddle and swim for it. Cameron hesitated, but then did as his father said, striking out for the island with jerky overhead strokes. The struggling horse swept past Hawkes, still ten yards shy of the island. But Cameron made it, dragging himself onto the sandy point, shivering from the cold and exhausted by the ordeal. Hawkes rushed to his side. He turned to shout for a blanket, but Le Due and Pretty Shield were already coming toward him, blankets in hand. Further downriver, Cameron's horse made its ungainly landing.

"Get him out of those wet clothes before he freezes," Hawkes told Pretty Shield. "Le Due, make us a fire back in the trees."

As Pretty Shield draped two blankets around Cameron, Hawkes searched the river for Thayer. Delayed in entering the water by his balky horse, the lieutenant was still a hundred yards upriver. Like Cameron, he was swimming alongside his mount, clinging to the saddlehorn. But the horse was not faring well. Hawkes could faintly hear its shrill whinnies over the roar of the river, could see that it was doing more struggling than swimming. It then made the fatal error of trying to turn and head back to the other bank. Hawkes knew then that Thayer was in desperate straits. He shook out the rope, looked around quickly, and found a stout piece of wood on the sandy shore. To this he tied one end of the rope just as Thayer, realizing what his horse was up to, let go of the saddle and struck out on his own for the island. Trapped in the middle of the river, its strength failing, the horse was swept pell-mell past the upstream point where Hawkes stood. Thayer wasn't going to make it, either. The mountain man hurled the piece of wood even as he shouted the lieutenant's name. As Thayer was carried past, Hawkes saw the piece of wood land directly behind the dragoon, the rope falling within his easy reach. Thayer saw it, grabbed it, and held on as Hawkes reeled him in. As the lieutenant reached dry ground his doomed horse struck the fallen tree. For a moment Hawkes thought that the natural bridge would break apart from the impact, but it held. The horse struggled briefly, but the force of the current pushed it beneath the fallen tree and under the surface. Trapped in the underwater branches and collected debris, it drowned there.

Hawkes helped the exhausted lieutenant to his feet and took him into the woods, where Le Due had a small fire going. Thayer shrugged out of his soggy coat and wrapped a blanket around his shoulders. Shivering uncontrollably, he huddled next to the fire as Le Due added more wood. Cameron sat there too, wrapped in another blanket, looking very pale.

"You two better shed those wet clothes before you catch pneumonia," said Hawkes.

"I don't think the Sioux will oblige me by waiting until my clothes are dry," said Thayer, "and I do not care to go into battle bare-ass naked."

"Nor do I," said Cameron, forcing the words through a jaw clenched tightly to keep his teeth from chattering.

"Suit yourselves," said Hawkes and turned to go.

"Gordon," said Thayer.

"Yes?"

"Thanks for saving my life back there."

Hawkes nodded and saw that Pretty Shield was making as though to follow him. "You better stay back here in the woods. Keep low and out of sight. They'll be along soon."

She shook her head adamantly. "I am coming with you. If these are our last moments I do not want to spend them apart."

Exasperated, Hawkes glanced at Thayer and Cameron and then back at Pretty Shield. "Okay, then, come on."

As they left the fire, Le Due following them, Thayer looked over at Cameron.

"I'd have to say she's in love with him, wouldn't you?"

"I reckon," muttered Cameron.

"I think he feels he owes her. For a man like your father, an obligation is a serious matter."

"He's in love with her. And if that is so, it means he doesn't love my mother anymore. Because you can't be in love with two people at the same time."

"You sure about that?"

Cameron nodded. He knew it had to be true. He was in love with Walks in the Sun and could not imagine ever loving another. In the past he had just assumed that his father and mother loved one another with the same kind of all-consuming passion and devotion. But now he realized that could not be so, at least as far as his father was concerned, because that kind of love never perished. He was living proof of that. And being separated from the one you loved had no effect on the intensity of that love. Once again, his experience proved that.

"Well, I'm no expert on the subject of love, God knows," said Thayer. "But I wouldn't leap to any conclusions where your father is concerned, if I were you. He's a complicated man. And he's only human, in spite of what you might have thought."

A shot rang out from the downstream end of the island, followed quickly by a flurry of gunfire.

"They're here," said Cameron.

Thayer nodded. The thought foremost in his mind at that moment was how tragic it would be if Cameron and his father died without being reconciled.

Chapter 20

When the Sioux arrived at the trees across the river, they could read from the tracks in the snow that their prey had taken refuge on the island. Dougherty fired the first shot, knocking one of the Oglala warriors off his horse. The others quickly faded back into the trees and dismounted. While some took their ponies and moved them further from the river, the rest of the Sioux found whatever cover was available and began returning fire. This forced He Smiles Twice and Broken Bow to abandon their hatchet work on the fallen tree. The two Absarokes found cover, taking up position near the tree, at the downstream end of the island. Dougherty and Le Due settled in about twenty yards upstream from them, while Hawkes found a good place up near the other end of the island. Long ago, perhaps the previous spring, when the river ran high from snowmelt, the Muddy had flooded and left a pile of debris caught among the trees. Hawkes and Pretty Shield found shelter behind this natural barricade, which stood four feet high in most places. He did not have to stand up and fire over the debris—there were several places where he could slide the rifle barrel through the tangle of deadwood and get off a shot. It was like shooting through a gun slot in a window shutter.

Many of the Sioux had long guns, but the majority of these were trade muskets, old flintlock smoothbores without much accuracy at any distance. And the Sioux rarely had sufficient powder and shot so that they could get in enough practice to become outstanding marksmen. But with about a hundred guns firing at once, there was a lot of lead being hurled at the island. Lead balls continually slapped into the barricade that concealed Hawkes and Pretty Shield, and many more whistled overhead, striking the trees behind them. The powder smoke from the Sioux guns thickened, obscuring the warriors. But there wasn't enough cover for all of them, and Hawkes managed to locate some good targets. He hit several Oglala warriors, killing two of them, and his companions were equally as effective. Within thirty minutes' time most of the Sioux had moved back beyond the trees, leaving only a couple of dozen near the river to continue a harassing fire.

As the shooting diminished, Thayer and Cameron made their way to Gordon's position, moving through the trees at a crouched run. Cameron had his rifle and the lieutenant carried only a pistol—his long gun had been strapped to his saddle during the river crossing. Both of them needed to reload, and Hawkes realized he had left all the extra cartridge pouches at the other end of the island.

"So what are they up to?" Thayer asked him, peering through the spaces in the deadwood.

"The one who must be leading them, Long Horse, is no fool," said Hawkes. "He knows it's unwise to lose too many men at the outset, so he's pulled most of them back."

Thayer nodded. "Bad for morale if you suffer heavy losses at the beginning. Look there!"

Two Sioux horsemen raced out of the trees, heading downriver.

"What's happening?" asked Cameron.

Thayer glanced at Hawkes. "Think they know something we don't know?"

"I hope not. I think they're just looking for a way across. If they knew of one already, Long Horse would have sent more men to get around behind us."

"You seem to know this Long Horse pretty well."

Hawkes looked at Thayer a moment, and the coldness in the mountain man's eyes sent a chill down the lieutenant's spine.

"I'm going to kill him," said Hawkes, "if it's the last thing I do."

Thayer glanced downriver at the fallen tree that connected the island to the bank. He noticed that Hawkes was looking in that direction, as well.

"Think they'll give it a try, then?" asked the lieutenant.

"I reckon. But he'll want a diversion first."

"Can't wait to find out what that will be," said Thayer dryly.

The Sioux firing was desultory now, and Hawkes decided it was as good a time as any to make his move.

"I'm going to the other end of the island. Check on the others."

"Bring back some cartridges if you can," said Thayer.

Hawkes nodded, and noticed that once again Pretty Shield was preparing to go with him.

"No, not this time," he said firmly. "I'll be right back. You stay put."

"I have told you before—I am going to stay with you."

"You're not coming with me this time, Pretty, and that's final. If I have to, I'll tie you hand and foot."

Pretty Shield opened her mouth to argue—but the look on his face gave her second thoughts, and she decided to say nothing more.

"Keep an eye on her, Lieutenant, if you don't mind," said Hawkes.

"You can count on it."

Hawkes glanced at his son. "Are you okay, Cam?"

"I'm fine. Don't worry about me."

Hawkes handed him his rifle and cartridge pouch. "Keep a sharp eye upriver. Long Horse might try to get some men to the island by putting them into the river upstream so they can float down to the point."

Cameron took the rifle without comment, and Hawkes left the protection of the deadwood pile on the run. The shooting from across the river picked up as he broke into the open, and he heard the angry buzz of hot lead as it whistled past him, too close for comfort. A bullet smacked into a tree trunk just as he raced behind it—if the tree hadn't been there, the ball would have found its mark.

He reached the position held by Dougherty and Le Due. An old log, partially decayed, lay here, and the river had covered some of it with sand. Billy Ring lay on his back behind the log, looking for all the world like a man just taking his ease. Dougherty was kneeling beside Le Due, checking the French Canadian's arm, which Hawkes saw was stained with blood. Dougherty cut open the sleeve with his knife, slitting it from the shoulder halfway down to the elbow. Hawkes dove behind the log, chased by a flurry of

Sioux bullets, and Dougherty had to stop what he was doing and duck down until the shooting had diminished.

"Is he hit bad?" asked Hawkes.

"Nah," said Dougherty. "Just a scratch. Le Due here is a tough old buzzard. Got himself a right thick hide. Ain't got the sense God gave a mule, though. He won't never learn to keep his head down when somebody's trying to shoot him."

"Get back to the fire," Hawkes told Le Due. "Heat up your ramrod and slap hot iron on that wound."

Le Due made hand signals and Dougherty chuckled. "He says he would, except he has to stick close to make sure I don't go and get myself kilt. That's funny, seeing as how he's always been the one who ends up bleeding. Hell, I ain't gotten so much as a scratch in nigh on ten years. Now git," he told Le Due gruffly. "Do what the man says. Reckon I can manage here by myself for a spell."

The French Canadian crawled deeper into the trees before getting up to run, clutching his arm, to the place where he had built the fire earlier.

"What are you trying to do?" Dougherty asked Hawkes as he laid his rifle barrel across the log and drew a bead. "Get yourself shot full of holes?"

"Need some cartridges. They're all down at the other end of the island."

Dougherty squeezed the trigger. His rifle jumped and spewed smoke and flame.

"Bring me a rifle while you're at it," said Billy Ring. "I'm getting mighty bored sittin' here waiting to have my scalp lifted."

Dougherty laughed as he reloaded his long gun.

"Give you a rifle? Do we look like we done just sprouted?"

"I am a better shot with one arm than anyone else on this godforsaken island," said Billy Ring, his one good eye fixed on Hawkes. "You need me."

"We'll manage," replied Hawkes.

"And if I give you my word? That I won't shoot nothing but Sioux devils until this is over?"

"He ain't fool enough to buy into that," predicted Dougherty. Then he glanced at Hawkes, concerned. "You ain't, are you?"

"No," said Hawkes. "But if the Sioux do reach the island, I want you to cut him loose."

"How about if I cut his throat instead? Then he won't feel a thing when some Sioux buck takes his scalp." Aware of the expression on Hawkes's face, Dougherty grimaced and looked across the river. "Yeah, okay. I'll cut him loose, if that's the way you want it."

Hawkes thanked him, then took off running again, heading for the south end of the island. Once again the Sioux firing grew more intense, but he reached his destination unscathed. He Smiles Twice and Broken Bow had taken cover some distance apart, the former closer to the fallen tree. It was there that Hawkes had dropped the extra cartridge pouches.

"They will try to cross here," said He Smiles Twice. "And they will try soon."

Hawkes nodded. "Surprised they haven't given it a try already. May be that they'll wait until dark. I've got to get some cartridges back to the other end of the island, but when it gets dark I'll come back."

He Smiles Twice nodded. Hawkes gathered up several of the pouches and made his way back. Once again the Sioux fire picked up. He didn't break stride as he passed Dougherty's position, tossing one of the pouches to the trapper as he raced by. Dougherty shouted his thanks and then got off another shot. Hawkes heard the man let out a whoop.

"Keep on a-runnin' back and forth like that," called Dougherty wryly. "I done kilt two of the heathen since you started. They be so eager to get off a shot at you that some are gettin' right careless."

Reaching the deadwood barricade, Hawkes sank to the ground behind it, winded, and handed Thayer the rest of the pouches. Pretty Shield moved to kneel beside him, laying a hand on his chest, concern knitting her brow. He gave her a reassuring smile.

"They never even came close," he lied.

"What are they waiting for?" asked Cameron, peering through the deadwood at the Sioux-infested shore. His voice was taut and pitched higher than usual.

"Just take it easy, son," said Hawkes.

"They're in no hurry," said Thayer. "It's not like we're going anywhere."

Hawkes glanced at Thayer, then downstream at the fallen tree that formed the bridge connecting the island to the riverbank.

"Maybe we could be, though."

Thayer stared at him, confused. "I seem to recall that you were the one saying we couldn't run for it, that we had to stay put and make a stand."

"Well, maybe some of us do." Hawkes smiled at the perplexed expression on the lieutenant's face. "I'll be back. I need to take a look at something."

"Wonder what the hell he's up to now," muttered Thayer, watching the mountain man disappear into the woods.

Reaching the other side of the island, Hawkes stud-

ied the angry torrent of the river that separated the island from the snow-covered opposite bank. At its nar-
rowest point the chute was perhaps forty feet across.
Hawkes spent some time measuring that distance
against the height of the trees that grew along the
steep banks on this side of the island. Then he made
his way to the downstream end of the island and rejoined He Smiles Twice.

"How far are we from Fort Union, by your reckoning?" he asked the Absaroke. "For a man on foot."

The Fox Clan warrior gave the question a moment
of careful consideration. "In this snow? At least two
whole days."

Hawkes nodded. "That's the way I figure it, too."
He took the Absaroke's steel-headed hatchet and retraced his steps to the other side of the island, where
he cut a deep notch into the tree he had already selected as the one best suited for what he had in mind.
It was a poplar that stood at least sixty feet high. Here
the river had cut deep embankments on both sides,
and the tree grew quite near the edge. To the mountain man's eye, the tree appeared to be leaning
slightly out over the river at its most narrow point.
Having clearly marked the tree, he returned to the
deadwood barricade to rejoin Thayer, Cameron, and
Pretty Shield.

"You find what you were looking for?" asked
Thayer.

Hawkes nodded. "Only question is, will the Sioux
find a way across the river to get around behind us?"

"I don't follow."

"Well, you said it before. Why should Long Horse be
in any hurry? He doesn't think we're going anywhere."

"I'd have to agree with him about that."

"So, what if we felled a tree and bridged the other channel? A couple of us could stay behind to make Long Horse think we're still here. The rest could cross to the other bank and head south for Fort Union. A long two days on foot should see you there."

"A couple of us stay behind?" echoed Thayer. "One of whom, I presume, would be you."

"Well, it's my idea," said Hawkes, with a taut smile.

"And you think a couple of men could hold out long enough for help to get back from Fort Union? That would be a good four days."

"You never know."

"Well," said the lieutenant dryly, "being a cavalry-man, I am not fond of the idea of walking through deep snow for two days. So if this is going to happen, I'd just as soon stay here with you, if you don't mind."

"No," said Cameron. "I'll stay."

"No, you won't," said Hawkes.

"I'm not a kid anymore. I'll do what I please. And I didn't come all this way just to go back to Ma and tell her I left you here to die. If you stay, I stay, and that's all there is to it."

"You're not staying. Two men with plenty of car-tridges can hold this island for a while. That will be me—and Billy Ring."

"Billy Ring!" exclaimed Thayer. "Are you mad? That man would sell his soul to the devil for the chance to kill you—or he would if he hadn't already made the sale. Gordon, between Billy Ring and those Sioux, you wouldn't stand a chance."

"I don't mind long odds. I've beaten them before."

While the three men were talking, Pretty Shield had been keeping an eye on the other side of the river, peering through a space in the tangle of deadwood. Now a sound of alarm escaped her lips, and Hawkes, hearing it, glanced at her just as she turned to look at him.

"They are coming!" she whispered.

Chapter 21

A hundred yards upstream, Sioux warriors were emerging from the woods to plunge into the freezing waters of the river. Hawkes counted five, ten, then a dozen. An instant later, a war cry split the air. He knew it came from He Smiles Twice, and he understood its meaning. Turning his attention downstream, he saw more Sioux warriors breaking cover to attempt crossing the fallen tree. At the same time, other Indians in the woods opposite the island quickened their fire, laying down cover for their brethren.

"Your friend Long Horse is a little short on patience, I think," said Thayer, and brought his rifle up to start shooting at the Sioux who were being carried downriver by the swift current.

Hawkes noticed that the warriors crossing the fallen tree moved swiftly and with remarkable agility through the branches, one following closely after the other. He Smiles Twice and Broken Bow were firing at them steadily. The first Oglala brave toppled into the river, and a second one fell, too, his lifeless body snagged by branches before it could be claimed by the raging waters. But the other Sioux kept coming. Hawkes made a snap decision. He could tell at a glance that some of the Indians in the river would not

reach the island. The current was too fast and strong
for them. The greater threat, then, was posted by the
ones crossing the fallen tree. The judgment made, action followed in a heartbeat. He was up and sprinting
for the downstream end of the island. As he passed the
position held by Dougherty and Le Due he saw that
the French Canadian was back in place, and he
shouted at Dougherty to follow him. He didn't look
back to see if the trapper was coming, but plunged on
through the brush at top speed. There wasn't a moment to waste.

As he drew near the end of the island, he saw that
the Sioux were nearly across the fallen tree. He Smiles
Twice and Broken Bow had accounted for six of the
enemy, but it wasn't their marksmanship that slowed
the attack. Rather, it was the tree itself, bowing under
the weight of more than a dozen men and shuddering
violently from the ceaseless onslaught of the river.
Other Sioux hesitated at the edge of the river, waiting
for their fellow warriors to get across, dubious about
adding their weight to the tree. As Hawkes broke
cover he saw one of the Sioux leap from the tree and
race toward He Smiles Twice, tomahawk raised, a war
cry on his lips. The Absaroke had just discharged his
rifle and had not finished reloading. Hawkes brought
his long gun up and fired, hitting the Sioux in mid-
stride. The next Sioux brave swung his rifle around to
fire at Hawkes, but Broken Bow's gun spoke first and
the bullet's impact hurled the Oglala into the river.

The next Sioux in line decided to get across the log
to the island before fighting, and as he got to the shore
Hawkes raced forward and drove the stock of his rifle
into the Oglala's face. The warrior dropped, but not
before Hawkes had cast aside his empty long gun and

jerked the Sioux's trade musket out of the unconscious Indian's grasp. Leaping up onto the fallen tree, he fired the musket at hip level at the nearest foe. A warrior jackknifed as the lead ball ripped through his belly— doubled over, he toppled into the river. The Sioux behind him let out a shrill war cry as he lunged at Hawkes, who gripped the barrel of the musket with both hands and used the gun to club the Oglala with such force that the musket shattered and the Indian was launched into the freezing waters. Off balance himself, Hawkes slipped off the log. He grabbed at a thick branch but it broke beneath him, and he fell up to his waist into the river.

Clutching desperately at other branches, he held with all his might as the current fought to drag him under the tree. If that happened he would become entangled in the underwater debris and would drown. It was all he could do to hold on—and when he looked up he saw a Sioux warrior raising his long gun to bring the stock down on his skull. But before the Oglala could strike, a rifle spoke, and the brave was hurled backward off the log. Those that remained suddenly lost their taste for the fight and withdrew. A moment later, just as Hawkes began to wonder if he could hold on any longer, He Smiles Twice was there, reaching down to wrap strong hands around the mountain man's wrists and hauling him up out of the icy torrent.

Though he had not been in the water long, Hawkes had lost nearly all feeling in his legs—they were like blocks of ice. He Smiles Twice had to carry him back to the island, with Broken Bow and Dougherty providing covering fire. Once he was on dry ground, Hawkes gripped his Absaroke friend's arm.

"Give me your rifle and then go help Cameron. Take

Broken Bow with you. Dougherty and I will hold them
off if they try to get across again."

He Smiles Twice nodded and, with a curt gesture at
Broken Bow to follow him, headed for the upstream
end of the island. Hawkes watched them go, worried.
He had a sense that his son and the lieutenant were in
trouble, and he wanted to go to their aid, but for the
moment he could scarcely walk, much less run, and
every second counted.

Hawkes was right. Of the twelve warriors who had
braved the frigid waters of the Muddy River, five had
been swept past the island. Of these, only two managed to climb up onto the fallen tree; Dougherty dispatched one of them, but the other reached the safety
of the riverbank. The others drowned. Several more
had been killed or wounded by the accurate shooting
of Thayer and Cameron. But four had reached the island. Two made landfall on the sandy spit, while the
other pair were carried further down, struggling
ashore beyond the deadwood barricade that concealed
Cameron, the dragoon, and Pretty Shield. Thayer
stood to shoot as they passed but missed his mark. Reloading, he checked to see how Cameron was faring
and saw that his young companion had turned his attention to the other two Sioux. Cameron dropped one
with a well-aimed shot, but before he could reload, the
second warrior made a dash for the woods behind the
barricade. Knowing he couldn't let the Indian get behind them, Cameron moved out to meet him. That was
all Thayer had time to see. Then he had to contend
with the other two Oglalas.

The Sioux had carried only knives or tomahawks
into the river, and the warrior confronting Cameron
clutched a blade in his hand as he lunged at his enemy.

Cameron reacted, trying to strike at the knife with his rifle, but it proved to be a feint on the Oglala's part. The Indian tossed the knife from one hand to the other and then struck. Cameron gasped as the blade bit into his flesh, grazing a rib. Twisting desperately to elude the knife, he lost his balance and sprawled in the sand. Seeing his chance, the Sioux uttered a triumphant yell and closed in for the kill. Suddenly Pretty Shield was there, launching herself at the Oglala, clinging to his back and clawing at his face. Snarling, the warrior shook her off, but it bought Cameron precious seconds, and before the Sioux realized what was happening, Cameron's own knife slid between his ribs and pierced his heart, killing him on his feet.

Cameron took Pretty Shield's arm and helped her to her feet. Together they ran for cover as the Sioux across the river continued shooting at them. Reaching the deadwood barricade, he pushed her down on the ground and stabbed a finger at her.

"You stay down!" he rasped. Almost as an afterthought, he gratefully muttered, "And thanks. You saved my life."

"I did it for your father, not you."

Cameron smiled tautly. "Well, at least you're honest."

He turned to scan the woods, wondering what had become of Thayer—and then he saw the lieutenant, along with He Smiles Twice, darting from tree to tree, trying to get back to the deadwood barricade. The Sioux gunfire slowly died down. Cameron checked downstream. There were no more Oglala warriors attempting to cross the fallen tree to the island. There were no more braves entering the river upstream, either. It seemed the attack was over.

"Is that it?" he asked in disbelief. "You mean they quit?"

"For now," said Thayer. "You're bleeding."

"It's nothing. Just a scratch. Is anyone else hurt? Is— is my father . . . ?"

"White Crow lives," said He Smiles Twice. "But Broken Bow has been killed."

"God, no," said Cameron, stunned.

"He died a warrior's death. No more need be said." He Smiles Twice was very curt and seemed almost indifferent. But Cameron sensed that this was a front. He could tell from his friend's eyes that He Smiles Twice was deeply affected by the death of the stalwart Broken Bow. So was Cameron. Though Broken Bow had been a taciturn and unsmiling man, Cameron had come to admire him as a paragon of the Absaroke warrior—loyal, courageous, resourceful, and fiercely proud. Broken Bow had been there for him, just as He Smiles Twice was, and Cameron had derived comfort in knowing that he could always rely on the Fox Clan warriors.

"There were two of them that got onto the island downstream," said Thayer. "They're both dead, but not before one of them got Broken Bow."

Without another word on the subject, He Smiles Twice turned to disappear into the woods. Cameron assumed he had only wanted to confirm that all was well on this end of the island. Now the Absaroke was going back to the other end to tell Hawkes that the island was secure, though the victory had not been won without a high price.

Within an hour, the sun had dipped to the western horizon, a ball of orange that seemed to melt slowly into the snow-blue plains. Back beneath the trees across the river, Long Horse and his Oglala warriors built their fires. An occasional shot rang out, a blossom of flame marking the location of the Sioux warrior who pulled the trigger. Thayer told Cameron that the shooting would likely go on all night, a tactic designed to prevent them from getting any rest. That didn't phase Cameron. He'd never been so tired in all his life, and he was quite sure that a gunshot or two every now and then would not be enough to keep him awake.

As night descended, Hawkes returned to the dead-wood barricade and told them that Le Due had made some coffee at the fire back in the trees. Cameron went to get some for himself and Thayer. On the way back he heard the distinctive sound of wood being chopped somewhere on the other side of the island. When he got back to the deadwood barricade he found that his father and Pretty Shield had gone.

"You hear that?" he asked Thayer.

The lieutenant nodded. "I think that would be He Smiles Twice. He and your father are taking turns try-ing to drop a tree over that channel on the other side of the river. Meanwhile, whoever isn't chopping can help Dougherty stand guard down there." He nodded in the direction of the fallen tree. Wrapping his hands around the tin cup and bringing the fragrant steam close to his face, Thayer glanced curiously at Cameron. "He's not going to let you stay with him. You know that, don't you?"

"How is he going to make me go?"

Thayer smiled. "I have to admit, I like you, Cameron. You've got courage, and a stubborn streak at least a mile wide. But when it comes right down to it, I'll put my money on your father."

"We'll see," said Cameron. His clothes were dry

enough to suit him. He finished off his coffee, then
ventured down to the river's edge. Sitting on his heels,
he took off his coat, raised his shirt and splashed cold
water on the knife wound in his side, gasping at the
pain. He gazed across the river at the dark trees where
the Sioux were lurking. He was trying to sort through
mixed emotions and figure out what he should do
abut his father, and about Pretty Shield. She had risked
her life to save his. *I did it for your father,* she'd said. Obviously her love was very strong. Cameron knew he
ought not to be resentful toward her. But he couldn't
seem to help it every time he thought of his mother,
and what the story behind his father's relationship
with Pretty Shield might do to her.

With a deep sigh he went back to the deadwood.
Thayer told him to try and get some rest. "I'll wake
you in a couple of hours," said the lieutenant.
Cameron nodded and curled up on the ground with
his rifle beside him. He went right to sleep in spite of
the bitter cold, the painful wound in his side, the knot
of hunger in his belly, and the occasional Sioux gunshot.

He opened his eyes, groggy and disoriented, when
Thayer shook him awake. It was still dark, and so cold
it made his bones ache.

"Come with me," said Thayer.

Cameron got stiffly to his feet and followed the dragoon into the woods. When they reached the fire he
saw that everyone but Dougherty was gathered there.
Even Billy Ring was present, sitting cross-legged on
the ground, leaning forward to be closer to the fire, his
arm still bound behind him. A body lay nearby, covered with a blanket. Cameron stared, knowing it had
to be the corpse of Broken Bow.

"We've got a couple of hours yet before daybreak," said Hawkes. "It's time for all of you to get started. There's a way off this island now."

"You're assuming we're all going to just walk away and leave you here. I don't care to go unless we all go," Thayer said.

"We can't all go. With luck I can keep Long Horse and his braves busy for a while."

"We *can* all go. We'll have the river between them and us."

Hawkes shook his head. "We don't know if there's a crossing downriver."

"What about Le Due? He's supposed to be familiar with this neck of the woods."

"I asked him. He can't say for certain."

"I think it's unlikely, as high as the river is running, that Long Horse will be able to get across," said Thayer.

"I've made up my mind. I'm staying. The rest of you are going. When you get to Fort Union you can send help back."

"That would be four, five days in coming," said Thayer. "You know as well as I do that you can't possibly hold out that long."

Exasperated, Hawkes stepped closer to Thayer. He had expected some opposition from Cameron, and perhaps from He Smiles Twice, but not from the lieutenant.

"Listen," he said, fixing his steely gaze on Thayer. "If we all stay, we'll all die."

"We all came up here to get you out. And now you want us to leave you."

"I'm grateful that you helped my son."

"Well, my orders were to stop him, not help him,"

said Thayer wryly. He glanced at Cameron and nodded. "Yes, that's right. Colonel Lovell sent me and Sergeant Landrum after you for the purpose of keeping you out of Sioux country, one way or another."

"Sergeant Landrum?" asked Hawkes.

"Yes. I told the sergeant to stick close but stay out of sight. Haven't seen a sign of him since we left Fort Union, but if I know Landrum, he knows where we are and the trouble we're in. Could be that he's even gone for help."

"I wouldn't count on that," said Hawkes. "But I *am* counting on you, Lieutenant, to get my son and Pretty Shield out of here."

Thayer glanced at Cameron and the Sioux woman, trying to read their expressions. "I don't think either one of them intends to leave you."

Hawkes turned to his son. "Cam, I'm asking you. Think about your mother and Grace. What will happen to them if neither one of us gets back? They need you there."

"Ma would never forgive me if I left you here to die."

"Who said anything about dying? I'm just going to keep the Sioux occupied for a day or two so the rest of you get a good head start."

"There's more to it than that, I'm guessing," said Thayer. "Revenge is part of it, isn't that right, Gordon? You don't like the idea of running away from Long Horse. You want to kill him so bad you can almost taste it."

"I know what that tastes like," said Billy Ring.

"Thing is," continued Thayer, "you're going to have to go through a hundred Oglala warriors to get to Long Horse. That's too big of a job, even for you."

His face like stone, Hawkes said, "Reckon I'll find out."

"You said revenge was part of it," said Cameron. "What's the rest, Lieutenant?"

Thayer was pretty sure he knew, but he didn't say anything. He didn't think it was his place to tell Cameron that his father was in search of redemption. The mountain man felt he had let his son down, not to mention his wife, by taking up with Pretty Shield. And he was right, there was no denying that.

"It doesn't really matter," answered Thayer. "We're wasting time. I'm going to Fort Union. There's a small detachment from my regiment posted there, Gordon. I'll bring them back, in case you manage to work a miracle and stay alive that long."

"I will not go," said Pretty Shield.

Hawkes didn't argue with her. That surprised Thayer. He was fairly certain Hawkes had made up his mind that the Sioux woman would leave the island. But the mountain man merely extended a hand to He Smiles Twice, then to Thayer, and Le Due, and finally turned to his son. Cameron took his father's hand, clasping it firmly. Thayer had a hunch that Hawkes and his son both wanted to wrap their arms around the other in a farewell embrace. But they were too proud, and neither could find words sufficient to express his feelings.

"There's something I've been meaning to give you," said Cameron. He reached under his shirt and took out the Crow wampum belt. "I found this down on the Yellowstone, where the Oglalas captured you."

Hawkes took the belt, deeply moved. "I always thought this brought me good luck. I'm glad to have it back. Thank you."

Cameron just nodded, unable to reply.

"Take all the food," Hawkes told the others, "but leave the extra guns with me."

"What about me?" asked Billy Ring.

"Oh, I forgot to tell you," Hawkes replied. "You're staying here with me."

He approached the buffalo runner, knife drawn. Ring watched him warily, wondering exactly what the mountain man intended, but Hawkes just bent down to cut the thongs that bound Ring's wrist to the back of his belt. Ring stood up shaking his wrist, grinning like a wolf at Hawkes.

"I know I've said it before," said the buffalo hunter, "but it's worth saying again. You got some hard bark on you, mister. It's almost a shame to have to kill you."

Hawkes picked up a rifle and tossed it to Ring.

"You can try me now," he said flatly, "or you can help me with the Sioux. But one way or the other, this business between us is going to be settled right here on this island."

Billy Ring checked the rifle. It was loaded and capped, and for a moment he gave his options a careful study.

"I got me a score to settle with them Dakota, too. So I'll save you for last."

"Fair enough." Hawkes turned to Thayer. "I'll go take over for Dougherty. Wait for him."

Thayer nodded. "Good luck."

With one last look at Cameron, Hawkes disappeared into the darkness, followed by Pretty Shield. Billy Ring hung back a moment.

"My crew is still at Fort Union, I reckon," he informed Thayer. "Tell 'em to give me the rip-roaringest wake this wild country has ever seen. God damn it, I deserve that!" He laughed and followed Hawkes and the Oglala woman into the night.

Thayer glanced at Cameron and thought the young man looked very pale and gaunt. There was a strange distance in his eyes. The dragoon put a hand on his shoulder and Cameron jumped at the touch, as though startled out of a daydream.

"So he really will end up dead," muttered Cameron. "Just like everybody told me he was all along."

"Come on, let's get going."

They gathered up the bags of hard biscuits, pemmican, and jerky. He Smiles Twice took the blanket-wrapped body of Broken Bow and put it across his shoulder. Thayer didn't think there was any way the Absaroke could carry such a burden in a two-day trek, on foot, through deep snow. But he wasn't about to try and talk He Smiles Twice out of it, and neither was anyone else. He Smiles Twice was not going to leave the body of a friend and fellow Fox Clan warrior in Sioux country if he could help it.

When Hawkes and Pretty Shield reached the downstream end of the island where Dougherty was guarding the fallen tree, Hawkes told the trapper that the others were leaving and that he needed to get moving himself.

"I don't cotton to the idea of turning my back on you," admitted Dougherty.

"Just be sure to tell Jim Bridger thanks for looking after Pretty Shield."

"What?" asked the Sioux woman.

Hawkes drew a deep breath—then turned and hit her squarely on the chin. He didn't hit her with full force, just hard enough to knock her out cold, and he caught her before she could hit the ground.

"And tell her I'm sorry I had to do that," said Hawkes.

Dougherty nodded. Hawkes swept Pretty Shield's limp form up in his arms and gave her to the trapper.

"Don't worry about a thing, hoss," said Dougherty. "I'll make sure she gets to Old Gabe, and I know he'll take care of her like she was his own daughter. Hell, it wasn't all that long ago when the Injuns carried off his own girl, and there's been no word of her since. I reckon he'll take to the task of lookin' out for this gal like a duck takes to water."

"I hope so. Thanks, my friend, for all you've done."

"Warn't nothing," replied Dougherty—and then he saw Billy Ring emerge from the darkness, and he all but dropped Pretty Shield so he could go for the long gun hanging by a strap on his back. "What in tarnation!" he exclaimed, seeing that the buffalo runner was not only free but armed.

"I forgot to tell you," said Hawkes, "but Ring here has volunteered to stay and help me keep the Sioux busy for a while."

"You must be right tired of living, old son."

"Nope. Just tired of having to look over my shoulder all the time."

Dougherty morosely shook his head. "It pains me to think of your topknot decoratin' a Sioux scalp pole." Then he glanced at Billy Ring. "I can't say the same about you."

And with that parting shot he was gone, leaving Hawkes and Billy Ring face to face with one another.

"Now what do we do?" asked the buffalo runner.

"Come with me. I need your help."

Hawkes led the way across the island. He took his time, and when they reached the tree that bridged the roaring chute, the others had already crossed. All that remained were their footprints in the snow. The hatchets were buried in the fresh stump, and the two men took them and hacked at the poplar until it was completely separated from the trunk. Then they put their backs to it, digging in their heels and heaving and pushing and groaning until they had shoved the trunk over the edge of the steep bank. It splashed into the dark waters, and the strong current caught it and carried it downstream, dragging the other end off the far bank.

Standing there catching their breath, the two men did not speak for a moment. Then Billy Ring grinned.

"By God, Gordon, they'll be spinnin' yarns abut us and our last stand on this damned island until the world dies of old age."

Chapter 22

When dawn finally came, Hawkes saw movement beneath the trees across the river, and soon the Oglalas were shooting again. Billy Ring propped his long gun across a log and took aim, intent on making a lethal reply. About twenty feet away, hunkered down behind a tree, Hawkes called out and told him not to shoot.

"And why the hell shouldn't I?" asked the buffalo runner. "I can convert one of them red devils with every shot, and that's a guarantee. Don't let the fact that I only got one arm fool you. I am still the best damned shot west of the Mississippi."

Hawkes sighed. "Yeah, so you keep telling me. If that's so, how come I'm still alive?"

Ring scowled. He knew Hawkes was referring to their showdown at Fort Union some months ago. " 'Cause you waited until I was fallin'-down drunk to pick a fight, that's how come."

Hawkes smiled coldly. "That's because you're a better shot than I am. But right now you won't be doing any shooting. If we return fire they'll figure out before long that something is up, since they'll only hear two rifles. If we don't shoot they'll think we're short of ammunition."

"And if they think that they'll come for us."

Hawkes nodded. "That's the general idea. How fast can you load and shoot?"

"I can get off two shots in a minute. Do it all the time. Used to be three, up until you took my other arm."

"Good. You'll get a chance to prove that soon enough."

Billy Ring shook his head. "Let me get this straight. You want them Dakotas to come at us? Now why the hell is that? You'd rather die early in the day instead of late?"

"No. I want to live."

"You have a funny way of showing it."

"I figure Long Horse has lost twenty-five, thirty men so far."

"So? He's got a lot more to spend."

"Sooner or later some of them will start wondering if they want to be spent that way."

"If that's how your thinking goes, how come you sent the others away? Six rifles are better than two."

" 'Cause this probably won't work out the way I want it to."

Billy Ring smirked. "I still think maybe I ought to kill you now."

"Do whatever you have to," said Hawkes, not taking his eyes off the far bank of the river.

In an hour's time the Sioux shooting died down. Here and there a warrior left his place of concealment, exposing himself to their guns, but Hawkes and the buffalo hunter refused to take the bait. Hawkes was certain Long Horse would send some men across the fallen tree. It was just a matter of time. As it happened, he didn't have long to wait.

Suspecting a trick, Long Horse sent five warriors to attempt a crossing. Hawkes told Billy Ring to hold his fire until all five men were on the fallen tree. He and the buffalo runner were well hidden, but once their rifles spoke, the Sioux across the river would respond with a withering hail of gunfire. When the first warrior in line was halfway across, Hawkes swept his rifle to his shoulder and fired. Billy Ring cut loose a split second later. As Hawkes ducked down to reload he heard the long crackling thunder of the Sioux guns, and the air around him was filled with the angry whine of hot lead. Rifle reloaded, he rose up coolly into this deadly hail, drew a bead on the next Oglala charging across the fallen tree, and squeezed the trigger. Billy Ring fired his second shot simultaneously—and two more Dakota warriors perished. That left one man on the tree bridge, and he hesitated, knowing that certain death awaited him if he advanced, and knowing as well that if he turned tail he would face the scorn of his peers and certain dishonor. So he moved forward, and Hawkes, preparing to shoot a third time, also hesitated, admiring the doomed Indian's nerve, and reluctant to take his life. Billy Ring had no such compunction, and he shot the Oglala dead.

With all five of the Sioux attackers dealt with, Hawkes stayed low and waited for the shooting to subside. He could only hope that at least some of the warriors who followed Long Horse were having second thoughts by now. If enough decided to quit the fight, the Dakota war chief would have no choice but to let them go. In spite of his captivity and all that he had suffered at their hands, Hawkes found he had no desire to kill any more of the Oglalas. He derived no satisfaction from taking their lives. And he wondered whether Billy Ring enjoyed the killing, if the buffalo hunter could snuff out human life with the same callous indifference that he exhibited when slaying shaggies by the hundreds. There was only one Sioux life that Hawkes wanted to take, and when at last the gunfire had died down, he shouted out the name of Long Horse. A Sioux long gun answered him, and then another, and after that all was quiet but for the rushing of the river. Steeling himself, Hawkes stood up, holding his rifle over his head.

"Long Horse? I am White Crow, and I would have words with you!"

Hunkered down behind the nearby log, Billy Ring stared at Hawkes and just shook his head in sheer wonderment.

"You're either the bravest man I've ever seen," muttered the buffalo hunter, "or the biggest damn fool."

"Long Horse!" shouted Hawkes. "Why do you hide from me? You said I and my kind were nothing compared to the Sioux. Then why are you afraid of me?"

He saw the Oglala war chief then—Long Horse emerged from the trees, carrying his rifle cradled in one arm, his face painted for battle, pride and defiance manifested in the way he carried himself as he came to the water's edge.

"Long Horse fears no one!" said the Oglala leader. "Least of all you, White Crow."

Peering over the log, Billy Ring said, "Drop the bastard, Gordon. Kill him now and maybe the rest of 'em will head for home."

"Shut up, Ring."

"Fine then. I'll do it myself if you won't."

"No, you won't. This one is mine."

"I am here!" shouted Long Horse. "Say what you have to say."

"You and me," replied Hawkes. "You want to see me dead. That's the only reason you're here. Twice before I have challenged you. I challenge you again now. Are you a coward, Long Horse? Is that why you send your brothers to kill me instead of doing it yourself?"

Long Horse shook a furious fist at Hawkes. "I will tear the living heart out of your body with these hands, White Crow"

"Then meet me halfway!" taunted Hawkes, pointing at the fallen tree. Casting his rifle aside, he drew his hunting knife from its sheath and held it up.

Long Horse threw down his rifle and, brandishing his own knife, ran for the fallen tree. Hawkes moved too, leaping onto the tree and advancing to the middle of the river. There he waited for the Oglala. He didn't have to wait long. Long Horse loped toward him, and as he drew near he uttered a piercing war cry and lashed out with the knife. Hawkes eluded the blade and lunged forward, thrusting his own knife at the Oglala chief's belly, but the Sioux caught his wrist, his strong fingers closing on it like a vise, holding the knife at bay while bringing his own blade downward in a stabbing motion. Hawkes reached up with his free hand and, clutching the Indian's arm halfway between wrist and elbow, stopped the knife from descending further.

For an instant they seemed frozen there, locked in a death struggle, balanced on the fallen tree that spanned the angry river, their bodies trembling with exertion. And then Hawkes fell backward, bringing one leg up to plant his foot in the Sioux war chief's belly and catapulting his adversary over his head.

Long Horse landed on his back in a thick tangle of
dead branches, which gave way under his weight, and
for a brief moment Hawkes thought the Oglala would
fall into the river. But Long Horse was quick and agile
and managed to get back onto the trunk of the tree and
regain his footing. He had lost his knife, but that
didn't stop him from launching himself at Hawkes.
The mountain man dropped a shoulder to take the
brunt of the Indian's charge, and as they fell he
plunged his knife to the hilt in Long Horse's side, then
withdrew it and tried to strike again. But once more
Long Horse clutched his wrist, while his other hand
closed around Gordon's throat, his weight pinning
Hawkes down. Hawkes tried to break the Sioux's grip,
but Long Horse was just too strong. Strangling,
Hawkes saw his world begin to darken, and desperately reached out and clawed savagely at the Indian's
eyes. Long Horse reared back, roaring in pain, and let
go of the mountain man's throat. Hawkes heaved his
body up and sideways and Long Horse rolled off the
trunk of the tree, into the brittle branches, which
snapped beneath him. As he fell, Long Horse grabbed
the front of Hawkes's hunting shirt, dragging him off
the trunk too. Up to his waist in the freezing, fast-running water, Long Horse snarled incoherent hate at his
enemy and did his best to take Hawkes into the river
with him. But Hawkes reached out with his free hand
to grab a stout branch at its base and at the same time
freed his knife hand from the Indian's weakening grip.
"This is for Plenty Coups," rasped the mountain man—
and with a savage thrust buried his blade in the Sioux
war chief's throat. Blood spewing from his gaping
mouth, his finger's relaxing their grip on Gordon's

shirt, Long Horse slipped, dying, below the turbulent gray waters.

It took all the strength Hawkes could muster to pull himself back up onto the trunk of the fallen tree. He looked to the riverbank and saw that many of the Oglala warriors had come out of hiding to watch the hand-to-hand combat. A few of them made threatening gestures accompanied by angry taunts or shouts of dismay—but no one took a shot at him as he got to his feet. Shifting his gaze to the island, he saw the barrel of Billy Ring's rifle laid across the log and the head and shoulders of the buffalo runner, and for an instant he believed that Ring intended to pick off another one of the Oglalas. But then, even as he opened his mouth to yell at Ring not to do it, the barrel swung toward him, and a heartbeat later he saw the muzzle flash—just as the ball hit him, the impact throwing him off the fallen tree and into the river.

He nearly blacked out, but the shock to his system caused by immersion in the frigid waters of the Muddy River revived him. He flailed to the surface, gasping air back into his lungs as he came up. The powerful current seized him and carried him away, and he tried to swim, but his strength failed him, and he went under. The icy embrace of the river began to weaken him, and he came close to surrendering to the inevitable. Then, despite the angry roar of the river that filled his ears, he heard a voice—heard it with remarkable clarity. It was a woman's voice, calling his name, and he clawed his way to the surface again and forced his numb arms and cramping legs to work as he swam with clumsy strokes. His body slammed into something beneath the surface, and he would have been swept on past except that the wampum belt

around his waist caught on something. It was a log
that had been swept downstream and lodged against a
cutbank where the river curled into a sharp bend.
Hawkes clung to it, and in a while managed to drag
himself along the log until he reached the shallows at
the foot of the cutbank. He lay there in the mud, while
the world and all the pain that was in it slowly faded
away.

Chapter 23

Cameron estimated that they had walked no more than six hours when they saw the horseman coming toward them from the south. But those six hours had felt like six lifetimes. His feet were blocks of ice, and every muscle and joint and bone in his body hurt, so that every step he took was pure torture. But the physical pain, as bad as it was, was nothing compared to the agony of his soul, for he knew he had found his father only to lose him again. And this time it was for good.

He stood there, staring wordlessly at the oncoming riders. The others did likewise, the same question on everyone's mind. Who were these horsemen? Could they be Sioux warriors? If so, it was finished. Cameron knew he did not have the strength left in his body to put up a fight. But they weren't Sioux. As the riders got closer he could see that they wore the blue caps and greatcoats of dragoons.

"I'll be damned," muttered Thayer in utter disbelief. And then he laughed, and couldn't stop. He laughed until there were tears in his eyes. All Cameron could do was stare at the lieutenant. He couldn't figure out what was so damned funny. His exhausted mind had difficulty grasping the idea that the appearance of the soldiers meant that they were saved, that the long ordeal was finally over.

When the dragoons reached them and checked their horses, Thayer looked at Sergeant Landrum and grinned.

"Well, I wondered what the hell had become of you, Sergeant."

"I stuck as close as I could, Lieutenant," said Landrum. "But those damned Sioux kept getting in the way."

Lieutenant Coopersmith dismounted. "Sergeant, get some blankets for these people."

Landrum turned to the dragoons behind him. "You heard the lieutenant. Get moving!"

Coopersmith shrugged out of his greatcoat and draped it around Pretty Shield's trembling shoulders. Then he turned to Thayer and extended a silver pocket flask. "You look like you could use a drink."

"Don't think I have ever needed one worse." Thayer uncapped the flask and took a swig. The whiskey burned like fire in his throat, and he gasped. Then he passed the flask on to Dougherty, who was staring at it the way a starving dog would stare at a bone. The trapper was almost drooling, and he accepted the flask with the reverence due some holy relic.

"The sergeant said you were in a spot of trouble," drawled Coopersmith, "so we thought we might come see if we could do anything to help."

"Coop, you're in Sioux territory. Were you aware of that? What are you trying to do, start a war?"

"Think Lovell will have me court-martialed? I should be so lucky."

"He might. And I expect he'll want to do the same to me."

As some of the dragoons shook out their bedrolls and handed out blankets, Landrum brought his own to Thayer.

"I seen how you was holed up on that island," said the sergeant. "So I got across the river downstream a ways and rode hard for Fort Union."

Coopersmith was looking at the blanket-wrapped body of Broken Bow. He Smiles Twice had laid it on the ground and was sitting on his heels beside it, so exhausted that he didn't seem to notice when one of the dragoons put a blanket around his shoulders.

"How many did you lose?" asked Coopersmith.

Thayer glanced at Cameron. "There are two men still back there on that island, Coop."

"Who?"

"My father," said Cameron, "and a buffalo hunter named Billy Ring."

"You mean they're still alive?"

"I sure as hell hope so," said Thayer.

"Then I had better go find out," said Coopersmith, turning to his horse.

"Wait," said Thayer. "I'm going with you."

Coopersmith looked him over. "Are you sure you're up to it?"

"I'm sure."

Coopersmith smiled wryly. "Well, I guess I ought to put you under arrest, shouldn't I? After all, you did desert."

"You would be well advised to keep an eye on me. So take me along."

"I'm going with you too," said Cameron.

Coopersmith peered at him speculatively, pursing his lips.

"I know what you're thinking," said Cameron. "You're thinking how could I have left my own father back there to die. Well, I shouldn't have. But he wanted me to go. Wanted me to live. And he was going to give his own life so that I had a chance to do just that. I made a big mistake. I treated him wrong." Cameron looked at Pretty Shield. "I misjudged him. And I want to go back and make it right. If it's not already too late."

Coopersmith looked at Thayer, who nodded.

"Very well, then. Sergeant, pick two men to stay here with the others. The rest of us will ride immediately for the island. I expect we'll be back before nightfall," he told Dougherty and the others.

"Don't fret over us," said Dougherty. "Just do me one favor—leave that there flask with us."

Coopersmith laughed. "It's yours, sir, with my compliments."

The two dragoons whose names Landrum called out brought their horses to Thayer and Cameron, who climbed into the saddles. Coopersmith and the other soldiers also mounted up. Pretty Shield stepped closer and looked up at Cameron. She did not have to say anything. He knew perfectly well what she was after—just as he knew he could not say no. He extended his hand and she took it; he pulled her up behind him, then glanced at Coopersmith, expecting the officer to protest. But Coopersmith said nothing to him, turning instead to his men to make sure they were ready to ride before spurring his horse forward.

They had traveled upriver about an hour when they saw the Sioux warriors, four of them, on the opposite bank. One was mounted, holding the horses of the others, while the other three stood at the river's edge. One had a rifle to his shoulder and got off a single shot before they noticed the column of blue jackets. It appeared to Cameron as though the Indian was shooting at something in the river. Coopersmith kicked his horse into a gallop and the others followed. The Sioux leaped to their ponies and sped off—all but one, who hesitated, checking his horse and raising his rifle overhead to hurl a taunt at the soldiers. Then he too was gone. Coopersmith reined in his mount and raised a gloved hand to bring the column to a halt. Thayer saw Landrum jerk his carbine out of its saddle boot and bring it to his shoulder, aiming at the fleeing Indians.

"The range is too long, Sergeant," said Thayer. "You won't hit your mark."

"Hell, I know that, Lieutenant, but I just want to get at least one shot at them Dakotas."

"Oh, you'll get plenty of chances in the future," predicted Thayer.

Landrum lowered the carbine, then spat a stream of tobacco juice. "Yeah, reckon you're right," he allowed. "And I can't say I'm sorry to hear it."

"Well, you might be," said Thayer.

"What was the Indian shooting at?" Coopersmith wondered aloud.

Cameron swung a leg over his horse's neck and slid to the ground, leaving Pretty Shield in the saddle. He ventured to the edge of the embankment and looked down at the swirling, gray-brown waters of the river. He noticed the log jutting out from the bank directly below where he stood. Then he saw the body—and his heart seemed to stop, because he knew it was his father. He went over the edge and slid down the steep, muddy bank, a twenty-foot drop with a soft landing in the river's shallows. Reaching his father, he saw the bloodstains on his hunting shirt. The fact that there wasn't a trace of color in Gordon's face scared him to death. Feeling his wrist for a pulse, Cameron muttered, "Please God, please God," over and over again—and when he finally found a pulse his eyes burned with tears of relief and gratitude.

Standing at the rim of the embankment with Coopersmith and Pretty Shield, Thayer called down to Cameron. "Is he alive?"

Cameron looked up and nodded, unable to speak.

Coopersmith barked an order at Landrum, and a rope was lowered down to Cameron, who tied it around his father's chest, under the arms. Landrum and Thayer hauled the unconscious man up to the top of the embankment. Cameron found a place where he thought he could climb to the top, but the muddy earth gave way underneath him and he had to wait until the rope was lowered again.

When Cameron got to the rim, Pretty Shield was on her knees beside his father, a hand resting on his chest, the other gently brushing the mud from his cheek. She was saying something in the Sioux tongue, speaking to Hawkes even though he could not hear her, leaning over him with her face close to his. Then Hawkes stirred, and his eyes fluttered open. Cameron knelt beside him in time to hear his father speak in a hoarse and barely audible whisper. He croaked a single name—"Eliza." A moment later he had drifted into unconsciousness again.

Cameron glanced at Pretty Shield and saw the anguish in her eyes, and all the resentment he had felt toward her vanished. So he didn't mind at all when the Sioux woman lay down across his father's body wrapping her arms around him, sharing her body's warmth with him. A dragoon brought up a blanket, and Cameron took it from him and draped it over both Pretty Shield and the man she loved so unconditionally.

"I should proceed to the island," said Coopersmith, "though I doubt that Ring fellow is still alive."

"I'm taking my father to Fort Union at once," said Cameron.

"You would be well advised to wait and go back with us," said Coopersmith. "No telling how many Sioux are out and about."

"I don't care about the Sioux. My father needs medical attention, and there's a company doctor at Fort Union. So I'm starting back right now."

Coopersmith took a long look at Cameron and could tell there was no need to debate the point. The young man's mind was made up and there would be hell to pay in trying to detain him. Deciding not to try, Coopersmith turned to Thayer.

"What about you, my friend?"

"I'll ride with you, Coop. Cameron doesn't need my help. He knows how to handle himself."

Cameron nodded at the lieutenant, grateful for the vote of confidence.

When the column of soldiers had moved on, Cameron walked about a hundred yards upstream to a small stand of willows. He selected the stout lower limbs of a dead tree, broke them off the trunk and used his knife to cut away the smaller branches. Using the rope and blanket that a dragoon had left for him, he made a travois and lashed it to the saddlehorn.

With Pretty Shield's help, he placed his father on the travois, and then put the Sioux woman in the saddle. Walking, he led the horse southward.

A couple of hours later he reached the place where Dougherty, Le Due, and He Smiles Twice waited with the two soldiers who had given up their horses to him and Thayer.

"Well, I'll be damned," said Dougherty, staring at the unconscious Gordon Hawkes. "I'm beginning to think this feller is unkillable. Either that or he's the luckiest man alive."

Cameron announced his intentions to ride to Fort Union.

"What about her?" asked Dougherty, nodding in Pretty Shield's direction. "Might as well leave her here with us. That way you'll make better time. I'll take her on to Jim Bridger, just like your pa asked me to."

"You're right, I would make better time. But she's not going to Bridger. She's coming with me."

As they left the others behind, Pretty Shield quietly thanked him. Cameron just nodded his head, saying nothing, and walked on.

When night fell they made camp in a hollow, out of the wind. Cameron went down to the river's edge and found some fairly dry branches at the bottom of a pile of driftwood. He made a hole in the snow, digging down to the frozen ground, and in this built a fire. There wasn't much left of what he'd departed Fort Union with weeks ago, but he did still have a few paper cartridges and a Hudson Bay fire steel and flint in the saddlebags on the army post. He unwrapped a cartridge, throwing away the lead ball contained within, then laid paper wrapping and powder under some kindling before striking the steel against flint to produce a spark, which in turn ignited the gunpowder. The kindling caught and Cameron blew on the tenuous flame until he had a strong fire going. He unlashed the travois from the saddle and placed it close to the fire so that his father might benefit from its heat. Unsaddling the horse, Cameron spread the saddle blanket on the snow by the fire and dropped the rig beside it, then bade Pretty Shield to sit there. He tethered the horse to the saddle, then covered his father with a blanket. The last blanket he put around his own shoulders, since Pretty Shield still had Lieutenant Coopersmith's greatcoat. They dined on some hard biscuits and jerky from a bag tied to the saddle.

"I want to apologize," said Cameron, suddenly breaking the silence between them.

"There is no need."

"What will you do now?"

"If I cannot be with your father then it does not matter what happens to me."

After a moment Cameron said, "But it matters to me."

She looked at him in surprise, but he kept his gaze glued to the fire between them.

After she had eaten, Pretty Shield went to the travois to lie beside Gordon Hawkes, draping an arm and a leg over him, once again sharing her body heat. Cameron kept the fire going for as long as he could, but sheer exhaustion eventually got the better of him. He fell asleep sitting up, his chin resting on his chest.

The bitter cold woke him an hour before dawn, and they were soon on the move again. Looking back on that day, Cameron never quite figured out how it was that he made it through. Every step was torture. Every breath was labored. Once he found himself on his knees in the snow, with Pretty Shield touching him and asking him if he was all right. She told him to ride for a while, but he refused, and insisted that she get back in the saddle. With her help he got back to his feet and trudged on.

As that long day finally drew to a close, he stopped at a low rise and stared at Fort Union in the distance, praying that his eyes did not deceive him.

Chapter 24

When Gordon Hawkes regained consciousness, the first thing he saw was Pretty Shield's face in profile. She was sitting in a straight-backed chair pulled up beside his bed, gazing out the room's solitary window, lost in thought. She looked, he thought, very pensive—and very beautiful. He opened his mouth and tried to speak her name, but all that issued from his throat was a hoarse croaking sound. Looking at him, her eyes came alive with joy and relief, and she shot to her feet, touching his face, murmuring heartfelt thanks in her native tongue to the spirits who had watched over the man she loved. Then she put her arms around his neck and rested her head on his chest. Hawkes lifted his hand—shocked that it required such effort—and gently stroked her soft, raven-black hair. A moment later, she reluctantly rose.

"I must go tell your son that you are awake."

"Where am I?" he asked, looking around at the small room. Apart from the bed and chair there was a barrel with an oil lamp on it, and an old parfleche trunk. A warm fire crackled in a stone fireplace.

"You are safe now," she said, and with one last smile at him, she left the room.

Hawkes searched his memory, trying to figure out

how he had gotten here—wherever here was. The last thing he remembered was seeing the muzzle flash of Billy Ring's gun. What had happened after that? Try as he might, he could not recall a thing from that point on. But he knew he had been shot. His chest and shoulder were tightly wrapped in bandages, and his body was very sore, throbbing in relentless pain. He felt extremely weak. He tried to rise up on his elbows to look out the window, but it was just too much for him, and he sank back onto the bed with a sigh of disgust.

A few minutes later the door opened and his son walked in. Cameron smiled, relieved to see his father awake.

"How do you feel, Pa?"

"Weak as a sick pup. Where am I, Cam?"

"You're at Fort Union. You've been unconscious for three days since we got here, and a couple of days before that."

"How did I get here?"

"I brought you. The day after we left the island we met up with Lieutenant Coopersmith and his dragoons. It seems that Thayer's friend Sergeant Landrum had followed us all the way up into Sioux country, and when he found out we were trapped on the island, he rode here and got the blue jackets. Thayer and Pretty Shield and I rode back with Coopersmith, and on the way we spotted four Indians on the other side of the Muddy River. They were shooting at something in the river. It happened to be you. You were shot and half drowned."

Hawkes nodded. "Billy Ring shot me. I must have fallen into the river. But I don't remember anything about that."

"Pretty Shield and I brought you straight here, and the others pressed on to the island. They got back yesterday. There was no sign of Billy Ring. No sign of the Sioux either. My guess is they took him alive and carried him off to torture him. Whatever happened, it's a sure bet that Billy Ring is dead."

Hawkes would have felt much better had the buffalo runner's body been found. But he had to concede that Cameron was probably right. Ring had to be dead. There could have been no escape for him. A one-armed man could not have survived in the river, and he could not have held off the Sioux for long by himself.

"And the others?" he asked. "Dougherty and Le Due and He Smiles Twice?"

"Dougherty and Le Due headed out yesterday. Said they wanted to spend the rest of the winter in Sante Fe. And He Smiles Twice left before that, taking Broken Bow's body back to his people. Thanks to you we all made it. Well, all of us save for Broken Bow."

"And I made it thanks to you, Cam, and the others."

"I reckon you would have gotten home on your own."

"I was coming home, son. But I know, too, that I stayed a little too long."

Cameron shook his head. "Pretty Shield told me that you tried to escape, and that you were nearly killed. And she told me what she said about being with your child, in order to save your life. She's quite a woman."

"Yes, she is."

"I can see how it would be easy to fall in love with her. But you . . . you didn't, did you, Pa?"

Hawkes smiled faintly. "What makes you say that?"

"Because I know you're still in love with Ma."

"And your mother. How is she? And Grace?"

"They're fine. They're still here at Fort Union, as the major's guests."

Hawkes desperately wanted to know what Cameron had told Eliza, and what his chances were of seeing her, but he couldn't bring himself to ask his son these questions. It wasn't pride that kept him silent, but fear. He didn't think he could handle the answers he would receive, not just yet.

Seeing that his father was troubled, and knowing why, Cameron laid a hand on Gordon's arm and said, "Ma came to see you the other day."

"She did!" Hawkes was surprised, but warned himself not to get his hopes up.

"She's right outside. Do you want to see her?"

"I've thought of nothing else for many months."

Cameron smiled, nodding. "I'll go get her."

He went to the door, opened it, and Hawkes caught his breath as Eliza walked into the room. Lingering at the door, Cameron watched his mother approach the bed, heard his father say in a hoarse whisper, "Eliza—Eliza, will you . . ." and saw her reach out and put a finger on his lips to silence him. And even though her back was to Cameron as she bent down to kiss his father, he had a hunch his mother was smiling.

As he turned to leave the room, swinging the door shut behind him, Cameron saw Pretty Shield standing there under an adobe arch, looking very small and cold and alone. Behind her was the Fort Union wagon yard, the snowdrifts piled high against the buildings that encompassed it. The winter sky was gray and as usual the wind was scouring the High Plains. Gusts picked up the snow and carried it across the wagon yard. From where she stood, the Sioux woman could see through the open doorway into the room where Hawkes lay, and Cameron knew she had seen the kiss.

"Reckon you're sorry now you didn't go south with Dougherty," said Cameron. The trapper had offered to take her to Little Sante Fe, where she could await the return of Jim Bridger. But Pretty Shield had insisted on staying with Hawkes.

"I will go away soon," she said, staring at the closed door and practicing the stoicism that Indians learned at an early age. But though she did not betray her feelings, Cameron could sense that she was deeply anguished. "I will stay until he is well. Then I will go."

"I wish you wouldn't."

Her eyes met his, full of surprise, and though he wanted very much to look away, Cameron didn't. Finding courage he didn't know he had, Cameron stepped closer and brushed the wind-driven snow out of her hair.

"Why do you want me to stay?" she asked. "Because you feel sorry for me?"

"No, that's not it. Because you're in my thoughts all the time." He shook his head, smiling wryly. "Don't ask me how that happened. Until a couple of weeks ago I didn't think I would ever love anyone else but Walks in the Sun."

"Walks in the Sun?"

He nodded. "An Absaroke girl I've known for a long time. But we could not be together, and now she is married to a River Crow. In spite of that, I thought I would never love anyone else as long as I lived. Funny thing is, it's you I think about all the time these days."

Pausing, Cameron studied her face, hoping to find some clue to her feelings as she heard his confession. But there was nothing, and he wondered if he was making a colossal fool of himself. There was no turning back now, though. He had to tell her. And he had to convince her, somehow, to stay.

"Look," he said. "I know you're in love with my pa, and you probably always will be. I'm not the man he is, that's for sure. I don't have much to offer, except that I want to be with you, take care of you. And maybe one day you'll look at me the way I've seen you look at him. If and when that happens I reckon I'll be the luckiest man this side of Maryland."

"Maryland? Where is Maryland?"

Cameron laughed. "I have no idea. But a friend of mine was born there."

His laugh brought a smile to her lips.

The door opened and Eliza emerged, pulling her plain woolen coat closer around her throat to ward off the winter chill. Seeing Pretty Shield gave her pause, but then she approached them. Cameron watched his mother warily. He did not know what to expect from her where the Sioux woman was concerned. All he knew for certain was that when he had told her the news, it had been a hard blow, even though he had tried to break it gently. He'd made no excuses for his father, or for Pretty, and had just presented his mother with the plain unvarnished truth because he hadn't been able to figure out a better way to explain Pretty's presence. Anyone with eyes could see how Pretty felt about Gordon Hawkes.

Eliza looked at Pretty Shield for a moment, her expression one that Cameron could not fathom, and the Sioux woman stood her ground. Then Eliza nodded, and, much to Cameron's astonishment, smiled.

"I want to thank you for everything you did for my husband. If it weren't for you, he would not be here today. It was your love that kept him alive through that terrible ordeal."

"No," said Pretty Shield. "It was his love for you. It was always there in his eyes. I hoped one day it would go away. But it never did."

"Thank you. You don't know what that means to me, to hear those words. But now, we have a . . . a situation. Because my son is in love with you." She glanced at Cameron and smiled at the shocked expression on his face. "I don't know if he's told you yet. He's rather bashful. And I suppose he might have thought I didn't know how he felt. But I'm his mother, and mothers have a way of knowing these things."

"He has asked me to stay with him," said Pretty Shield.

"And I hope you will," said Eliza. "I would be very happy for him if you chose to."

Pretty Shield made no commitment one way or the other, but she was there in the days to come as Gordon Hawkes quickly recuperated. Cameron thought his father's remarkable recovery was due solely to the fact that his mother had forgiven him. In no time at all, Hawkes was back on his feet, and though the American Fur Company doctor who resided at Fort Union urged him to stay in bed for at least another fortnight, Hawkes refused to listen.

When Cameron told him that Lieutenant Thayer was still at the fort, Hawkes went to the encampment of the Second Dragoons detachment, his first trip beyond Fort Union's walls. Pretty Shield was opposed to his exerting himself to that extent, but he insisted, and she went along with him. He found Thayer with Coopersmith in the latter's tent. Pretty Shield waited outside, even though Coop invited her in. When she

politely declined, he told Sergeant Landrum to get her
some coffee. Landrum escorted her to the fire, poured
her a cup, and, at her request, added some sugar. She
liked her coffee sweet. Several of the dragoons came
over to talk to her, and Coopersmith, watching from
the tent, saw that they were treating her with respect.
Word of what she had done, of how much she had
risked to save the life of the man she loved, had gotten
out, and the dragoons were in awe of her.

Hawkes was happy to see Thayer and shook the
lieutenant's hand warmly. He also commented on the
fact that Thayer was back in uniform.

"Surprised, are you?" laughed Thayer. "Well, to tell
you the truth, so am I. I thought I'd be headed for a
court-martial. But it doesn't look like that will happen."

"No? How come?"

"Because he's a hero," said Coopersmith. "News of
your capture, your ordeal as a prisoner of the Sioux,
and the daring rescue has spread like a grass fire, Mr.
Gordon. I guarantee you that in a matter of weeks it
will be in all the newspapers back East. You're famous.
And so is every man who rode to save you."

"Famous," said Hawkes. It was the last thing he'd
expected—or wanted. By nature he was inclined to
shun publicity; as a fugitive from the long arm of the
law, he knew it was entirely too dangerous.

"Poor Colonel Lovell," said Coopersmith wryly. "As
much as he would like to nail our hides to the barn
door, his hands are tied. You can't court-martial a hero,
you know. It just doesn't look good."

"What about next spring, if the Sioux attack a
wagon train on the Oregon Trail?"

"With any luck we'll be there to stop them," said

Thayer. "And Sergeant Landrum will finally get his chance to shoot at a Sioux warrior."

Hawkes nodded, thanked them both, and took his leave. As he headed back to the fort, accompanied by Pretty Shield, he saw his son emerge from the main gate.

"There you are," said Cameron. "I was looking for you."

Hawkes smiled. "For me? Or for Pretty?"

Cameron's cheeks reddened, and it was not entirely because of the blistering cold wind sweeping across the plains. "Well, I have to admit she does occupy my thoughts, Pa."

"She has a way of doing that," agreed Hawkes, looking fondly at the Sioux woman.

"You must be chilled to the bone," Cameron told her, shedding his coat and putting it around her shoulders, for she wore only her doeskin dress and long moccasins. She thanked him, and the way his eyes lingered on her caused her to look shyly away.

It was then, just as Cameron turned to lead Pretty Shield back to the gates, that Hawkes happened to glance out across the snowy plain and see the lone figure stumbling toward the fort. Even at a distance of two hundred yards, Hawkes knew immediately who it was, this gaunt, bearded apparition in tattered clothes, using a rifle like a staff to support himself as he trudged through the snow. It was the empty sleeve blowing in the wind that gave Billy Ring away.

Cameron glanced back to see how his father was faring, and then followed Gordon's gaze. He, too, knew right away the identity of the lone man. "My God," he breathed, and drew a pistol from his belt, but before he could advance further, Hawkes took the pistol from him.

"Get her to safety," Hawkes told his son. There was steel in his voice, so Cameron knew there would be no debate, and he turned to take Pretty Shield by the shoulders even as she moved to be at Gordon's side.

Once Hawkes was certain that Pretty and his son were making for safety, Hawkes turned and advanced to meet Billy Ring.

When they were a hundred yards apart, the buffalo runner cast his rifle aside and dragged a pistol out of his belt. "Gordon!" he shouted, his voice hoarse and raspy. "You're a hard man to kill, God damn you! But today I'll get the job done!"

"I thought you were dead, Ring."

"I am dead! I went into the river and drowned. Then I crawled out of the river and froze to death. But I ain't goin' to hell alone, you son of a bitch."

Hawkes kept walking. He needed to get closer to make his one shot count. "By God, Ring," he shouted, trembling with rage, "I've had enough of you!"

When forty yards separated them, Ring stopped and raised his pistol. "This is for my brother!" he roared and pulled the trigger.

The pistol spit flame and smoke, and Hawkes heard the shimmy of the lead ball as it passed inches from him, but he did not flinch or break stride. Infuriated, Ring growled something incoherent, flung the empty pistol away, whipped a knife out of his belt, and broke into a shambling run. When he was forty feet away Hawkes stopped and raised the pistol and drew a bead and fired. The bullet hit Billy Ring squarely in the chest. His legs flew out from under him, and he landed on his back in the blood-splattered snow, and thrashed briefly. Then, with one last roar of supreme rage, the buffalo runner died.

Hawkes approached the body, and nudged it with his foot. When he was certain that Billy Ring was no more, he dropped the empty pistol in the snow and drew a ragged breath before turning back toward Fort Union. Halfway there, he looked up to see that a crowd had gathered at the main gate. He saw Cameron, his arm around Pretty Shield, and he thought the Sioux woman made a movement as though to break away and come to him. But she stopped herself when Eliza pushed through the on-lookers and ran toward him, the wind catching her pale yellow hair and the plain woolen coat he had bought for her long ago. It was a bitter-cold wind that blew across the High Plains, but Hawkes didn't feel it. All he felt was the warmth of Eliza's love—even before she reached his waiting arms.

PENGUIN PUTNAM INC.
Online

Your Internet gateway to a virtual environment with
hundreds of entertaining and enlightening books from
Penguin Putnam Inc.

*While you're there, get the latest buzz on
the best authors and books around—*

Tom Clancy, Patricia Cornwell, W.E.B. Griffin,
Nora Roberts, William Gibson, Robin Cook,
Brian Jacques, Catherine Coulter, Stephen King,
Jacquelyn Mitchard, and many more!

Penguin Putnam Online is located at
http://www.penguinputnam.com

PENGUIN PUTNAM NEWS

Every month you'll get an inside look at our upcoming
books and new features on our site. This is an ongoing
effort to provide you with the most up-to-date
information about our books and authors.

Subscribe to Penguin Putnam News at
http://www.penguinputnam.com/ClubPPI